Trials Of Saints And Glory

FAE OF REWYTH BOOK 4

EMILY BLACKWOOD

Copyright © 2023 by Emily Blackwood

All rights reserved.

No part of this book may be reproduced in any form or by any electronic or mechanical means, including information storage and retrieval systems, without written permission from the author, except for the use of brief quotations in a book review.

Cover Design by Moonpress | www.moonpress.ca

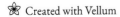 Created with Vellum

CHAPTER 1
Malachi

The violent, icy mountains taunted us on the horizon ahead. A challenge approached with each frozen step we took. My tired feet had well surpassed the point of pain. They were numb with the increasing amounts of ice we walked over.

I traveled through the mountains once before. *The monster mountains*, some had called them back then. It was decades ago now, yet I still remembered the path.

Saints. I had been so ignorant back then. If I knew then what I knew now, maybe I never would have left. Maybe I would have been living deep in these mountains all along.

But that time I spent in the bitter, biting cliffs had taught me how to turn them off; those pesky, vexatious emotions. Silas, the leader of the Paragon, had been my teacher. He taught me how to carry myself like a king. He taught me how to drop an entire army with my magic. I had loved him like a father at times, and yet he treated me like a wild animal.

His wild animal.

But he had taught me how to be dangerous. He had taught me how to be feared.

How to be a weapon.

I clenched my fists. *He was going to do the same thing to Jade if I didn't stop this.*

Silas was the most powerful fae alive. He possessed magic that terrified most, even the powerful witches could not compete with him. The Saints, for whatever reason, had gifted him with an outrageous amount of magic. He could freeze a grown man where he stood, could shield himself from anyone else's gift, including my own. He likely possessed magic that I hadn't seen yet.

Which is why it was impossible to kill him. Silas could see an attack coming from miles away. He had an uncanny ability to protect himself, and he would kill any attacker before they had a chance to protect themselves.

When I was younger, I thought he was a Saint himself. He sure acted like it at times.

But now...

My power flared under my skin, and it took everything in me to will it back down. The last two days had been a constant pattern of that; of controlling my temper. Of reminding myself that I would need to save my energy for later, for when we reached the temple.

I carried Jade through the path for hours until my arms ached. She insisted she could walk, but the life-ending wound on her torso still hadn't healed completely, even with Silas's healer working diligently to stitch her wound closed with magic. We were all exhausted, though, even the powerful healer. Healing her wound entirely would drain him during our travel.

Two days. Two days since the battle in Rewyth, and two days we had been traveling toward the Paragon's mountains.

Esther's waist-length, silver hair nearly blended with the white powder around us. She had come along with the group, even though she could hardly look at me. She, too, was weak. After bringing Jade back from death's wicked grasp, she had nothing left. Each step on the icy terrain seemed to drain her further.

I forced a surge of my power back down again. The memory of what had happened remained fresh in my mind, replaying like a torturous loop of consciousness that I couldn't escape from.

The blade slicing Jade's torso. Her slim, fighting body falling to the ground. Esther at my side, chanting something I couldn't understand.

Jade coming back from the dead.

And I knew from the moment Jade's eyes closed, cold and lifeless, that I was going to find a way to kill him.

If Silas really wanted Jade to compete in the Trials of Glory, I would end his life for it.

She was a human, for Saints' sake. She might have special abilities that we were just beginning to understand, but she wasn't a *fae*. The Trials of Glory were made for special circumstances, special powers. They were made to test and to break. Jade, as strongly as she fought and as stubborn as she was, was not *inhumanly* strong. She wouldn't survive a set of tests built to destroy the strongest fae and witches.

And even if she did, she would never be the same. The old Jade, the Jade that we all knew, would be gone forever.

Jade and I walked behind the rest of the group, far enough to attempt at least an ounce of privacy. At first, I worried that I might accidentally kill one of them out of pure spite if I got too close. For what they did back in Rewyth, they deserved it. Each and every one of them deserved to die by my hand, if not by Jade's.

"How are you feeling?" I whispered in Jade's direction.

She looked at me with tired, dull eyes. Dirt and blood smeared her face from the battle in Rewyth, and I could only imagine how much worse I looked.

"If you ask me that question one more time," she whispered back, "I'll have to move to the front of the group to get away from you."

I fought a smile. At least she still had her attitude.

"Fine, fine," I said, holding my hands up in surrender. "I'm just worried about you. I mean, you *died*, Jade. That blade cut deep. There's no way you're feeling up for a hike through the mountains."

She pressed her hands against her thighs as she walked, using more energy than necessary to shift her weight from one foot to the other. "The healer has been working hard. I feel fine, Mal. I mean that."

She lied, but I understood. Showing weakness in front of them wouldn't help us win this fight.

"I'm going to get you out of this," I whispered, quiet enough to ensure nobody else could hear. The howling wind around us helped disguise my voice. "I'll find a way to end this. You don't owe the Paragon anything, and you certainly don't deserve to go through those damned trials after everything else you've been through."

She stopped walking and faced me, her chest rising and falling with each labored breath.

"Don't I, though?" Her voice cracked. "That's the whole reason I'm here, isn't it? Maybe even the whole reason I was born. The Paragon keeps the peace between humans and fae. I am the peacemaker. If this is what I was born to do..."

"You were not born to be viciously slaughtered in the trials. They're out of their minds if they think you'll pass." A silent beat passed between us. My words came out cold and harsh, but it was only my worry for Jade's safety that put me on edge. She deserved better than this. Much, much better.

If she was insulted by my outburst, she didn't show it.

Another frigid breeze hit my face.

"You doubt me that much?" she asked as she turned and continued walking. "After everything we've been through, you don't think I would survive?"

"It's not you I doubt." Her limp was growing more severe with every minute that passed. I reminded myself not to stare, it would only set her off. "It's them. They have no honor, Jade. If they think for even a second you're a threat, they'll eliminate you."

She scoffed, clearly not as concerned about her own safety as I was. "Then I suppose I'll have to avoid appearing as a threat."

Something was going on in her mind. I had pried and pried around in her thoughts as much as possible over the last two days, but she was only just beginning to speak up more.

She had seen something when she died. Or gone somewhere. Either way, the subtle glimmer of light that used to glow in her deep eyes had disappeared.

The old Jade would have thrown a fit over the Trials of Glory, even when she didn't fully understand what they were. She would have blasted the entire world with her magic before going with the Paragon. She wouldn't have cared about being the peacemaker, about having this weight on her shoulders.

But then again, so would I. That was before *her*.

I would risk everything for her. I was willing to lose it all to save her life. But I couldn't tell her that. Because deep down, I knew she was willing to risk it all, too. But not for me.

She was willing to risk it all to save the world.

"You can't trust him," I whispered to Jade. She turned to look at Silas, who stopped near a half-frozen stream a few yards ahead. I watched as he knelt down to cup the water in his hands, pulling the liquid to his lips. Such a mundane task for a deadly, horrendous man. "He'd suck the power out of you and use it for himself if he could. He'd make every single kingdom bow to him again, he'd control every fae. Every witch."

Jade placed a hand on my arm, returning my gaze. "I'm growing tired of all the people we cannot trust." Her face flickered with sorrow, only for a second, before she was able to recover. "We're being alienated out here."

And she wasn't wrong. Esther, Silas, the entire Paragon. All I knew was that we couldn't trust them. Any of them. Jade and I only had each other.

"I won't leave your side," I admitted. "I don't care if I have to tear the mountains down myself to get to you. I'm not leaving."

"Until the trials?" she asked.

My jaw tightened. "Maybe even not then."

The smile that grew on her face was the warmest thing I had felt in days. I knew I would have to leave Jade at some point. I would have to let her show the Paragon just how powerful she was.

She didn't need my help for that. She never did. Jade had become more powerful than I had ever been. I would protect her with my life, yes, but I also knew she could protect herself from any threat, even if that threat was Silas.

"Get comfortable," Silas yelled from his crouched position near the stream, pulling my attention from Jade's face. "We'll camp here for the night, and we'll climb the mountain in the morning."

A chill betrayed me. Jade and I both adjusted our gazes to the towering mountains that now stood in front of us. There was nowhere else to go. We had made it to the base of the mountain, and all we had left to do was climb.

And then we would be stuck there, forced to live with the Paragon in the temple until Jade proved just how powerful she really was.

The frigid temperatures made flying dangerous, although not impossible. I could fly myself, but with Esther and Jade, we couldn't risk the extra weight. The cold weather and the thin air made flying an exhausting task even for one fae.

Jade and I, fresh from battle and with her still-healing wound, would have to hike through the monster mountains.

Esther, although not a Paragon member, practically kept herself glued to Silas's side. I watched the way she followed him, even going so far as to sleep next to him on the forest ground.

And the others...

Serefin's objections were endless when he couldn't join us on this journey, but I needed him in Rewyth more than I needed him here. If he were with us, he would be one more person I had to watch over, and I couldn't handle that right now. All of my attention needed to be focused on Jade.

Jade and those damned trials.

Our other companions were members of the Paragon, the same ones who were trying to kill my people just two evenings ago. We didn't speak. They didn't even look in our direction, although they knew who I was.

The King of Shadows was not to be challenged.

And neither was his wife.

Still far away from the group, I kicked a few sticks out of the brush beneath us and pulled off my cloak. "Here," I said, laying it down beside Jade. "You should get some rest."

Those big, brown eyes stared up at me. "You'll have to sleep at some point, Mal," she whispered. Her tired voice cracked again.

I had to look away. How could I tell Jade that I couldn't sleep? That I couldn't close my eyes? That I couldn't stop watching over her, not even for a single second?

Because those four minutes where she laid lifeless in my arms were the worst four minutes of my entire life.

And I never wanted to feel that pain again. I wasn't sure I would survive it if I had to.

I didn't *want* to survive it.

Those few moments with Jade lying lifeless before me, I decided something. Something I knew from the moment I met her, but never fully realized. I would end the world before I lost Jade. I would overcome any obstacle, tear down any enemy. These trials? They were merely a stepping stone. An obstacle.

I wasn't going to let them touch her, Paragon or not.

Jade held her breath as she lowered herself onto my cloak, only exhaling when she reached the forest floor. She leaned back onto the cold ground, grimacing with every movement.

"Come here," she whispered once she settled in. "Come lay with me."

"I have to keep watch," I replied. My eyes flickered to the group ahead, arranging themselves in a small circle for warmth. There was no way I could sleep with our enemies so close.

"You've been keeping watch for two days and nights. You can lay with me for a few minutes. Please, Malachi, at least to keep me warm."

The forest around us *was* frigid. And I did crave being close to her, even if for a few moments, but the hair on the back of my neck stood up at a single movement in the forest around us.

This wasn't Rewyth. It wasn't Fearford, either, or Trithen. We were in new territory, and we faced very new enemies. Some of them camped beside us.

But Jade's eyes stared into mine with a need that included more than just keeping watch.

"Just for a few moments," I replied. I lowered myself next to her, keeping a few inches between us as I splayed my black wings around our bodies.

Jade only shifted her body closer, pressing herself against me as if I were the last thing she had in this world to cling to. Her head rested on my shoulder, her hands finding their way up my tunic and around my bare waist.

The slightest brush of her skin against mine sent my power into a feral spiral. I shuddered at her touch, and a small smile on her lips told me she knew exactly what type of effect she had on me.

"Careful," I growled.

"What?" she replied, faking her innocence. "I'm only warming myself up."

For the first time since we left Rewyth, I allowed it. I wrapped my arms around Jade and pulled her to my body, careful not to apply pressure on her healing wound. She exhaled deeply, taking in the warmth of my body just as I did to her.

My instincts flickered from the forest around us to the Paragon members that settled into sleep nearby. Certain that everyone was quickly falling asleep, I dragged my hand up to Jade's chin and tilted her head up to mine.

"I never wanted this for you, Jade," I whispered in the darkness. "If I could trade places with you, I would."

She exhaled slowly. "None of this is your fault. I don't blame you for any of it, Mal. I hope you know that."

She should blame me, though. I was the reason she got forced into this mess. My father forced me to marry her, yes, but I should have protected her more, shielded her away from the chaos of this world.

"I wish you would blame me," I admitted. "It would make me feel much better about dragging you through all of this."

Jade lightly hit my chest. "You're ridiculous," she replied. "We're in this together, okay? No blame, no hatred. We make it out of here alive and then we'll talk about hating one another again."

I couldn't stop the smile that formed on my face.

"You are my light, Jade Weyland," I whispered. "For so, so long, I was stuck in the darkness. Not anymore."

Jade smiled, warm and genuine, before settling her head back onto my chest. I ran my fingers through her black hair, soothing her in any way that I could. It wouldn't be enough. With the chaos that surrounded us, it would never be enough.

I listened to her heartbeat until it slowed. And just when I thought she had fallen asleep...

"I'm afraid, Mal," she whispered in her breath, barely loud enough for me to hear. "They want me to be strong, but I am not."

I let my body relax around her, giving her the comfort I knew she craved. "You are strong," I said. I pressed my forehead to hers and held her tightly in the privacy of my black wings and the lowering sun. "You are strong, capable, and resilient. You've died and come back from the darkness. You've lost so much and yet you're still standing, Jade. You are one of the strongest people I know. You can do anything, you can overcome anything."

A single tear slid down her face. I quickly brushed it away. "I don't want to be strong," she said. "I'm tired. I'm so tired."

Jade shifted against me, muffling sobs in my thick, ripped tunic. "We're almost to the end," I said. "I'll find a way out of this. I'll find a way."

CHAPTER 2
Jade

Sleep was nothing like dying. Sleep was sometimes terrifying, sometimes delightful. Sleep was healing and replenishing. It was necessary for daily functioning.

Death, on the other hand, was something else entirely.

To me, death had been the hands of a lover welcoming me to bed. It was so hard to say no, and saying yes seemed too easy.

So I said yes. And then the darkness followed.

Malachi explained that I was only gone for a few minutes before Esther brought me back, but that wasn't what it seemed like. That wasn't how it felt.

It felt never-ending. It felt like I had lived many, many lives in that darkness. It felt like I belonged there all along, but also like I had an eternity left to spend in the nothingness.

There was no fire. There was no punishment. There were no Saints.

Just...nothingness.

And then I re-awoke inside my own body, with Esther chanting over me and Malachi holding me in his arms.

And seconds later, I was here, being whisked away into the Trials of Glory that I couldn't win, to be someone I could not be.

But how did I tell them that? How did I tell them all that I would fail them?

How was I supposed to tell *him*?

There were no words to describe the pain on Malachi's face when Esther brought me back, in those few moments between life and death.

He thought he had lost me, and he was utterly, mercilessly broken.

And I never wanted to see that again. Not from him. He deserved better than me, he deserved better than someone who would die before they completed the Paragon's Trials of Glory.

I barely had magic. How was I supposed to complete the ancient trials from the Saints?

I reveled in the warmth of Malachi's body and tried to forget. I tried to forget the war. I tried to forget the darkness. My father. Serefin. Everyone we left behind. Tessa.

I tried to forget it all and focus on his arms around me. His wings keeping me safe. Sleep didn't come easily. I had dozed off a couple of times, but even though Malachi held me while I slept, I knew he would be wide awake. He wouldn't drift off for even a second.

His strong arms held me to him, close enough that I felt

safe, but not hard enough to put pressure on my half-healed wound.

"I wish we could leave this place," I whispered, more to myself than to him. I gave up on sleep, but I didn't dare move from the warmth his arms provided. The forest was pitch-black now, and the nightlife created an array of noises around us, each one fueling the adrenaline in my veins.

His chest rumbled with a small laugh. "Trust me, Jade. I would carry you out of here and never come back if I could."

"Somewhere warm. With sunlight and plenty of nature."

"And no wars. No kingdoms."

"Can Adeline come?" I asked, tilting my face up so I met his gaze in the moonlight. "And Serefin?"

He moved forward and placed a warm kiss on my forehead. "You can bring anyone you want."

I tensed, and I knew Mal felt it. I couldn't stop my mind from wandering to my father. After everything, he had tried desperately to save me. Was he any match against a fae? No, not in the slightest.

But for once, he had fought. For once, he had tried to protect his family.

What was left of it, anyway.

"They'll all be okay," Mal whispered, brushing his fingers against the side of my face. "We'll be back home before anyone can cause any trouble. My brothers will keep things in line, and Serefin won't let a single thing happen."

"I know, I just... I hate to think of him in a kingdom of fae, all alone."

"He's not alone. And maybe it will be good for him."

A shaking breath escaped me. "I can't see how that's possible."

I ran my hands down Mal's sculpted chest. "I shouldn't care. If I cared about everyone's wellbeing, I would drive myself crazy."

His chest rose and fell. "You care because you love so much. And that's part of what makes you so marvelous."

His fingertips slowly grazed my body, settling on my lower back. I couldn't help but shiver. Being this close to him still made me feel this way, like it was my first day with him all over again.

"*Marvelous*," I repeated. "That's an interesting word for it."

He moved his hand, inching his fingers under the loose fabric of my shirt so the rough, calloused skin touched my bare back. My breath hitched. "You should get some sleep," he whispered.

But I could hear the grin on his face as he said the words.

His index finger began moving in circles over that sensitive spot on my lower back, sending chills erupting through my body.

"Malachi," I grumbled.

"Yes, my queen?"

He then traced his finger along my spine, all the way up to my shoulder blades. He hovered lightly, kissing the skin with a delicate touch.

I shut my eyes, reveling in the sensation. "How am I supposed to sleep with you touching me like that?"

"Like what?"

He moved his hand to my bare side, caressing my ribs. Again, I shivered. "Like that." He then traced the curve of my hip, lingering on the waistband of my filthy trousers.

"Would you prefer it if I didn't touch you?"

I took a long, shaking breath. His hand lingered in a silent question. "No, *my king*," I answered. "I would very much *not* prefer that."

I pushed myself into him, gently pressing my lips to his. It had been days since he held me like this, since we kissed like this. A low growl rumbled in Mal's chest as he kissed me back. He moved slowly at first, gently maneuvering his mouth against mine. As if he were taking it all in. As if he were kissing me again for the first time.

His black wings blended with the night sky, shielding us from the outside world. Mal's hands were hot against my ribs, gripping my waist and holding my body tightly to his. I did the same, sliding my hands up his shirt and pulling him close to me.

I moved to slide my body on top of his when a piercing pain came from my abdomen. I hissed and pulled away.

"Are you okay?" Mal asked.

I pulled back and slid my tunic up, finding the bandages holding my wound together covered in dark red blood.

Again.

The healer had been working diligently to heal me every few hours, but the cut was deep, and he had to save most of his energy for our travels.

Malachi pushed himself up, immediately calling for the healer. "She's bleeding!" he yelled to the group that lay sleeping by the river bank, startling half of them with his booming voice. "Come help her!"

Mal knelt behind me, lifting my head and supporting my body as the healer woke up. He wasn't a pleasant man, and his hands were very, very cold. But I had to admit, a small amount of healing was better than none.

"You're moving too much," the man said as he approached. He had silver wings, but they were smaller than most. He clearly didn't do much flying, and I wondered if it had something to do with his old age. Fae were nearly immortal creatures, but this fae in particular was covered in history and wrinkles.

And whatever life he lived, it didn't teach him to be gentle.

His hands were cold as he peeled away my red bandages. The chilled air replaced the warmth of my own blood, causing my muscles to tense. The healer placed his hands on my torso, on either side of the wound.

I flinched.

"Careful," Mal hissed from behind me.

The healer only shot Mal an annoying glare with his blue eyes before closing them in focus.

I closed mine, too. Not because it hurt. It was a feeling that was hard to describe. Warmth immediately radiated from his cold, lifeless hands, and the pain in my wound dulled as a tingling sensation took over my torso. This happened every time, and it was almost as if I could feel the tendrils of my flesh mending together once more.

Malachi's hands held on to me tightly. Saints, I much preferred Mal's hands over this old hag's.

A few more seconds went by, and the healer opened his eyes once more. "Lay still tonight," he warned. "We climb the mountains tomorrow, and I won't be able to heal you any more during the journey. We must wait until we reach the temple."

"Great," I mumbled. "Can't wait."

The healer stood up and returned back to his position with the others, who were now beginning to stir. In the shadows of darkness, I could see Silas staring at us.

I stared back at him. I wasn't sure what all went down between him and Malachi, but I didn't like it. Not one bit. Silas made Malachi stiffen when he was near. Mal treated him differently, looked at him differently.

What had happened between them in these mountains all those years ago? Who *was* Silas? And what was he going to do to me?

Mal explained very few details. Silas was a powerful fae, that much I knew. More powerful than Malachi. More powerful than anyone. That's why he was able to claim himself as leader of the Paragon. Nobody was ever able to kill him, nobody's power matched his.

I could tell Mal tried to hide the hatred in his voice when he spoke of Silas. For what? I still wasn't sure. I knew Silas was the one that trained Mal to kill, to use his own power. He was the reason Malachi became so powerful to begin with.

But what happened after that? Why would Silas attempt a war with one of his own friends, one of his own mentees?

Mal moved away, leaving me lying alone on his cloak. I

immediately missed the warmth from his body. "Where are you going?" I asked.

"Get some sleep," he said. "You need to conserve your energy for tomorrow."

The heat I had been feeling in my body dissipated with his words. He didn't even look at me. His dark curls hung around his cheekbones as he sat on the cold ground next to me, ready to keep watch for the night and once again not getting any sleep.

I couldn't say I blamed him. I had died. I had left him, like each of his wives before me, I was lost.

I couldn't imagine how he felt now.

I settled into the darkness, enveloping myself in Mal's cloak. "Sleep well, my queen," he whispered.

But his voice was hollow.

I closed my eyes and drifted into an eerie, chilling sleep.

The sun woke me.

It began to rise in the distance, and the shreds of sunlight flickered in through the thin trees above us. I pushed myself up, feeling stiff from yet another night sleeping on the ground.

Today was the day. The day we climbed those damned mountains and arrived at the Paragon's temple.

"Are you feeling okay?" Malachi asked again, just like he had done hundreds of times yesterday. I nearly jumped at the sound of his voice, but he was leaning against a tree with his legs stretched before him.

"Good as new," I grunted. I glanced over to where the others were also waking up. "You up for this?" I asked.

His eyes were dark. "I don't think we really have a choice," he answered.

I waited for him to say more, but he sat there staring into the forest like I wasn't even there. I knew he was nervous. I knew he was afraid of his past, whatever that entailed.

But all we needed to focus on today was climbing the mountain.

Climb the mountain today, and deal with saving the world tomorrow.

Easy enough, right?

I left Mal and limped over to the stream to splash the freezing water on my face. I was no longer a fan of streams, not after almost being killed by the kraken. But these days, I had much worse enemies than those disgusting sea monsters. I had men wanting to put me through trials that were designed to break me. I had fae and witches trying to steal my power.

Much worse enemies than the kraken. At least I knew those creatures wanted me dead. The worst type of enemy were the ones you couldn't see coming, the ones that tried to protect you first before stabbing you in the back.

"The climb isn't so bad," Silas said. His deep voice made me jump. I stood from my kneeling position by the stream.

"It's not the climbing that keeps me up at night," I replied, rolling my shoulders back and lifted my chin. "It's what comes after."

He smiled and looked down at his feet. In his all-black cloak, he seemed small. Not terrifying. Not dangerous. Just...simple. He had to squint to make eye contact with me, which was amusing enough coming from the most powerful fae of our time.

"I think you'll find the temple to be quite welcoming. Just because we are the Paragon doesn't mean we don't enjoy the simple luxuries of life." He finished the sentence with a forced smile.

"I've heard otherwise," I spat. "And I'm not sure it's the luxuries of life that have earned you your reputation."

He considered my words. "What are you afraid of, Jade Weyland?"

"*Afraid* of?"

He took a step closer. His pale skin seemed iridescent, even in the morning sun. His eyes were sunken in against his cheekbones, and I could barely see the white hair growing against his shaved head.

"Yes, child. Tell me what you fear."

Child. I hated when Esther called me that, and now Silas?

"Why would I tell you such a thing? I don't know you."

"Not yet," he answered. "But you and I will be getting to know each other very well over the next few days."

I placed a hand on my hip. "And I can't tell you how excited I am for that." I couldn't keep the attitude out of my voice. Silas was trying to intimidate me, and it wasn't going to work.

He dropped his smile. "If you are who you claim to be,

peacemaker, you'll have no problem completing the Trials of Glory."

"I don't see how that's true, considering I'm human."

He looked me up and down. His gaze was cold and eerie, but I didn't look away. I didn't step back.

"Humans don't possess magical gifts, Jade. Humans do not die and come back to life. Humans are not chosen to become the peacemakers of our world."

He turned on his heel and walked back to the group before I could ask what he was talking about, but my mind burned with his words like fire.

Was I not human?

CHAPTER 3
Malachi

I despised him.

I despised that he was here, that he was still alive. I despised that he looked at Jade. That he talked to her. That he existed.

Even watching them converse near the stream put a fiery anger deep in my chest.

I had always been protective of Jade, but this was different. If he dug his claws into her, I was afraid she would never escape. And neither would I.

"What was that about?" I asked as Jade returned.

She was paler than usual, even with her face dripping in the cool water from the stream. "He doesn't seem to think I'm human," she answered.

I stood up from the tree base. "What?" I asked. "Why does he think that?"

Jade shrugged. "He said humans don't possess magic. And they can't come back from the dead."

That bastard. I had suspected whether or not Jade was

truly human for quite some time, ever since we learned that our magic was connected. Why would the Saints give a human such a special gift, only to give her the life duration of a human?

But that wasn't Silas's place. He could keep his damned opinions to himself.

"I don't like it when he talks to you," I said. "He should leave you alone."

"You really hate him, don't you?" she asked. "What did he do to you, Mal?" She glanced at the crowd again before stepping closer to me and lowering her voice. "What are we about to walk into?"

I shut my eyes and shook my head. *That was the past*, I reminded myself. That was the old Silas, the old Malachi. That was decades ago now, and so much had changed. I changed. I was sure Silas had changed, too.

I had to tell myself that. If I let fear control me, I would become paralyzed. And that's not what Jade needed right now. She needed strength. She needed fearlessness.

"It's nothing," I answered.

But I could tell she wasn't buying it. "I'll find out at some point," she said. "And do you believe him? About me not being human?"

"I don't know," I said. "But I think we'll be finding out very soon."

"Everyone ready?" Silas yelled. Jade and I approached slowly, still lingering in the back of the crowd. "This will be a difficult journey. If we're lucky, we'll reach the temple before the sun falls. If we aren't lucky, we'll have a rough night of camping in the winter. Stay close and keep your wits about you. We don't know who's watching us out here."

Jade glanced up at me. "Should I be worried?"

"Stick with me and we'll be just fine," I answered.

For the first couple of hours, the climb was fairly simple. The cold forest ground turned to snow-covered rock, and then fluffy, freezing snow. For as far as we could see, snow.

I had given Jade my cloak to wear, but the sound of her teeth chattering still sent a feral anger down my spine.

"We need to move faster!" I called forward to Silas. "We're not making fast enough time."

"We're moving as fast as we can!" he yelled back, although his voice trailed off with the howl of the icy wind.

"Well, it's not fast enough." I caught up to Jade, who was only a few paces ahead of me. "Are you feeling okay?" I asked. I felt like I had asked her that every ten seconds for the last three days.

"I'm fine," she answered through gritted teeth. "Please tell me the path doesn't get worse than this."

I couldn't lie to her, so I stayed silent.

Two more hours passed like that, with the winds increasing and the snow growing deeper.

Until we reached the first passage.

"No way," Jade said before we even made it to the edge. "There's no way I can climb over that."

A rope bridge connected the two cliffs together, creating a pathway. One that I never wanted to cross again. And unlike Esther and Jade, I had wings.

"I'll be with you the entire time," I said. The group of

us now congregated near the bridge while Silas brushed some of the ice from the first plank. "The others will go first, and you'll see it's not that bad. Right, everyone?"

The others prepared to cross, but I felt a pair of eyes lingering. I looked up to meet Esther's gaze. Her face was red with burns from the fierce wind, but her eyes were strong and angry.

Always strong and angry.

I waited for her to say something. Anything. These silent glances between us had been happening often, ever since she saved Jade's life. But we hadn't spoken. Not a single word.

What was I supposed to say? How could I possibly thank her for saving Jade's life when she was also the one who put it in danger?

"I'll cross first," Silas spoke. "Take your time following. The cliffs are too sharp for any of us to dive down after you."

Jade's jaw tightened.

"He's lying," I whispered, low enough for only her to hear. "I won't let you fall, Jade. Ever."

"I want to believe you," she hissed back, "but my hands are frozen and I'm not confident I can even grip the rope."

I grabbed her cold, stiff hands and cupped them together in front of my mouth. Her eyes widened as I exhaled on them, warming her with my breath.

But she didn't pull away.

"Better?" I asked.

"Not really," she replied. "Although I don't mind your

mouth warming me up. I have a few other areas that are cold, you know."

I rubbed her hands between mine once more before letting go. "All in due time, my queen."

Ahead of us, Silas gripped the rope bridge. He put one foot on the first wooden plank, and we all watched in silence as it squeaked beneath his weight. A chunk of ice fell beneath him. He didn't move for what felt like a full minute.

But then he took the next step.

He slid his hands across the wooden rope, and a few steps later, he stood on the other side.

One had crossed. Six to go.

My faith in the bridge hardly existed, but at least the entire thing wasn't going to fall under the weight of a man.

And Jade was half the weight of Silas. She would be fine.

I would make sure she would be fine.

Silas's men went next, one after the other. With each step taken across the wooden planks, I found myself holding my breath. I angled my sharp ears in Jade's direction and found that she was doing the same.

Esther was next.

"Be careful," Jade said to her softly. I had to admit, I was surprised. That was the first time Jade had spoken to Esther.

But Esther just returned a grateful smile. "I'll be okay, child. There's nothing to fear."

Jade smiled, too, and then Esther turned to the bridge.

She gripped each rope with her small, frail hands. I wondered how stiff they were, if they were as cold as Jade's.

Silas watched intently from the other side, tracking her every move.

The bridge creaked as she stepped forward. It swayed in the wind, her weight not quite heavy enough to keep it from moving. But she held her head high and continued gripping that rope.

She took another step. Slid her hands forward. Took another step.

A few seconds later, she jumped onto the other cliff and into Silas's arms.

Jade and I were the only two left.

"You can do this," I said to her. "The bridge is strong, and you have me watching you every step of the way."

"Come with me," she pleaded. If she was hiding her fear earlier, she wasn't anymore.

I shook my head. "The bridge isn't strong enough to hold us both. You go first, and I'll be right behind you."

She stared at me for a second more before she turned back to the bridge. She stepped forward, and then she looked down.

"Don't look," I reminded her. "It'll only make you nervous, and you have no reason to be nervous. Look at the other side." She did. "Now take one step."

I held my breath, too, as Jade shifted her weight onto the wooden plank beneath her. Similar to Esther, she was too light to keep it from swaying.

But Esther had made it.

"Good," I said. "Now keep looking ahead of you."

She kept her head up, but I could see how tightly she gripped the rope. Saints, it felt like we were already in the Trials of Glory.

Jade was nearly across.

She had one more step to take when she slipped and lost her footing, her worn black boots sliding on the ice-covered planks. "Jade!" I yelled out, but I was stuck on my side of the bridge. The entire thing would collapse if it were holding both of us.

Esther launched herself forward and clamped a tight grip onto Jade's arm.

"I've got her!" she yelled.

Jade clung to that wooden plank for her life.

And Esther clung to her.

Silas and the others stepped in, pulling both Esther and Jade to safety on the cliff's edge.

As soon as they were away from the bridge, I crossed it without so much as holding the rope.

"Jade," I said again as I sank to my knees next to her. "Are you alright?"

Esther still held onto her, as if she were afraid of letting go all together. Jade nodded.

"I'm okay," she said. "But I never want to do that again."

"Deal," I replied. I helped her to her feet first, then I reached a hand out to Esther.

"That's twice now I've saved your wife's life. You could at least look me in the eye, son."

Jade began walking with the others. "I'm aware of how I am so indebted to you, mother," I replied.

"There is no debt," she corrected me. "You owe me nothing. I just wish you could see that I am on your side."

I stepped closer to her and dropped my voice. "*Are* you? Are you on my side? What about him?" I motioned to Silas. "Are you on *his* side? Because you can't be on both. Not with this. Not with what's about to happen to her."

"You don't need to worry about the trials," Esther whispered. "Jade can survive each one with ease. She's a fighter. You know she'll be okay."

A cruel laugh escaped me. "You really believe that blood-thirsty bastard is going to make this easy for her? He wants her dead. You're blind if you don't see that."

"If he wanted her dead, he would have killed her back in Rewyth."

"And I would have ripped his head off where he stood."

She held her hands up in front of her. "Enough with the scary alpha contest, okay? Silas isn't your enemy."

"You have no idea what Silas is to me. And why are you so sure you know his character? There's something you aren't telling me."

She took a long, shaking breath. In the distance, Jade called back to us, yelling for us to catch up.

"Tell me. Now," I demanded.

"I knew Silas very well, but that was decades ago. I hardly recognized his face when I saw him again. But I lived with him in the mountains for a very long time, long before you were born."

No way.

"You lived with Silas?"

She nodded, but glanced down at her feet. "I didn't want you to know. I know how you feel about him."

"How I *feel* about him? He turned me into a weapon!"

"Malachi!" Jade yelled, waiting for me a few paces ahead.

Anger burned inside of me. Esther had consistently been a lying, mischievous witch. I still didn't trust her, and I didn't care how many times she saved Jade's life.

"This discussion is not over," I hissed at her. I began stalking through the snow, back to Jade. Back to the one person in this entire group that I trusted.

"We're not your enemy, son!" Esther called from behind me. I didn't so much as turn my head.

"What was that all about?" Jade asked as I stepped closer.

"Esther being untrustworthy. Nothing new."

Jade gave me a sideways glance. "Untrustworthy? If my memory serves me correctly, she's the one who brought me back to life."

"She needs you. For what, I'm not sure yet. But she was using you before. I wouldn't be so sure that she's not doing it again."

CHAPTER 4
Jade

We climbed higher and higher through the mountains. The temperature dropped until I was positive that my nose was frozen on my face.

Sometime before the sun began to set, Silas stopped us. "We're here," he announced. I looked around us. There was no temple. No city. Not a single sign of life anywhere in the distance.

"Here?" I repeated. The pain from my abdomen slowly began to return, adding to the edge in my voice. After nearly falling off the bridge, my wound had all but ripped back open. My fingers were numb with ice, and I wanted nothing more than to be done with this horrid trip. "There's nothing here."

Silas turned and began walking into the side of the mountain, literally *into* the side of it.

A slight shimmer on the surface was the only thing I saw as Silas's body disappeared.

"Is that…"

"Glamour," Mal answered for me. "They use it to hide the entrance to the temple at all times. It's how the Paragon is able to stay hidden from the rest of us. Even if intruders managed to find their way through the mountain's paths, they would have no way of finding the temple."

"Isn't that exhausting?" I asked. "I mean, wouldn't it be tiring for someone to use their glamour all day long?"

Mal put an arm around my shoulder and squeezed. "This is the Paragon. The strongest fae in existence live here, and a handful of witches, too. For them, it's nothing. They could hold this glamour in their sleep."

The weight of those words hit me like a punch to the gut. "That's terrifying."

"You have nothing to fear," he said, but his voice wavered. I knew Mal was worried about what would happen here. He was right to worry. Still, I didn't argue with him. "You're the peacemaker. You are powerful beyond any gift these witches and fae might possess. They should leave you alone."

I couldn't help but scoff at the thought. *Peacemaker.* That still meant nothing to me. I didn't feel powerful. I didn't feel protected. "Until they see how *not* powerful I really am."

"Don't say that," Mal argued. "It isn't true."

"I have power, sure. But there has to be some other explanation. I mean, what *exact* type of power am I supposed to possess?"

Malachi shrugged. His calm, collected exterior didn't

fool me. Not for a second. "I suppose that's what we're here to find out, my queen."

I watched the hidden passageway ahead of us. "What's on the other side, Mal?"

He gripped my hand tightly. Through the cold that infiltrated every ounce of my body, I could hardly feel it. "We'll walk through together. I'll be right by your side the whole time."

My teeth were still clenched together, but I could no longer tell if it was from the cold or from the nerves. We had finally arrived at the Paragon's temple.

It was now or never, and I didn't seem to have much of a choice. Surely Silas wouldn't drag us all the way up the mountain to ambush us.

Malachi matched my steps as I inched forward, closer to the glamour-covered entrance of the temple. Closer to the trials. Closer to answers and questions that I didn't even know to ask yet.

This was it.

I shut my eyes and stepped into what seemed to be the side of the cliff, and suddenly we were inside the temple.

Mal and I stood there, hand in hand. I squinted at first until my eyes adjusted to the dimly lit space. I was unable to move, completely encapsulated by what I saw.

We were... we were *inside* of the mountain.

"Holy Saints," I muttered. "It's...it's beautiful."

"The Paragon has had decades of hiding down here. It's impressive, isn't it?"

Impressive didn't even begin to describe the sight laid out before me. We stood at the apex of the room, which seemed to be the connecting point to dozens of underground tunnels that dispersed underneath the mountain. In the center, beautiful gold pieces of furniture and fire lanterns flickered through the dim lighting. Everything was elegant in a way that made me wonder how they got all of it here and under this damn mountain.

"Welcome to the temple," Silas announced, interrupting my thoughts. "We'll spend the week preparing you, answering any questions you may have about the trials. One week from today, you will start the first test."

"What's the first test?" I asked.

Silas stared at me with those large, vacant eyes. I noticed now that they had a hint of red in them. "You'll learn more about the trials tomorrow. Why don't you and your husband get some rest and warm up for the evening. It's been a long few days."

"I don't want to rest," I answered. I was unable to keep my annoyance out of my voice. I didn't feel tired anymore. I didn't feel like I needed to warm up. What I wanted was answers. I needed to know what I was walking into. "I want to know what the damned trials are."

Silas looked at Malachi for the first time since we had been talking. "I'm sure your husband can answer any questions you have. First, we need to finish healing your wound."

Silas waved toward the healer. "Do whatever it takes to finish closing the injury," he ordered. Now that our journey was over, I supposed the healer could afford to use more of his healing magic on me.

The healer only nodded, stepping toward me with his

arm extended. My first instinct was to flinch away, but Malachi's hand on my lower back urged me forward.

"Come," the healer said. "Sit over here."

With Malachi following closely behind me, I did as I was told. My feet glided across the stone floor tiles as I approached one of the many gold-trimmed benches in the center of the room. A few Paragon members—all dressed in black cloaks—glanced my way, but quickly returned to their meals as I took my seat.

Saints, it felt good to sit.

The healer sat next to me, but not Malachi. He stood in front of us, wings flared and eyes vigilant. My stomach twisted at the sight of him on edge. I hated that he had a past here.

"Roll up your tunic, please," the healer ordered. I ignored the burning in my muscles long enough to reach down and lift the edge of my shirt that now dripped with blood, melting ice, and dirt. The healer didn't hesitate, pulling back my bloody bandages and revealing the half-healed wound.

"This won't take long," he said. His voice was stern, but I could have sworn I heard a hint of pity in his words as he leaned closer to the wound. "Sit still."

Like I had a choice.

The man's hand hovered over my torso, just like he had done before. Except this time, I could actually feel the warmth radiating from him. Warmth and...something else.

Magic.

When I looked at Malachi, he was staring at the man's hand, unblinking.

We sat like this for a few minutes until the healer gasped and pulled his hand away.

"What is it?" I asked. "What's wrong?"

The healer shook his head, eyes wide as he continued to stare at my wound. "Nothing, I–"

"What?" Malachi chimed in, stepping closer.

"I could have sworn I saw..." The man shook his head again, as if shaking the thought from his mind. "Never mind," he said. "It's been a long journey. I'm tired. Your wound should now be healed, peacemaker. If you experience any more pain, come find me."

Before we could ask any more questions, the man scurried away.

"Did you see anything?" I asked Mal, who had been watching the healer the entire time.

"Not a damn thing," he answered. We both surveyed my wound, which was now nothing but dried blood and smudged dirt. Whatever the healer had done worked entirely. Not even a slight cut remained on my skin.

"Well," Silas clapped, reminding us of his presence. I pushed myself from the bench to stand beside Mal. "Now that we've taken care of our peacemaker, you two should get some rest. Follow me, I'll show you to your rooms."

I kept my mouth shut as Silas began walking, his black robe trailing behind him as he moved, almost as if he were floating.

Malachi's hand on my lower back reminded me to move my feet.

"We aren't your prisoners? We're free to roam as we

please?" I asked. Malachi remained suspiciously quiet next to me.

"For now, yes. Things will change once the trials begin."

"Isn't that a bit of a risk for you? What if you wake up one morning and we're gone?"

Silas stopped walking to answer me. "If you are foolish enough to think that you can evade the most powerful individuals of our time, you are not as smart as I believed you were, Jade Weyland. You can try to escape, but you will not be successful. Isn't that right, Malachi?"

Malachi stiffened. I could nearly feel the coldness from him on his light touch against my back.

Had Malachi tried to escape from the Paragon before?

"Just show us to our room," I interrupted. I hated the way Silas looked at Mal, as if he were a toy.

Silas nodded and began walking again. We walked through the tunnels until I thought there was no possible way they could continue, but then they did. We turned dozens of times, and I silently hoped Malachi had a great memory because there was no way I would remember the path. When I glanced up at him, though, his face held an unreadable expression.

We passed a few others in the tunnels, but each of them wore the same black cloak as the Paragon members we had already met, and not a single person looked at us. Not a single person met our gaze. I wondered if that was because of Silas, or if looking people in the eye was a rarity around this temple.

"Here you are," Silas said. He stopped in front of a small opening in the mountain edge. A door fit perfectly within the small curve of the stone. "Food is served in the main room at sunrise. We'll talk more then. Bathing is that way." He pointed down the tunnel. "Rest well."

And then he was gone, scurrying back down the tunnel the way he came, his black robe hiding him in the depths of the under-mountain shadows.

"Cozy," I said.

Malachi had to tuck his wings behind his back to duck through the doorway of our room. I followed closely behind him.

The room was small, but it was equally as elegant as the rest of the temple. A bed with solid-gold posts and white silk sheets sat in the center of the room, and a small table in the corner held a stack of clean clothes.

Not the black robes, to my surprise, but black trousers and tunics for both Mal and I.

Malachi still did not relax. His black wings expanded, but he looked smaller than I had ever seen him. He stared at the bed, and slowly shifted his focus to the moisture that dripped down the stone mountain wall. He wasn't really paying attention, though. He had gone somewhere else, somewhere distant.

I shut the heavy stone door behind me before I walked over to Mal. The echo of the tunnels disappeared, finally leaving Mal and I alone. "Hey," I whispered. I slid my hands up his back, narrowly avoiding the base of his wings. He flinched when I touched him. "Tell me what you're thinking."

His head dropped, hanging in a rare glimpse of defeat.

"Being back here is more difficult than I thought it would be."

Malachi had mentioned that he had lived here with Silas. For how long? I wasn't sure. I also wasn't sure what exactly happened, or what Malachi endured. "This is temporary," I reminded him. "Once I complete the trials, we'll be out of here."

He turned to face me. "There's something you need to know about the trials," he said. "Something I haven't told you before."

An icy chill ran down my back, and it wasn't from the tundra we had just escaped from. "What is it?"

"Decades ago, before I became the Prince of Shadows, I completed them."

My breath hitched in my throat. "*You* completed the Trials of Glory? But that doesn't make any sense. Why? And how?"

He delicately placed both hands on my shoulders, over my cloak that was now damp from the melted ice. He picked at the loose strands of my hair that had escaped my messy braid. "I was young. Impressionable. Silas seemed like...he seemed like he wanted to take care of me. So I let him."

"And Silas made you do it?"

Mal met my eyes. I saw something deep, then, something animalistic. *Rage.*

"It was my only way of surviving. I was to complete the trials and then I would become the Prince of Shadows. The only non-Paragon member to ever attempt them and live. It was a death sentence."

I shook my head. "But you survived them? How, I mean? Why would Silas even want you to do that?"

"He saw how powerful I became. He knew I would never join him in the Paragon, not when my kingdom needed me. It was his way to eliminate the threat."

"Threat?" I repeated. "But he helped you. He saved you. He's the reason you stepped into your powers."

Malachi shook his head. "When Silas first approached me and offered me an escape from my father, I was more than happy to go with him. I had wanted nothing more than to get away from that foul bastard."

"What changed? What did Silas do?" I swallowed as I waited for an answer.

"He did exactly what he promised me he would do. He changed my life. Him and the rest of the Paragon taught me how to kill. How to harness my power in ways that I never knew possible. It took years before I could bring a man to his knees. Decades before I could use my power on my own will whenever I pleased. Silas was there the whole time, protecting me like I was his own son. Until he suggested the trials."

Malachi took a deep breath.

"He told me I could be just as strong as him. Just as powerful."

"If you passed the trials?"

"Yes. If I passed the trials."

"So you're telling me Silas passed the trials, too? And so did everyone else in the Paragon?"

Malachi turned around and pulled his own wet layers

off. His skin was damp and sculpted underneath. I tried not to stare.

Tried and failed.

He sat on the edge of the bed. I dropped my wet cloak on the floor and did the same.

"The trials aren't the same for everybody," he explained. "Silas and the Paragon members passed them, yes, but they won't be the same trials you have to pass, nor were they the same trials I passed. They're mind games, Jade. They get into your thoughts and create a brand new reality."

I swallowed. I wanted to ask him to explain more. I wanted to ask him exactly what he had to do in his trials, exactly what was so traumatizing for him to be back here. But I didn't. I could see how difficult this conversation was for him already. He would tell me on his own time. When he was ready.

"Who decides that?" I asked. "Who decides what the trials are?"

"Silas. Silas decides."

The hair on my arms stood up. "Well," I stuttered. "That hardly seems fair."

"It's not fair at all. Each member passes three trials—one of the past, one of the present, and one of the future."

"Past, present and future? What's that supposed to mean?"

"It means something different for everyone. The trials are laced with magic from the ancient witches. Magic and power from hundreds of witches and fae that lived before us come together to create experiences that—" His voice cracked.

I gripped his bare arm. "You don't have to tell me now," I said. "We can rest, and you can tell me all about it this week."

His nostrils flared, but he wrapped his strong arms around me and pulled me onto his lap in one swift motion, burying his head into me. "We'll get through this," he whispered. "I promise you, we'll get through this. I won't let him hurt you."

I hugged him back. Malachi's arms had become my only home lately, after losing Tessa, after everything in Rewyth. "I know you won't," I said back.

We sat there for a while, holding each other. I silently thanked the Saints that Malachi had come with me on this journey. He had an entire kingdom at home, a kingdom that had just been through a battle, and here he was.

With me.

I wrapped my arms tighter around his broad shoulders. His hands slid up my back, keeping me sitting firmly on his lap. I could have stayed there for hours.

"Do you want to head to the baths before we sleep?" he eventually asked.

"As much as I would love bathing with you in the middle of this underground temple," I joked, "I think we both need as much sleep as we can get. Especially you. We'll worry about cleanliness tomorrow."

"Sleep," he repeated. "I don't deserve sleep. My men died in battle. I left them to take care of themselves after an attack."

"Shhhh," I whispered, pulling him with me to lie back

on the clean bed. "Don't worry about any of that," I said. "Serefin and your brothers will deal with it all."

"I couldn't leave you," he said. "I couldn't let him take you. I couldn't live with myself if I didn't know what had happened, especially if—"

"I know," I interrupted. I rested my head on his chest, listening to his rapid heartbeat. "I know."

His hand fell onto the back of my head, as if ensuring I was really there. Mal hadn't slept in days. I had no idea how he was still functioning, but I *did* know he needed sleep. How this place of nightmares would grant him as much as an ounce of peace, I wasn't sure. But at least we were in the stone underground of the mountains and not on the exposed cliff side. Our enemies were known, and they were calling a ceasefire for now.

For now.

"Goodnight, my queen," he breathed. I listened to his heart rate until the beats slowed, until mine matched his, and until the warmth of his body pulled me into a deep, dreamless sleep.

CHAPTER 5
Malachi

I didn't want to wake her up. I wanted her to stay in her peaceful sleep, ignorant of the chaos she would endure while in the presence of the Paragon. The chaos we would both endure.

It was hard, explaining what had happened. How could I possibly make her understand? I couldn't tell her that Silas would discover her weaknesses, bit by bit, and expose them. Torture her with them.

The trials would be her own personal nightmare.

Yes, I was seen as a threat to Silas.

But in Silas's eyes, Jade was a threat to the whole world.

She stirred in my arms. "Rise and shine," I whispered. She mumbled something, still half-asleep, and nuzzled herself into my chest. I could have stayed right there forever, knowing Jade was safe in my arms.

Last night was the only night I had managed to get an ounce of sleep, although I couldn't stop my dreams from wandering to my past. To those trials. To Silas.

It was easy to brush the memories away when I was awake with Jade. *She* became my focus, not the past. Those things didn't matter. All that I cared about now was keeping her safe. And if I had to put my past behind me in order to do that, I would.

I could be civil with Silas.

Even though he brought war to Rewyth.

Even though he threatened Jade.

Who was I kidding? His very presence threatened Jade. He might have held a noble stance to anyone else, but to me? I could see right through it.

He was a scheming, vindictive, power-hungry monster.

But I was a monster, too. I wasn't the young boy he had trained all those decades ago. I was the King of Shadows.

He wasn't going to touch what was mine. Not again.

"We should eat something," I said.

"No," Jade grunted, tightening her arms around my bare waist. "We should stay here. Just like this. Forever."

I held her chin and tilted her face to meet mine. "You need your strength. You haven't eaten a solid meal in days." Whatever argument she was thinking of slowly dissipated in her deep brown eyes. "Just imagine a bowl of steaming hot stew waiting for you."

She moaned, and I had to fight the urge to shut her up with a kiss. "Fine," she said. "What are the odds that nobody else is awake, and we'll be the only people in this entire temple eating?"

"Hmmm." I ran a thumb across her cheek. "I'd say those odds are pretty low. But if you don't feel like talking to anyone, let me know. I'll be your personal bodyguard."

"Personal bodyguard?" She smiled, and for a split second of time I forgot where we were and what we were about to endure. "That sounds enticing."

"I think I've been your personal bodyguard since the day we got married."

"Before that, even."

I smiled. The memory of Jade, all that time ago, fighting off a pack of wolves with nothing but a knife played clearly in my mind. "Yes, even before that."

Jade pushed herself off of me and stepped out of the bed. "I do, however, believe you and I both smell. Badly."

I jumped from the bed behind her and wrapped my arms around her waist. "You smell of cinnamon, it's delicious and intoxicating and torturous as always."

Jade gripped my arms and pulled them tighter around her, pressing her back into the front of my bare chest. "Is that so?" she teased.

I pulled her black hair away from her neck and kissed the skin there, slowly dragging my mouth up to her jaw. She leaned further into my chest, and I couldn't help the possessive growl that came from me.

"Breakfast," I muttered. "Breakfast, or I'm afraid I'll throw you back into that bed and never let you leave."

"Don't tempt me," Jade replied.

I only released her from my arms when she reached for the clean black clothes on the table and began dressing herself. I did the same, swallowing the memories that came with the dark linens. A few moments later, Jade was fully dressed and stepping into the tunneled hallway. I followed.

The temple was almost exactly as I remembered it, only now, it buzzed with hundreds of residents.

I couldn't tell if they were all Paragon members, but I didn't doubt for a second that each person under this mountain held great power. Normal fae, witches, or human did not live here.

"I hope you know where we are," Jade whispered. Even with her voice lowered, her words created an eerie echo against the dewy walls. "This place is a maze."

But I had memorized these tunnels from the inside out. I knew every twist in the darkness, and could find my way back from the depths of the underground no matter where we were. "This way," I said.

We walked for a few seconds before a cloaked figure stepped into the tunnel ahead, staring directly at us.

I clenched my jaw and kept walking. There was no way I was going to let someone mess with Jade on her first day here. She at least deserved the *respect* of the Paragon members.

It wasn't until I got closer that I recognized the jutted hip and the long, sharp fingernails.

I remembered this woman from my time here decades ago. The way she casually leaned against the stone tunnel wall only confirmed my suspicions. *Cordelia.*

"What do you want?" I asked. I attempted to brush past her, but she side-stepped me and blocked our path.

She reached up and pulled back her hood, just as dramatic as she was back then. She looked at me and smiled, but it was more of an amused smile and less of a happy one.

I didn't smile back, especially not as she slid her gaze over my shoulder to Jade, who still held tightly onto my hand.

I flared my wings, blocking Cordelia's view.

"Relax," Cordelia said, trailing out the end of the word to a low hum. Just like all those years ago, she had a voice that could slice flesh. "I only wanted to meet our special guest before all the fun began."

"Who is this?" Jade asked from behind me.

Saints. We were actually doing this.

I tucked my wings back behind my shoulders slowly, allowing Jade to look at Cordelia again. Cordelia wasn't stupid. She wouldn't try to hurt Jade right in front of me.

At least, I hoped not. But time in the Paragon was not kind. I may have known Cordelia back then, but I wasn't so sure anymore.

"I'm the one who will be training you this week," Cordelia said, reaching a hand out to Jade. Jade shook it with confidence, meeting the woman's sharp stare without a second of hesitation.

Good girl.

"If you don't mind," I interrupted, "we're in the middle of something here."

This time when I pushed past Cordelia, she let us through. I didn't miss the way her eyes scanned Jade as we passed, her dark eyebrow raised with intrigue.

There was no way I would be leaving Jade alone with her for training.

"You know her?" Jade whispered as soon as we were far enough away.

I grunted. "Something like that. We worked together

for Silas when I lived here. She's powerful, I'll give her that. But keep your guard up around her until we know where her loyalties lie."

Jade nodded in agreement and didn't ask any more questions. I was grateful for that. In time, I would explain it all. The people, the trials. Jade deserved to know what had happened to me under this mountain.

But not now.

With her hand tight in mine, we walked to the dining room.

For being beneath a snow-covered mountain, the underground was uncomfortably warm. Even in my clean black trousers and linen tunic, my forehead grew damp with sweat.

Jade walked with an uncomfortable silence. She held her chin high, though. Not once dropping it. Not once looking away. Even as we weaved through the underground maze and eventually arrived at the dining hall.

And no, we were not the only ones there.

A dozen rectangular slabs of wood littered the room, glistening slightly under the golden chandeliers of low-burning fire.

Jade stalled, and I fought the urge to reach out and grab her hand. But she needed to show them she was strong. Independent. She didn't need me to protect her.

She could do that on her own.

"I hope you slept well," Silas stepped into view on our left, dressed in a brand new black robe that covered even the tips of his fingers.

"Good enough," I replied.

Silas held my stare for a second too long before sliding his snake eyes over to Jade. She stilled. "When do I find out what my trials are?" she asked.

The bastard had the audacity to laugh at her. My power became a caged animal inside my body, begging to be let out.

"You'll find out soon enough," he said.

"Why don't you stop with the riddles and tell her? She's here, isn't she? This is what you asked for."

"She's here because she is the peacemaker, Malachi. Not because I asked for her to come. The Saints require this."

The tiny, unsealed crack in his exterior began to shine with anger.

"She came here to complete the trials like you requested," I reminded him. "The sooner we get this over with, the sooner we can all go home."

Silas's smile fell. "Eat," he said. "I'll explain over breakfast."

Jade and I followed him through the room of lingering eyes and found ourselves at a table with Esther.

"You have a habit of showing up places," Jade said as she slid onto the stone bench next to Esther.

Esther smiled. "I'm always where I need to be, child. Always."

"If I'm completing the trials, don't you think it's time to stop calling me child?" Jade asked.

"Hundreds of years ago, I might have considered it," Esther replied.

Silas and I slid onto the bench on the opposite side of the stone table. "What's changed?" I asked. Esther's eyes widened when I talked, like she was surprised I was speaking to her at all. I didn't blame her, though. I was surprised by it myself.

"Life changed. Enemies happened. You two think you have problems now, but I've lived through worse."

"You've lived through worse than the peacemaker? Than your own son being threatened?" Jade asked.

"Yes," she answered without hesitating. "I have."

A woman dressed in the same black robe brought more food to our table, setting it in front of Jade and I. I waited for her to take a bite before I even glanced at my own. She was too skinny. Too weak. She needed her strength if she was going to have any chance at surviving the trials.

A chance. Flashing, violent memories of my own trials came crashing to the surface. They had been doing that, lately. Too often.

And I couldn't push them all away. Not anymore. Not when I was here, back in this dungeon. Back in this prison.

"One week," Silas started. "One week until your first trial. Today you'll be able to rest, explore the temple–"

"I don't want to explore the temple," Jade interrupted. I was the only one who noticed the way Silas's grip tightened on his fork. "I want to prepare for my trials. And that's awfully hard to do when I don't know what they are." Silas didn't reply. Jade pushed on. "Malachi tells me you design them."

Silas looked down at his food while he answered. "I don't design them," he said. "The Saints design them. I am a mere vessel of their wishes."

I could have laughed at those ridiculous words.

"A vessel? Are you trying to tell me the Saints speak to you?" Jade asked.

"Yes," Silas met her deadly stare from across the table. "That's exactly what I'm telling you."

It was just like him to come up with such an absurd lie, nobody would question it. But I knew the truth. The Saints did *not* speak to Silas. Saints were not that cruel.

Still, I bit my tongue and attempted to keep a straight face.

Jade scoffed. "And you cannot tell me what the Saints have planned for me one week from today?"

"That's what we'll be learning over the next week, Jade Weyland."

Jade picked at a piece of her food with the fork before setting it down and running her hands down her thighs. "I did not ask to be the peacemaker, Silas. Do you understand that?"

He cocked his head to the side, looking at her with curious eyes. "I understand just fine."

"Then you also understand that I have absolutely no idea what I'm doing here, or what completing these damn trials is going to prove."

"Well," Silas began, "the trials have been around for centuries. Designed by the Saints, they are a way to determine the gifted over the non-gifted or the average-gifted."

"Average-gifted?" Jade rolled her eyes. "You're kidding."

"I'm not kidding in the slightest."

"You mean it's up to you and the Saints—who speak to you—to determine who is powerful enough to survive the trials?"

"Like I said, Jade, the Saints speak to me. I am merely a vessel. They tell me what each opponent's weaknesses are, and what they must overcome to become closer to the Saints."

"Closer to the Saints?"

It was Silas's turn to set down his fork. "We have much to learn this week, Jade. You know very little about the Saints, about their origin and about where they come from. You must learn these things. Malachi can teach you some, I have tutors in the library that can teach you the rest."

"What will a history lesson do to help me survive?"

Silas leaned in over the table. I did the same, making sure he knew to keep his distance. He was already too close to her. "The Saints have gifted you, child. Just like they have gifted us all."

"Some gift," I muttered.

Silas retreated to his seat. "Your husband is a skeptic. He denies his connection to the Saints. It is a pure gift, you know. Even a gift that kills. Even one so deadly. It is pure, gifted from the most powerful. The most good."

I clenched my fists to stop from shifting in my seat. I wasn't going to show him any weakness, any discomfort.

Of course, I had heard this speech hundreds of times. The speech that I was special, that I was somehow chosen by the Saints.

It made no sense. I didn't believe it for a second. If I was so special, why did the Saints make me a killer?

I was not special. My black wings meant nothing. My wicked power meant nothing.

Jade, however, had a gift. She had something more than

a deadly talent. She was a force so powerful, I had a feeling we were only beginning to see what she was truly capable of.

"Your power is magnificent," Esther interrupted, saying what I had been thinking. "You must learn to wield it properly if you are going to be the peacemaker."

"Not this again," Jade muttered.

"And what exactly are you doing here?" I asked Esther. "Or did you simply ride along to get a front row seat to what you've been trying to do all along—kill Jade?"

She tossed her head back and laughed. "If I wanted your precious wife dead, son, I wouldn't have brought her back from the depths of death. Or did you already forget that part?"

I didn't answer. I couldn't. I was beginning to miss the days when I thought Esther might be dead, when I believed my father had been holding her hostage. Life was easier back then; when I didn't have to decide on any new day whether or not I could trust my own mother.

Jade's leg brushed against mine under the table. It was enough to snap me out of my own spiraling thoughts.

When I looked at her, she wore a tiny grin. One that sliced through the growing hatred in my heart and actually made me want to smile back.

"Well," Jade announced to the table. "I can't say this breakfast has been enjoyable, but I smell. If you'll excuse us, I believe Malachi and I will go wash up."

"Meet me in the study this evening," Silas replied as Jade and I both stood. "We'll have your first round of trial preparations then."

"Where is the study?" Jade asked.

"Your husband can show you."

He turned back to his breakfast and resumed eating, obviously done with the conversation. Jade turned on her heel and began walking out. I followed tightly behind her.

Yes, I could show her where the study was. I could show her where anything in this damned temple was. She knew that. But Silas wanted to make sure I wouldn't forget my time here. He wanted me to suffer during these trials just as badly as Jade suffered.

"Has he always been such an arrogant asshole?" Jade whispered once we were out of the dining hall.

"Fae ears," I reminded her. "He can still hear you."

"Good. I hope he heard that. Is he even a real fae?" Our footsteps echoed again through the underground tunnels as we continued back the way we came.

"Unfortunately, yes, he is. All that shit about him being a vessel for the Saints, though, I'm not too sure about."

Jade scoffed. "I can't imagine the Saints choosing someone so arrogant to speak through. And I certainly can't imagine what the Saints want from me."

"Yeah," I agreed. "That seems to be the big mystery."

"And if the Saints really do speak through Silas, wouldn't they know what type of power they gave me? Why do I have to complete the trials to prove I am who they made me?"

The dull ache in my head began shooting pain down my temples. Jade was right to be suspicious. I had been thinking the same things now for decades. "I don't know."

"Whatever," Jade mumbled. "I guess there's not much

we can do about it. I have to pass these trials to survive, whether Silas is full of shit or not."

We made it to our room before Jade turned around and met my eyes. "You're coming with me, right?"

"To where?"

"The baths. I don't want to be alone here. I don't trust any of them."

I reached out and tucked a piece of her black hair behind her ear. She leaned into my touch, just enough to make me want to push her back into the bedroom.

"Of course I'll come with you," I answered. "I'm not leaving your side."

"Good," she smiled.

I decided then that I would give anything to keep Jade safe. I would do whatever it took. Jade was my wife, and I loved her so fiercely, the thought of ever losing her again was something I could not bear to think about.

I followed Jade toward the baths, stalking behind her. I was her bodyguard, her husband, her protector. I didn't care who tried to hurt her.

I would save her at all costs.

CHAPTER 6
Jade

Inside the Paragon's temple and surrounded by my enemies, all of my senses locked on Malachi following behind me.

Following me to the baths.

Being intimate with Malachi hadn't exactly been on my radar. Though I knew the one night we spent together was special to us both, we never had time to discuss it. War loomed over our heads.

But here, in the underground tunnels of the mountains, I felt connected to him. I had felt connected to him throughout the long journey here, actually. I wasn't sure if it was because he was the only one I trusted, or because he had been the one holding me when I came back from that darkness. Either way, I felt much closer to him than ever before.

And it wasn't just my magic.

I hadn't told Malachi, but my magic felt different. It felt new, almost as if it had been refreshed. Before, I couldn't feel my power. Not in the slightest. It had been hard enough for me to use it when it was absolutely necessary.

But now, every ounce of my being was aware of that ball of power sitting inside my chest. I could feel the source like a ball of light summoning energy with every breath.

I wondered if Malachi could feel it. Our powers were connected, anyway. That's what Esther had told us.

Could he feel how strong I had become? How different I was now?

The young, innocent version of me had died when that sword pierced my body. I was new. Stronger. I didn't feel like a frail human, I didn't feel afraid.

I felt, for once in this entire life, like I had a chance.

At least, that's what I had to tell myself if I wanted to survive. There was no room for weakness. Not anymore.

"To the right," Malachi directed from behind me. His voice was low, barely over a whisper. I heard the same emotion that I was feeling, that heat-filled longing that we had both felt for days now.

"It's dark," I replied.

Malachi stepped forward and placed a hand on my lower back to guide me. I had been spending so much time with him, it was easy to forget how advanced his senses were. How advanced all of the fae senses were, actually.

"This way," he said. "They keep the baths dark, but your eyes will adjust after a few minutes."

"How do they even get water down here?" I asked.

"It's run-off water from the mountain. Originally, there was a natural stream that ran right through these parts. With a little manipulation, they were able to create dozens of natural bathing spots. Enough to give privacy, but it's completely natural."

"Everyone shares the same bath?"

"You won't be able to tell. This way."

Malachi didn't move the hand from my back as he led me through the shrinking underground tunnels. After another minute of walking, I began to hear the faint trickle of water running against rock.

And soon, the glistening surface of the water came into view. My eyes adjusted, just like Malachi said they would, and I could see at least a few feet in front of me.

"Are we the only ones here?"

Malachi nodded. "For now. There's a more secluded bay around that bend." I followed his instruction once more, leading us to a quiet pool of water that slowly spilled over the rocks below us.

As we got closer to the water, I could feel a tiny bit of steam rising from the surface. "How is this hot?" I asked. "Isn't the mountain water freezing?"

"Us fae and our magic," he teased.

If the Paragon was using their power to heat the water for baths, I wasn't going to complain.

I gripped the edge of my black tunic before I realized Mal watched me.

"Turn around," I said. I could hardly see Malachi's face, but I could feel his eyes on me all the same. Lingering, dripping in that same heat of an expression I had seen before.

"Whatever you say, my queen," he replied. *Always with the voice of a king.*

I waited until he was fully turned around before I peeled off my clothes.

Malachi wouldn't turn around. Not until I asked him to, anyway. And these days, it was getting harder and harder to keep my distance.

After I dropped all of my clothes into a pile, I stepped closer to the water. The bath was inviting, and somehow held the slightest scent of mint.

I dipped my toes in first, feeling for the smooth yet rocky surface below.

And then I sank my entire body in.

I couldn't help the sound of relief that came from me as I submerged my shoulders and relaxed into the heat.

"You better not continue to make sounds like that," Malachi growled. "Not while I'm standing over here."

"You can turn around now," I said, ignoring his comment and the hunger that laced each word.

He did as I said, and I watched the reflection of his eyes as he scanned the pile of my clothes and then slid his attention over to me.

He froze completely. I could see him taking heavy breaths, his chest rising and falling.

"I'll wait out here," Malachi said.

"Don't be ridiculous," I argued. "You're my husband. I think we can both bathe at the same time."

"You believe me to be stronger than I am," he replied, and the sound of his words sent a chill down my body.

"Get in here," I said with more finality in my voice.

He laughed quietly. "Yes, my wife." He replied with a

wicked grin. Again, I couldn't see his face, but I could hear it in his voice.

I heard the sounds of him slipping his clothes off, dropping them on the ground.

And then I heard the sounds—torturous and slow—of Malachi dipping into the water next to me. Both of our breaths became audible then, as if we were back outside climbing that damned mountain.

I leaned my head back against the stone ledge. Malachi moved closer to me until his arm brushed against mine.

"Jade," he half-whispered, half-growled.

"Yes?" I replied, just as breathless.

His fingers came to my arm, brushing the skin beneath the water. He trailed his delicate touch from my wrist all the way to my shoulder, gently moving across my collarbone. I gripped his arm, splashing in the quiet stream.

"We should probably talk about the trials," he whispered. I pulled onto his arm, but that only resulted in me pulling myself closer to him. My thigh became flush against his.

"Probably," I replied.

"We should talk about a lot of things, actually," he said. His lips were close to mine, plump and firm.

"We really should."

The silence between us filled with our breath and the echo of the water. Mal's eyes scanned my face, lingering over each feature as if he were looking at me for the first time.

"Or," Mal said, "I could kiss you." My heart pounded against my chest. The heat that filled my stomach was a wicked, torturous mixture of my magic and my need for Malachi.

I swallowed. Malachi had a way of bringing this side out of me, the side that still lit up at his every word. He always had that effect on me.

"Kiss me," I demanded.

Malachi obeyed. In one swift motion, he hooked an arm around my waist and hauled me onto his lap. He held me tightly to him and his mouth found mine in the darkness of the baths.

I fit perfectly into his lap, and I tried not to think about how exposed I was; how naked we both were. Malachi kept his hands on my waist, though, until he wrapped them around my back and pressed me deeper against his chest.

"I've missed you," Malachi mumbled in between kisses.

"We've been together for days," I reminded him.

"I've missed touching you, kissing you. A woman like you deserves to be kissed."

He kissed me again. I didn't stop him. His hands moved back and forth from my back, my hair, my waist.

Malachi was my husband. He was my everything. At this point, he was all I had left.

"Someone could come in here," I said after I realized what we were doing.

Malachi replied by pulling my mouth back to his and running his tongue against my lower lip.

His wings splayed around us, adding to the darkness of the shadowed water. It was as if the entire place had vacated just for us, our secret hideout in the depths of this hidden temple.

Malachi kept kissing me, kept holding onto me like his lifeline. I did the same. My body was flush against his, but neither of us cared about hiding our bodies anymore. Not from each other.

Malachi was mine, and I was his.

"I want you," I whispered before I could process the words.

Malachi growled a low sound of approval, his sharp teeth moving to nibble on the delicate, exposed skin of my neck. Between the chilled mountain air and the steam of the hot water, my body erupted in sensations that sent goosebumps down every inch of my skin.

He seemed to notice this, too.

"I want to be the reason every inch of your skin raises in goosebumps," he muttered, "but I'm afraid we have company."

Just as he finished the words, footsteps echoed down the dark tunnels. I scrambled to climb off of Malachi's lap, although I wasn't sure why. He was my husband. I didn't care in the slightest what anyone in this damned temple thought of me.

And Mal's wings still splayed widely around him, also protecting me from any peering eyes. Although we were already hidden from view by sneaking around the corner of the bathing house.

I sank back into the warm water, somehow still feeling the chill of where Malachi's body had been.

"Don't worry," Malachi said. He was still sitting close enough that I could nearly feel the vibrations of his voice when he spoke. "Nobody will touch you. Nobody will even approach you, not when I'm here."

More questions began spiraling in my mind. Who was this man that I had married? I mean, I knew who he was. Deep down, Malachi had a kind heart and a protective soul. He had been hurt by more people than I could count. He had killed. Some deserved it. Some didn't. And above all, he was willing to risk every single person in this world to save me.

Did that make him a good guy?

I wasn't sure. But that did make him my...my something. My protector, my husband.

My king.

To everyone else, maybe he was bad. Maybe he was the killer, the enemy. From talking to Silas, he seemed to be the one that escaped the tight, sharp grasp of the Paragon.

But they didn't see him the same way I did. Malachi had reasons for hurting people. He had reasons for everything he did in his life.

"Tell me what you're thinking," he whispered. Splashing in the distance told me our visitor had just arrived to bathe themselves. They wouldn't be bothering us.

But I still couldn't resist glancing around at the tunnels every few seconds.

"I'm thinking I don't know that much about you," I half-lied.

Malachi smiled. "I prefer remaining a mystery."

"I'm serious," I said. "You know everything about me. You might even know more about me than I know about myself. But you? You have an entire past. You have lives that

I've never even heard about. I mean, who were you when you lived here with Silas? Who is the Malachi that these fae know?"

His smile flickered before it disappeared entirely. It pained me to take away that gorgeous, tempting smile, but I needed to know the truth.

"I told you," he started. "I came to the temple as a lost boy looking for a way out. I left the temple a killer."

"But what does that mean?" I pushed. "Did Silas make you kill?"

An uneven breath escaped him. "Yes."

"Who?" I tried to keep my voice soft. "Who did you kill when you lived here?"

His brows drew together, and I could imagine his mind rebuilding the massive stone wall, piece by piece.

"Don't do that," I interrupted.

"Do what?"

I pushed myself over to him and placed both hands on the sides of his face. "Don't lock yourself away like that. Don't shut me out. I'm right here, Malachi, and I love you. We need to lean on each other if we're going to make it through this. Please, talk to me."

He stared at me unblinking for what felt like a century. "I had killed many people before Silas came for me," he said. The pain in his voice instantly weighed me down, holding me close to him.

"Because of your father?" I asked. I barely remembered the stories now, but I did remember Malachi telling me his father used him as a weapon. Time and time again, Malachi was the one killer for Rewyth.

"Not when I was younger," he explained. "When I was younger, it happened to be a consequence of my temperament. I was hot headed back then."

"Now that, I believe," I said. My poor attempt to lighten the mood only barely worked. Mal's smile was a quick one.

"My father had been quick to cover it up before. He always had some sort of looming excuse as to why another soldier was dead. He never blamed me. Not in front of the others, anyway. Silas was the one who made me face what I had done. He forced me to stare at myself in the mirror and see myself for what I truly was. A killer."

"You're not a killer, Mal."

"That's exactly what I am. Silas made sure of it. He taught me how to take down any enemy, any opponent. He trained me and created a weapon." Mal drew in a long, shaking breath before continuing. "He is the reason the Prince of Shadow was ever born."

CHAPTER 7
Malachi

I scanned the study, which was just as old and rustic as I remembered it to be. Aisles and aisles of books lined the dark room, and barely enough light for Jade's non-fae eyes to see lit up the table before her as she read.

I stood behind Jade, lurking in the shadows and giving her the space she needed. We had been there for hours now, but there was no chance that I would leave her alone, especially not with Silas sitting across the table. I fought to keep my mouth shut every time he broke the silence, adding to something she read.

Jade, to my surprise, did not make any snarky remarks as Silas explained each of the Saints and what they were capable of. Jade knew of the Saints, but there was no way she knew that much.

Nobody outside the Paragon knew that much.

Silas spoke of the five forces that once guarded the magic of this world. They were strong—the strongest to ever walk amongst us. They were not fae or witches, but something else entirely. Something pure, even if not all of them used that purity for good.

Anastasia, the Saint of life, was the most loved of the five Saints. She was caring and wise, the first Saint to be recognized for her mighty gift. She was known as the healer, the one to save lives and bring dying children back from the darkness. In many ways, she brought balance to the world of witches and fae.

Erebus was the most hated. Not at first, of course. He began as all other Saints did, by having a special gift. His gift, though, was not pure and helpful like Anastasia's. His power was terrifying and brutal. He wiped out armies. He flattened kingdoms. With the gift of death, Erebus used the power of fear to subdue the witches and the fae who caused problems.

Phodulla, the Saint of air, could be temperamental at times, but she was nothing compared to the wrath of Erebus. Phodulla would conjure storms and winds that would shake any kingdom to their core. Where she walked, wind would follow. She was both a great asset and a mighty curse to her friends and enemies.

Detsyn was the Saint of love. Her compassion was one that balanced the power of the Saints. She was a guard in many ways, always making sure the other Saints used their power for good and not evil.

Rhesmus, the last of the five, was the Saint of war. Rhesmus did not crave chaos like Erebus, but he was just as fierce. Just as aggressive. Rhesmus would whisper into the minds of those on the verge of war, beckoning them for a fight. Beckoning them for blood. His mind-whispering abilities were ones that many of the other Saints envied.

Many of the humans only knew of the Saints as the world-saving individuals who protected them for so long. Being the most powerful creatures themselves, they were able to keep lands at peace. Fae, witches, humans. They lived together in harmony.

When the Saints decided to leave this world, after they began to lose control of the power of the world, they took most of the magic with them. It was the best for everyone at that time. To have magic running rampant would be detrimental to all species, not only humans. *It was for our own good.*

For decades, fae and witches had no magic.

Now, only a few gifted individuals could possess magic. Some say it was a gift from the Saints, a reminder of what once was. Either way, the Saints never returned.

Jade's eyes scanned page after page, drinking up this information until she slammed the book in front of her shut and cursed under her breath. "This isn't helping," Jade muttered.

Silas waited a few seconds before responding. "It's important that you know the history of the Saints."

"I know plenty about the Saints. What I need to know is how my power is supposed to make me the peacemaker. I need to know how to survive the trials, how I'll be tested. This is a waste of my time."

Again, Silas took a long breath. I was beginning to remember just how infuriating he could be, especially late nights in this library. Silas would push and push until Jade couldn't take it any more, until her eyes glazed over and she begged for sleep.

I clenched my fists. Being here brought back memories I wished to suppress forever.

Jade leaned back in her chair and crossed her arms.

"I told you, Jade," Silas started. "The Saints have chosen you for a reason. It is respectful, at the very least, to try and learn more about them. Learn about the ones who chose you for this destiny."

"Did Malachi? When he was here completing the trials, did he spend hours and hours memorizing useless information from books? Please enlighten me on how studying these pages made Malachi the Prince of Shadows."

I stiffened in the darkness.

"Malachi did as I instructed him," Silas barked. My power screamed under my skin, recognizing the threat in his words before they even reached my ears. I cursed under my breath as a small tendril of magic escaped my grasp.

"Careful, boy," Silas sneered, turning his attention to me in the back of the room. "We wouldn't want your bride getting hurt."

I scoffed. "Hurting Jade is not a concern for me."

Silas's eyes darkened and slid back over to Jade. "Is that so?"

Jade stared back at him, unanswering.

I quit caring entirely. We hadn't outright tried to keep it a secret, but Silas had been looking at Jade as if she were nothing but a useless human that happened to possess a singular ounce of magic. Magic he wasn't even helping her cultivate.

"My power doesn't hurt her," I said. "And hers doesn't hurt me, either."

"That's—" For the first time since I had ever known Silas, he looked genuinely surprised. His eyes widened as he looked at her again. "That's magnificent. Unheard of, actually. Malachi's power is so strong. How long have you known this, that you could not hurt each other?"

Silence filled the room. Water dripped somewhere in the distance.

Once.

Twice.

"I've suspected for a while, but we knew for sure a couple of weeks ago," I finally answered. "Esther helped us confirm it."

I recalled the way Esther practically threw our magic at each other, the way my heart stopped when I thought I had hurt her.

And the relief that flooded my entire damn body when I found out she couldn't be hurt. Not by me.

"You are immune to each other's powers." His eyes flickered frantically between Jade and I.

"Yes," I replied. "So, if you'd like to threaten Jade's safety, using my power against her will not work."

Jade stood from her chair. "I'm tired," she said. "If all you have in mind for me tonight is reading through ancient books, I can do that alone."

Silas didn't say anything. He continued staring at us in a way that made the hair on the back of my neck stand up. My wings flared out instinctively, but that only seemed to interest Silas more.

I turned to follow Jade out of the room when Silas added, "Do you know why your husband has black wings, peacemaker?"

Jade froze. So did I.

"He is the King of Shadows," she answered.

Silas laughed, dry and humorless. I stepped forward, inching closer to Jade.

"King of Shadows, yes. He is, indeed, that. But he had black wings before he was ever given the title of a king. Before he was ever given the title of a prince. He was born with these wings, with this mark. In a world full of silver-winged fae, his are black." Silas clicked his tongue.

The room grew so silent, I could hear Jade's rapid heartbeat. She was just as eager as I to hear what Silas had to say next, although I still couldn't trust a single thing that man said.

"Malachi Weyland, King of Shadows and ruler of Rewyth, has the blood of the Saints. One particular Saint was known for his black wings, a killer among fae and as ruthless as any of them. Can either of you tell me which Saint that is?"

"You're lying," I said. I moved my body to stand before Jade, blocking her from Silas's view. "My father was no Saint."

Silas laughed again. Each time he laughed, I grew more and more tempted to rip his vocal cords out of his throat. My power flared in my veins, wanting the violence just as badly as I.

"No, your father was no Saint. But you have the black wings of Erebus. You have a deadly gift, one that is unmatched amongst most fae." Silas shook his head. He stood from the wooden table slowly and walked closer to us, staring at me with wide, wondrous eyes.

My mind spun, sending my thoughts through tunnels of possibilities. Each one of them came up short. "It's not possible," I replied. "I would know if I were a descendent of a Saint, especially if that Saint were Erebus."

"Is it so absurd of a thought?" Silas asked. He looked at me now like he were seeing me for the first time. "To think that you might have the blood of a Saint pumping through your veins? It would explain so much, would it not? Your wings, your power. Your rare abilities."

"Erebus was not simply a Saint. He was a killer that nearly took over all humanity," I replied. I hated the way my voice shook. I hated that Silas had the ability to shake me.

"He was powerful," Silas explained. "He wielded a strong magic and he didn't care who got in his way. That sounds awfully familiar, doesn't it, peacemaker?"

I turned and looked at Jade, who just stared at me with wide eyes. I knew she was thinking it, too. If it were the truth, it would explain so much…

But my father had not a single ounce of magic. Esther was a witch. That was where my abilities came from. That was where my black wings came from.

Not from a Saint's blood.

Not from Erebus.

"If you're trying to distract us so that Jade is unsettled for the trials, it won't work," I stated.

"I'm not trying to distract anyone," he said. "I'm only piecing together what we have been seeing before our very eyes. Now you say that the peacemaker's power does not affect you. It makes sense."

"We don't have time for this," I argued. I grabbed Jade's hand and began pulling her out of the study. "When you want to be useful to Jade and help prepare her for the trials, come find us. We don't need you filling our minds with useless riddles."

Silas didn't stop us as we stormed out, although he was more than capable of doing so.

"What was that all about?" Jade whispered once we were alone in the tunnels.

"I have no clue," I answered honestly. "But I'm not going to sit around and pretend like I trust a single thing Silas says. I didn't trust him back then, and I don't trust him now. He's trying to get in our heads."

And it worked.

Jade tugged on my arm, forcing me to stop. Her eyes were rimmed with pink clouds and her face had grown pale with exhaustion. Even so, I was certain she looked much better than I did.

"Do you think it's possible?" she asked. "That you're a descendent of a Saint?"

With Silas out of sight, I could actually consider those words. *Was* it possible? I had been confused for so much of my childhood. I didn't understand why I was so different, why I was the one with the black wings.

Erebus had been famous for his black wings, of many things. But over the years of history, there had been many fae that wore the oddly-shaded wings. It was ridiculous to think each one of them were descendents of Erebus.

And my father's wings had been silver as day.

"Not entirely impossible," I answered. Jade's small hands lingered on my wrist. "It doesn't make any sense. Why would he bring this up now? I lived with that man for decades. He never mentioned the possibility of Erebus's bloodline."

Jade's brows drew together in concentration. "Maybe you're right," she replied. "Maybe this is all part of a distraction. To shake us up before the trials."

"Maybe. But why me? Why would he want to shake *me* up? You're the one going through the trials. He should be drilling you about your lineage if his goal is distraction."

She gave a weak smile, and it reminded me of our wedding day. She had been so brave then, too, standing alone in a kingdom of fae she didn't trust. She was just as brave now, with just as many people she did not trust.

"I think he was trying to bore me to death with those lessons," she whispered. The playful glint in her eye had returned, even if it only lingered for a few seconds. "It was about to work, honestly. He would not shut up about the Saints."

"Your magic is a gift from them," I said. "It wouldn't kill you to learn about who wants you to be so powerful."

She slid her arm around mine, tucking herself into my elbow. "Now you're sounding like Silas. We better get out of here before I really get bored to death. The Paragon wouldn't be happy if they didn't get their precious Trials of Glory."

I reveled in the warmth of her body next to mine. "I have a feeling the rest of the week will be anything but boring."

We made it back to the bedroom without running into any other Paragon members. I silently thanked the Saints for that. I couldn't handle pretending to be polite to anyone else.

I wanted to be alone. Truly alone. I wanted to grab Jade around the waist and fly her out of this temple, away from the Paragon and into the middle of an abandoned field where we could live without any threats.

Maybe one day I would.

"We need to get plenty of sleep," I said as soon as we were inside. "You'll train with the most powerful witches in the world tomorrow. You want to be ready."

I had turned to give Jade some privacy when her hands found themselves on my back. I flinched at first before relaxing into the warmth of her touch.

"I'll be ready," she breathed. Her breath tickled the back of my wings. Heat from her hands expanded, igniting every inch of my skin as she slid her hands under my tunic.

"Jade," I muttered. "We really should sleep."

Her hands slid around my bare waist, running over my torso as she stepped closer. "We should," she agreed.

I didn't stop her as she lifted her hands, taking my tunic along with it.

Leaving me shirtless in the darkness of our secluded, stone room.

I turned around to face my gorgeous, powerful wife. "There was a time when you were afraid to be in the same room with me," I reminded her.

A grin full of mischief flickered across her features. "I remember," she said. "You were deadly and intimidating and wickedly handsome."

"*Were*?" I repeated.

Her hands slid up my chest. I sucked in a breath of air. Her touch still had that effect on me, could still leave me breathless as if this were the first time she had ever laid eyes on me. She was that beautiful, that magnificent.

"I suppose I still find you wickedly handsome," she whispered. She leaned up on her toes and placed a hot kiss under my jaw.

"What about deadly and intimidating?"

Her finger slid up my chest to my collarbone, following the sharp line there.

"King of Shadows," she breathed, brushing her lips over where her finger had just lingered. "You are nothing if not deadly," she said. My stomach sank. "You bring each of our enemies to their knees," she breathed, kissing me again.

A predatory, feral instinct washed over me. In one second, I gripped Jade around the waist and flew us to the bed. She let out a surprised yelp, one that made the heat in my body grow hotter.

Jade was *mine*. She was my wife, my voice of reason. She was my lifeline. I was beginning to realize just how much of me belonged to her now, too. Just as she was mine, I was hers. I would do anything for her. Be anything for her. I would scour the ends of the world if it meant ensuring she was safe.

I wasn't losing her again. Ever.

"You could be the most powerful weapon any kingdom has ever seen," I said. My black wings splayed around us, creating a secret space where we could pretend we were alone. We could pretend we were anywhere else but these damned mountains.

"I'm no more powerful than you," she breathed.

"You are so much better than me, Jade. Your power is... it's something different. I can feel it. It belongs to you. It runs in your veins for you, as if it is loyal to you only."

The smile faded from her face as she searched my eyes with her own. Something sad lingered there, something dark and distant.

"What is it?" I asked.

"We could destroy them," she whispered. "We could destroy this entire mountain if we wanted to. We could end all of this."

I closed my eyes and rested my head against hers. "Our enemies will never stop," I reminded her. "They won't stop coming for you. They won't stop trying to take what runs inside your body."

Her brows drew together. "But why? Why me?"

"I don't know why it has to be you," I answered honestly. "But I'm glad it's you. I'm glad you're here with me, Jade."

Her hands found either side of my face and held me gently, forcing my eyes to meet hers. "I'm not going anywhere," she said. "We're in this together, now."

I knew that. I had known it for some time, now, that she would choose to stay with me. She was no longer entrapped. She was no longer forced to be my wife.

She stayed with me because somewhere deep inside of her, she wanted this, too.

She belonged with me.

I lowered my head and kissed her, slowly. Delicately. The blind lust that had pulsed through my body earlier was overtaken by love, by protectiveness. Jade was so much more than a weapon to me. She was so much more than the peacemaker.

She was mine. She had my heart.

And I didn't want it back.

I kissed her as long as she let me, until I forgot where we were. Until I forgot about Silas. Until I forgot about Erebus.

And I held her tightly in my arms as we both drifted to sleep.

Memories of my past trials morphed my dreams into nightmares.

A scream woke me up.

I was no longer in my bed next to Jade, though. I was in the middle of a forest, a forest that was littered with red trees and black dirt.

Where was I?

Not a single sound rustled the air around me. The silence

was so strong, I could hear my own heart beat growing louder and louder.

But I refused to give in to the panic. That was what panic always wanted; for me to give in.

I was the King of Shadows. I feared no one. I feared nothing.

"Who's out there?" I demanded.

No one replied.

I stood up, wearing nothing but my black trousers. The sun rose in the distance, and the red trees began to sparkle with something wet.

Something murderous.

It was blood, I realized, dripping from every tree in the forest. As if it had just been soaked in a fresh rain.

Blood covered every inch, every ounce of life.

My bare feet were stepping in it, too, as I took a few steps further into the forest.

And then I heard the scream again.

It was a boy's scream, one laced with pain and anguish.

I began running, filled with the need to find this person. They needed help. They needed my *help.*

I ran and ran, even as the bottoms of my feet were sliced open by the rocks on the floor of the forest.

I didn't stop. The boy screamed again, and again.

"Where are you?" I screamed.

"Help me, Malachi!" the boy yelled.

The voice morphed, turning from one voice of a boy to hundreds, echoing around the forest and into my brain like a storm of chaos.

I ran and I ran, and when I could not run any further, I took to the skies.

My wings beat against the stiff air. He was here. I was close. Someone needed my help.

Who was he? And why was I here? Why were we both here?

My eyes desperately scanned each of the treetops in the forest until I found a small opening, large enough that I could see a morphed figure lying below.

I tucked my wings and dove downward, only splaying my wings again right before I landed heavily on the forest floor.

One young boy stared up at me, tears in his eyes.

He had black, curly hair and his face was smeared with dirt. His clothes were ripped, his feet bare like mine.

And then, in the rising, glistening morning sun, I saw his wings. Those black, damned wings.

"Are you going to help me?" the boy asked.

I stared at him a second longer. "Who are you?"

The boy swallowed, but something inside of him seemed to change. He stood from his crouched position on the forest floor and he rolled his shoulders back.

"I," the boy stated, "am Malachi Weyland. Prince of Rewyth and heir to the fae throne."

My heart sank. No, this couldn't be happening. This couldn't be possible. Standing before me, with bloody hands and knees and wings black as night, was myself.

I staggered backward. There had to be some sort of explanation.

"What is it?" the boy—myself—asked. "Don't leave me,"

he pleaded. "I thought you were going to help me! Help me, please!"

"Why are you here?" I asked.

"I don't know," the boy cried. His shoulders sagged in utter defeat, sobs muffling his words. "I don't know why I'm here."

A sword appeared in my hand. I didn't remember carrying one.

"No," I said out loud, knowing what the world was trying to make me do. Nobody told me, but I felt it. I felt death approaching, urging me forward. I gripped the handle of the sword until my knuckles turned white. "I will not hurt him."

The sword grew heavier in my hand, along with the pressure to wield it. To act.

I would not hurt the boy. I would not—

My arms began to rise over my head, sword along with it. I wanted to scream. I wanted to tell the boy—myself—to run, to hide.

I was a danger to him. I was a danger to myself.

I couldn't stop my arms from lifting. I no longer controlled them.

At the very last second, the boy with big, dark eyes looked up at me.

We both screamed, the sound of it so cruel, so horrific, that all I could do was shut my eyes and give in to the darkness.

CHAPTER 8
Jade

"Hey," I shook Malachi's shoulders, but he had drifted deep into unconsciousness. His face twisted in fear and he woke me up with a half-cry. "Malachi, wake up!"

His eyes shot open, and he immediately flipped me over in the bed, covering my body with his with a predatory hand on my throat.

"Malachi," I squeaked through gritted teeth. "Mal, it's me. You were having a nightmare."

His eyes frantically searched my face before he realized who I was. He pulled his hand back as if he were gripping fire itself. "Jade, Saints, Jade I'm so sorry."

He scrambled off of me and pressed his back to the stone wall. His chest rose and fell as he panted, his forehead glistening with sweat.

"It's okay," I reassured him. "Everything's fine, I'm fine."

We spent the next few seconds staring at each other, not knowing what to say.

"That seemed like some nightmare," I offered after a few moments.

"Yeah," he breathed. "It was."

"Have you been having them often? Nightmares?"

He relaxed a touch but kept his distance in the room. His shoulders hung heavily around his body. "No," he said. "I haven't had a nightmare in years."

I pulled my knees up to my chest. "Well, do you want to talk about it?"

"It was nothing," he answered. I watched as he ran his hands through his thick head of wild curls, something he usually did when he felt nervous. "It must be our time here that's bringing back old memories. It was just a stupid dream. Nothing to worry about. Go back to sleep."

I waited for him to say more. Instead, he said nothing.

"Are you sure?" I asked. My chest tightened at the way his jaw flexed. Malachi was many, many things. But fearful?

He finally stepped forward and slid back into bed, but he kept his distance. Even as he leaned in and pressed a cold kiss to my forehead. "I'm sure. Sleep."

I tried to fight it, but exhaustion overtook my body. Malachi was still awake when I drifted off into the darkness once more.

The next morning, we met with Esther for more magic training.

"Good to see you again," I said to Esther. Our encounters had been nothing but awkward since she managed to save my life in Rewyth. The few encounters we had consisted of hushed tones and hidden messages.

Malachi could barely look at her. Esther kept her distance. I didn't blame her. We all had too much on our minds. With the Paragon and the Trials of Glory, bigger issues were at stake.

"You as well, child," she said. Cordelia pushed herself off the stone wall behind Esther, finally acknowledging our presence in the training room.

"Jade," Cordelia said. She reached her hand out to shake mine. She had beautiful dark skin and braided black hair, and she stared at me with a rebellious, hungry tint in her eye. The same tint that Sadie used to have. "I'm Cordelia. It's a pleasure to formally meet you."

I accepted her hand again, similar to the last time we met. Her long, bright red fingernail claws scratched my skin as she shook it.

Many people had attempted to intimidate me in my life. My father, the fae king, Malachi's brothers. I wasn't sure exactly when, but somewhere over the last few months, I quit backing down so easily.

If Cordelia wanted me to be afraid of her, she would have to give a reason.

"We have a lot to get done today," Cordelia said. "We might as well get started."

"I'll be back in a few hours," Malachi said from behind me. We hadn't spoken since his nightmare last night, and he hardly looked into my eyes when we woke up in the morning.

I didn't push him. I could see the storm brewing behind Mal's eyes. If space was what he needed, I understood that. Even if it caused my chest to tighten.

"You're not going anywhere," Cordelia argued. "Esther tells me your magic is attached to Jade's. We need you here to learn the full abilities of her power."

"You're kidding," Malachi replied. I physically flinched at the harshness of his voice, even though I knew it wasn't directed at me.

"I'm very serious," Cordelia said. She stepped forward. She had a style that reminded me so much of Sadie; dark and different. Like she didn't care what anyone in the world thought of her. I instantly felt a wave of regret for my old friend.

And I prayed to the Saints that she was okay on her own out there.

"Let's just get this over with," I interrupted, refocusing my thoughts. I heard Malachi breathe behind me, but I didn't turn to look.

We had arrived in a small room of the underground tunnels near the baths. A stream ran through the ground on the other side of the room, filling the space with the echo of the trickling water.

"We can start with the basics," Cordelia stated. Esther followed behind her.

"Okay," I agreed. "What are the basics?"

Cordelia stopped and looked at me with a straight face. "Summon your power."

"You—" I glanced at Esther, but she stared back at me with a blank face. "You want me to summon it here?"

"Yes."

"And what if I lose control? What if I blow up this entire mountain?"

"Then you won't have to compete in the Trials of Glory, and it'll be your lucky day. Come on. Let's see what we're working with here, peacemaker."

I could feel Malachi behind me then, I could feel his temper. My power responded to his, as hidden as it might have been.

Yes, I was afraid to use my power. I had used it in Rewyth and it almost cost me everything.

"You have no reason to be afraid," Cordelia added. I snapped my attention to her. "What happened in Rewyth won't happen here. You're safe with us."

Yeah right, I thought. *Like she knew anything about what happened in Rewyth.*

"I know more than you think," Cordelia said. When I met her gaze, she stared at me with a grim smile.

"Are you reading my thoughts?" I hissed.

"I can infiltrate whatever I'd like," Cordelia replied. "You're in my temple now. I only read your thoughts so I can help you. When I know what you're afraid of, I can help you overcome it."

"Get out of my head!" I yelled.

Cordelia took a step forward. Even with her flat shoes, she towered over me. It was a power move, a step of dominance.

"Watch it." Malachi growled a warning at Cordelia from behind me.

"Stand down, boy. Show me your power, peacemaker."

Wild emotion and a small, cascading feeling of helplessness washed over me. It was enough to remind me that I hated feeling helpless. Feeling trapped.

And I didn't have to feel that way. Not anymore.

I held my hands out in front of me. "Come on, Jade," I whispered to myself. "You can do this."

Cordelia flashed before my eyes. She moved from standing across the stone room to standing directly in front of me. She gripped my biceps, her claw-like nails digging into my skin.

I screamed—half from the pain, and half from the surprise.

"I said show me," she demanded through gritted teeth.

I shoved her backward, but she hardly budged.

Malachi moved behind me. He descended on us in an instant, grabbing Cordelia by the back of the neck. "Let go of her," he growled.

She only smiled, flashing her perfect white teeth. "Very protective," she sneered. "That's cute."

Cordelia released her grip on me and used both hands to shove Malachi backward. I didn't think for a second that she would be strong enough to move him, but he stumbled back, catching himself on the wall.

"Enough of this fighting," Esther sneered. "We have actual work to do here. We're wasting precious time."

Cordelia flipped her black braids over her shoulder. "That's right," she announced. "Where were we...oh yes. Jade was just about to show us her lovely, peace-making power."

"What are you?" I whispered. I hadn't realized I said the words out loud until all three pairs of eyes glued to me. "I mean...are you a witch? How are you that strong? How are you reading my mind?"

Cordelia smiled, but it was not a smile of delight. It was one laced with malice, one laced with pity. "Oh, darling," she started. "I am half witch, yes. But I am also half fae."

"Witch and fae? But I thought Malachi was the only–"

"You've been told a lot of things, it seems," Cordelia interrupted.

I stood there, speechless, like a blindsided idiot. How was I supposed to know what was and was not the truth? Malachi had told me that his heritage—being half fae and half witch—was unheard of. Witches could rarely get pregnant, which meant they rarely had children—much less children with fae, who had spent decades being their enemies.

"I am not your enemy," Cordelia said, clearly reading my thoughts again. Saints, that was getting annoying. "But many of your enemies *are* here. Believe me, you are powerful. I can see it already. You have something great and strong running in your veins, just as your husband does. But you will never discover it if you are not pushed to the limits. If you are not forced beyond your breaking point.

Although…" She stepped forward and reached her hand out.

I flinched away instinctively, and Malachi's power rumbled a warning once again.

Cordelia seemed to ignore all of this. She pushed forward again and gripped my chin tightly, forcing me to look into her eyes. "It seems as though you were already pushed pretty close. Your sister died." I tried to rip my chin from her grip, but it was no use. "And so did you."

"Let go of me," I sneered. "You don't know anything."

To my surprise, she did let go of me. She turned around and faced Esther. "You risked a lot by bringing her back." Her tone hinted at an accusation.

Esther lifted her chin, and I noticed the way she stole a glance at Malachi.

"What is she talking about?" Malachi asked. "What did Esther risk?"

"Nothing," Esther replied. "It's done, Cordelia."

Saints above, this was getting more and more interesting. "Esther brought me back to life," I said. "That was dangerous? How? What are the risks?"

Everyone spent the next few seconds staring at each other, like enemies waiting to see who would draw the first weapon.

"There is a delicate balance," Cordelia answered without looking away from Esther. "Life and death, there are two sides. Good and bad. Pure and evil. Pulling a soul from death and bringing them back to life is not natural."

"What does that mean?" Malachi asked. Only I could hear the hint of desperation in his voice. I wanted to reach out and comfort him, but I stopped myself. *Not here. Not now.*

"It means there will be consequences. You cannot bring one back from death and expect life to continue as normal."

"But she's been totally fine. There haven't been any changes at all. Right, Jade?"

All eyes shifted to me. What was I supposed to say? *Was I okay?* In all honesty, I was the furthest damned thing from okay. I had died, for Saints's sake. My sister had died. My father had nearly died. My mother was long dead, and who knew what type of secrets she had been keeping about me, about my identity.

I was not okay. But I wasn't sure how much of that had to do with dying, and how much of that had to do with living.

"Your past haunts you," Cordelia said.

"Are you going to crawl through my thoughts every time we're together?" I sneered.

"That depends," she replied. She stepped closer, raising one of her sharp eyebrows and pursing her lips before motioning to Malachi. "How much of your thoughts revolve around shadow-boy here being naked? I could hang around your thoughts for images of that all day long, peacemaker."

That did it.

I launched myself at her with full force, tackling her to the ground. I didn't realize I was screaming until we were both rolling across the cold, damp floor. Cordelia flipped me over and pinned both of my shoulders beneath her, holding me there with her weight.

Another yell of frustration escaped me as I thrashed beneath her.

"Good," she hissed. "Get angry. Show me how angry you are. Show me how powerful you can be."

I felt the power, the pure anger building inside of me.

And then I released it. At that moment, I didn't care if I hurt Cordelia. I *wanted* to hurt her, that bitch needed to learn her place with me, and there was no way she was going to get away with talking about Malachi like that.

My husband, my king.

She deserved it.

The light of my power flashed around us. I didn't flinch away, not this time. I didn't even squint as the blinding light erupted.

When it finally settled, Cordelia stood in front of Esther, a shield of what looked like glamour protecting them from my power.

Malachi stood on the other side of the room, completely able to protect himself.

"Good start," Cordelia said, still catching her breath. She turned to Esther with a grin. "You didn't tell me the girl had *life* magic."

"I wasn't sure," Esther replied. She looked at me in a way that made me want to cower. "I wasn't sure until now. It's been so long since–"

"Life magic?" Malachi repeated. "How is that... I mean, that isn't possible."

"What's *life* magic?" I asked.

"Life magic hasn't existed since the Saints walked these

grounds," Cordelia explained. "It's extremely rare, and can be very dangerous."

I stood up, brushing the dirt off my trousers. "Why do they call it life magic if it's dangerous?"

"This explains a lot," Esther said. "It was easy to bring her back from the other side. If she didn't have life magic, it would have taken my entire essence to bring her back."

"What are you talking about?" Mal asked.

"Your wife possesses the magic that is so rare, only one of the Saints was known to possess it. Anastasia. This Saint was able to create life with nothing more than the touch of a finger, and when motivated the right way, she was able to take it away."

"Take away life?" I repeated. I certainly didn't remember any of her stories that involved taking life. "You mean kill. My power can give life and it can kill people."

"I didn't think that part was a surprise."

"It's not..." I struggled to find my words. *No*, it wasn't surprising that my magic could kill people. It was destructive and dangerous, yes, but to outright kill?

Nobody had said it that way before.

"Teach her how to use it," Malachi snapped. "That's why we're here, isn't it? So Jade can use her special magic?"

When I looked into Cordelia's bright green eyes, she was staring at me. No, not *at* me. *Into* me. Like she could see something deeper, something I couldn't even see myself.

I suddenly felt more exposed than ever.

"Are we doing this or not?" I pushed.

Esther also glanced between Cordelia and me with her eyebrows drawn together.

"Oh, we're doing this," Cordelia finally answered. "When I'm done with you, you'll be the most powerful creature alive."

With a scream of pain, Malachi fell to his knees beside me.

CHAPTER 9
Malachi

Blinding, white agony ran through my veins, as if my blood itself were rising into the sky through my skin.

"What are you doing to him?" I heard Jade scream, but it sounded distant. "Stop it!"

"That's enough, Cordelia," Esther snapped.

The pain lessened, but the force lingered. Cordelia had her claws in my mind. I had felt it before, with her.

Decades ago.

I forced myself to my feet, still recovering from the pain.

"What's your game, *witch*?" I asked through gritted teeth.

"I have no game. You are Jade's biggest weakness. If you hurt, she hurts. Am I the only one who sees how much of a problem this is?"

Cordelia reached her hand out in my direction again, and I braced myself for impact.

But I never felt the pain.

Jade took two steps to the right, positioning herself in front of me.

"You want to fight?" she asked Cordelia. "Let's fight. Malachi is not my weakness. He is my lifeline."

"Is that so?"

"He's the reason I'm still alive," Jade said with clenched fists. "He's the reason your boss didn't kill me the first time he laid eyes on me. You call that a weakness?"

Cordelia stepped forward. "Your power is connected," she stated.

"It is," Jade answered. My own magic flared within me in response, as if listening to her words.

"Show me."

Jade stalled. "Show you how?"

"Show me how your magic is connected."

"That's not how it works," I barked. I didn't know why Cordelia was trying to get under my skin. She had always been this way; a vindictive, bratty witch.

But she was strong. And she *was* powerful, as much as I hated to admit that. Esther was a powerful witch, but Cordelia's special blend of fae and witch blood created something dangerous.

I would know.

"It's not something I can simply show you on command. I can feel his power when he is near or when he is angry, and he can feel mine. It's like a tether."

"Well," Cordelia said. "Let's see how much of that is really true."

Cordelia closed the distance between herself and Jade, and before I could process what had just happened, her silver wings flashed and they both disappeared.

"Jade!" I yelled. It took one glance around the room to know that they had left. Vanished. Cordelia had taken them somewhere else, and I would be lucky if they were still under this mountain.

"She wants you to come for them," Esther said, almost sounding bored. "To see how strongly you two are connected."

"That crazy bitch," I snapped. "I should have never trusted her with Jade. I should have never trusted any of you!"

"She won't hurt Jade," Esther stated. "You know that, don't you? She's here to help her. To help you both. Cordelia can be trusted, Malachi."

"Is that what you'd call this?" I asked. "You'd call disappearing in the enemy's temple *helping*?"

"Find her," she said. "Relax, tap into your power, and find your wife. Follow that tether."

"I'm not the one doing the damn trials here." Irritation flooded my senses. I couldn't focus on that damned tether when I was this pissed off.

Esther stepped toward me with fierce, focused eyes. "You need to listen to me, son," she said. For what felt like the first time since I begged her to save Jade's life, she looked me in the eyes. "I pulled Jade back from death. She had passed that line, and she was never supposed to come back. She may seem like the same Jade, but she is not. Something is different. I can feel it, and I know you can feel it. Silas may not know it yet, but..." she glanced around the empty room before finishing, "she may not be a mere mortal anymore. You need to have your guard up. You both do."

My heart raced in my ears. None of this was surprising to me, but coming from Esther? "What do you mean she's not a mere mortal?"

Esther opened her mouth to reply, but quickly closed it, shoving away whatever thought first came to her mind. "I can't say too much. Not here. If Silas found out..."

"Found out what? What will he do to her? He already suspects she is not human. He told her so himself."

"There are things you don't know," she replied. Her voice came out as a hushed whisper. "Things I can't tell you. But once you complete the trials, you need to get as far from this temple as possible."

"Great idea," I mumbled as I ran a hand through my hair. "I was planning on sticking around for a few more decades."

"This is no joking matter. If Jade completes the trials without raising any red flags, it will be a miracle from the Saints."

She began stepping toward the entrance of the room. "Where are you going?" I hissed. "You drop that riddle on me and then leave?"

"Find your wife," she said. "And keep your distance from Cordelia. You two don't need to bicker any more than you already do. I have work to do. We'll talk more later."

And she was gone, her silver hair trailing behind her as she went.

My breathing echoed off the stone walls of the cave. *What in the Saints was going on here?* Cordelia had my wife somewhere in this damned temple, and my mother was, once again, speaking in mysterious riddles.

I wasn't the one going through those damned trials.

I didn't wait another second before I stormed out of the room. The temple was an underground maze, and Jade could be anywhere. It would take me days to scavenge the entire place, and that was assuming she stayed put.

I really hated Cordelia.

Our connected power was the only way. I closed my eyes and sank into that feeling, into that presence of hers that was always there. That was always inside of me. My anger slowly dissipated, clearing my body of those foggy emotions. I let my power flare—just a small amount—like a predator searching for its prey.

Jade was here somewhere.

It didn't take long before I felt it; that warm, calming presence. It was Jade, I knew it was. Her power, at least, which was now part of her.

She wasn't far.

"I'm going to kill that witch," I mumbled as I began walking through the tunnels again. My black wings tucked tightly behind me as I stormed through the halls. I passed a few Paragon members, none of whom I felt particularly excited to see or speak to.

I kept my head down, focusing on that small tether. Focusing on Jade.

Focusing on our connection.

I didn't feel any pain or panic through that tether,

although I hadn't been able to focus that much on it before. I wondered if I could feel her pain, or if I could feel other things from her, too.

Maybe with time I could. Maybe with time, Jade and I would be able to communicate through our magic.

Life magic and death magic. *How great of a pair we were.*

"Where are you, Jade," I whispered to myself. I came to a fork in the tunnels when I began to feel a pull to the right. She had to be that way. She had to be searching for my magic, too.

So I followed it. I followed that slight, pulling feeling that guided me down the tunnel.

And that connection that I felt deep within my chest grew stronger and stronger.

I knew I was getting closer.

I followed the pull through the narrow stones and down a set of jagged stairs before I heard it; the faint, rapid flutter of Jade's heartbeat.

It was a sound I had grown fond of, and I was damn relieved to be hearing it now.

"Jade," I called out.

"Mal, I'm back here."

I made it to her in a flash, following her voice and my fae instincts in the darkness.

Jade was against the wall with a rope across her chest, shackled to the stone wall behind her, keeping her there.

"I'm going to kill her," I sneered. "I'm going to kill her for laying her hands on you."

My eyes quickly adjusted to the darkness to find Jade smiling at me. A wide, childish smile.

"What?" I asked.

"Nothing, it's just..." Her smile grew. "It worked."

"Of course it worked," I said. "I wasn't going to let you stay down here all day."

I ripped the rope away from her in one swift motion. "Now, tell me where that witch went. I need to talk to her."

"You're not killing Cordelia," Jade argued.

"Why not?"

"Look," she started, "I don't like her either, okay? But we *need* her. She's trying to help me."

I couldn't help but bark a laugh. "She keeps saying that, but I wouldn't be so sure. She's worked for Silas for decades now. We can't be certain where her loyalties lie."

Jade's hands found the tops of my shoulders in the darkness. She could barely see a thing, and my heart fluttered as I watched her eyes search blindly in the shadows.

"You hate her because she's powerful."

"I hate her because she's dangerous, and clearly has no respect for you. We can't trust her."

"I'm not saying she's my new best friend or anything," Jade said, "but she seems to know what she's talking about. I was able to pull you to me with my power. That's something, right?"

"That's something," I agreed. My hands found her waist as I pulled her to my chest.

Jade's arms wrapped around my shoulders. She drew in a long, calming breath. I did the same, feeling her chest rise and fall against me.

She pulled back just enough to ask, "What do you think she meant? About the balance between life and death?"

I debated telling her about my conversation with Esther, but it was still a mystery. Jade and I weren't lucky enough to get straight answers, especially in the depths of the Paragon. Everything either made no sense, needed more information, or turned out to be a flat out lie. I would have to dig to find the truth.

"I don't know," I answered truthfully. "I don't think we'll know for quite some time. Are you feeling okay? Are you feeling normal?"

Jade blinked and looked away. "I haven't noticed anything out of the ordinary, but considering how ridiculous my life has been lately, that's not saying much."

My hand on her back kept her pinned to me. "How long do you think we can hide down here without Cordelia finding us?"

Jade smiled again. "I think we have some time. She didn't seem to have much faith in your abilities to find me."

I leaned down and kissed her lips, leaning myself against the stone wall behind her. Jade wrapped her arms around my neck and pressed further against me, which only excited my power. Her mouth moved perfectly against mine, hot and needy in the darkness of the tunnel.

Heat tickled my stomach, and I was beginning to realize that as Jade's power flaring my own.

I needed more. So did my power.

I slid my hand under her shirt, feeling her flexing muscles underneath as she held herself against me.

She smiled against my mouth, and I pulled away just enough to ask, "What?"

"I can feel it," she said.

"Feel what?"

"Your power. I can feel your magic." She slid a hand down my chest. "Can you?"

"I've been feeling your magic since you blasted those damned deadlings in that cage made of bone."

And I kissed her again, hungrier this time. Like I needed her. Like she was meant just for me, here in the darkness. My tongue slid against her lower lip, and Saints, she tasted good.

She always tasted so damned good.

Footsteps approached behind us. I pulled away, barely, as they grew louder. Jade froze, too, her lips pausing mid-kiss.

It wasn't Cordelia. I could identify her footsteps from anywhere. It wasn't Silas, either. He never walked that fast. Someone was scurrying through these tunnels, and by the sounds of the random pauses at every turn, they were looking for someone.

Jade's eyes frantically searched mine, looking for guidance. Watching for my next move.

"What do you want?" I yelled into the tunnel, loud enough that my voice boomed off the stone walls and echoed through the caves.

The footsteps stopped.

"I'm looking for the peacemaker." A small, boyish voice echoed through the tunnel.

"What do you want with her?"

He waited a few seconds before answering, "I have a message."

I turned around and extended my wings, putting Jade behind me. By the sound of it, the young boy wouldn't be a threat, but I learned long ago to never underestimate any member of the Paragon. "We're in here."

The boy scurried closer to us, and I was surprised at how small he was when he entered.

"I need to speak with her," the boy said. He was young, maybe one decade old, with tattered clothing and dirty hands. His dark hair had been recently shaved, which made him look even younger.

"Speak," I demanded.

"Mal," Jade placed her hand on my back and stepped beside me. "It's okay. What's your message?"

He looked at us with wide eyes. Wide, terrified eyes.

"Is it from Silas?"

"No," he answered, shaking his head. "Silas can't know we spoke."

Now I was interested.

"What is it?" Jade asked again.

The hair rose on the back of my neck.

"Here," the boy said. He reached deep into his pocket and pulled out a letter. Not any letter, either. I recognized the deep blue seal on the envelope. The letter came from Rewyth.

I took the letter from the boy and immediately ripped it open. Serefin's handwriting scattered the page.

"Our enemies lurk. Your throne is in jeopardy. Your brothers

are fighting to keep Rewyth safe, but they are lost without their king. Come home as soon as you are able. Stay safe."
–S

I read the letter twice before passing it to Jade so she could read it. "Where did you get this?" I asked the boy. "Why are you hiding it from Silas?"

"He can't know I gave this to you," the boy stuttered. "He doesn't want you receiving messages here."

Of course he doesn't. He wanted to keep us here as long as possible, and if that meant not running back to Rewyth when they needed me, he'd do whatever he could to intercept our messages.

"Why are you helping us?" Jade asked.

The boy shrugged. "My grandmother told me the peacemaker would come one day. I wanted to help the peacemaker. I saw you when you arrived."

Jade's posture instantly softened beside me.

"Thank you," I told the boy. "Now go."

He did without a second of hesitation, his small footsteps disappearing in the distance.

"Our enemies..." I thought aloud once the boy had left. "Saints, if only that narrowed it down."

"At least we know it isn't the Paragon," Jade sighed. "We can check one off the list."

"Who would threaten my throne? They know they will pay with their lives once I return."

Jade thought on this for a second, her brows furrowing in focus. "Maybe that's it," she said. "Maybe they don't think you'll return in time to stop them."

I was already shaking my head. "Don't think that way, Jade Weyland. I'm not leaving you here, and that's final."

She opened her mouth to argue, but I interrupted her with, "Final."

"Fine," she said. "But we need to figure out who's trying to steal your throne."

CHAPTER 10
Jade

I stared up at the dark, stone ceiling while Mal breathed heavily next to me on the bed. We had been there for hours, not moving. Just breathing.

"Each day is a day closer to the trials. Each day is one day closer to possibly dying. Again." I didn't look at Malachi when I said the words. I didn't think I would survive the look on his face.

We hadn't returned to training with Cordelia. Instead, we snuck away to our bedroom, where we had been silently staring into the darkness.

"You're not going to die," Malachi replied. "I won't let that happen."

My chest tightened. "I know you think that," I said, "but if Silas wants me dead in those trials, I think it will be hard for you to stop him."

"He won't kill you," Malachi stated. I finally looked at him, but his eyes had focused somewhere in the distance. "He needs you."

"Yeah," I agreed, "he needs me to disappear from this world. He needs me to stop being a threat. He needs all the power for himself."

Malachi let out a long breath. "As much as I hate to say this, I think we need to talk to Esther. She promised she could help us, and it's time she actually did that for once. She knows something."

I shifted in bed. "I think she's done plenty to help us already." I hated disagreeing with him, but Esther had saved my life. More than once. If it weren't for her, I would have been dead right now. Esther may have hid things from us, but she clearly had her own secrets under this mountain.

We had bigger problems to handle than Esther.

He scoffed. "Like what? Antagonizing her witch friends during your training?"

"Like bringing me back from the dead. Or are you still choosing to forget that part? She's part of the reason I'm still alive, Mal."

Malachi's dark eyes snapped to mine. "No, Jade. I will never forget that. You dying is the one thing that I can't seem to burn out of my memory. It's the one thing I see at night, and it's the one thing I can't get out of my head as I'm falling asleep."

His words were harsh, but I understood. I felt that same pain when I worried about Malachi. It was the reason I couldn't sit back and let him fight that war alone. It was the reason I had disobeyed him time and time again when he told me to stay put.

I couldn't lose him. I couldn't live with myself if I did.

"I'm sorry," I whispered. "I know you've been through a lot with her."

"Oh, Jade," he said, shifting his body closer and holding my face with his hands. "You have nothing to be sorry for."

I relaxed into his warmth and let him wrap his arms around me. My head always fit perfectly against his chest. "Do you think that *Erebus* thing is true?"

"What Erebus thing?" Mal asked nonchalantly, as if the fate of his heritage didn't linger in the air.

"Do you think you're his descendent?" I asked.

Malachi took another long breath. "I think I'll add that to the never-ending list of things my mother needs to answer."

My mind wandered to Esther. She *had* been acting different lately. Softer. Kinder. She defended me during the training, but I had to admit I was surprised. Esther was a powerful witch. Her coven was one of the most powerful that ever lived, yet Cordelia walked around like she owned the place.

Half witch, half fae. Just like Malachi.

But Cordelia's gifts were different. Malachi couldn't read minds.

At least, not that we knew of.

"This place is starting to creep me out," I admitted. Malachi laughed, and I rolled over to wrap my arms around his torso. "I mean it. The people, the black robes. I can't believe you lived here."

"In my defense," Malachi stated, "the robes were quite comfortable."

"Oh, shut up," I spat.

Malachi ran his hands up and down my back. "You're tense," he said.

"Not any more tense than you."

"Lay on your stomach," he demanded. He moved himself off the bed, giving me room to follow his orders.

I obeyed.

I couldn't help the nervous uptick in my racing heart.

"This is going to help you relax," Malachi said, lowering his voice to a sultry whisper. He peeled my tunic up and over my head, beginning to work his hands across the knotted muscles.

I hadn't realized how tense I actually was until each muscle started to relax beneath him.

"I hate this," he said after a few minutes. It took me a second to realize what he meant, but he was running his hands along the long, healed scars on my back. The ones his father's men gave me.

The ones he risked everything to avenge that day in Rewyth, standing up to his own father.

"I know," I whispered.

Malachi leaned down and placed a kiss on each scar, tracing the delicate skin of my back with his lips. I shuttered.

"I never wanted any of this for you," he said. His voice cracked.

"I know you didn't," I said. "You're too good, you're too kind. You shouldn't have gone through any of that, either."

He laughed, but it was humorless. "People like you don't deserve the things they go through. These things happened to you, and you're nothing but an innocent victim."

"And what about you? You're equally as innocent as I. You may have more blood on your hands, Malachi, but you did what you needed to do to survive. I would do the same."

When he didn't respond right away, I sat up in bed. I didn't care that my tunic was gone, or that Malachi could see me. I wanted him to see me. I wanted him to understand. I took his face in my hands and pulled him onto the bed.

"You are good, Malachi. You are kind and strong and vengeful. You are powerful, but you are also generous and caring. You are nothing like Erebus. Not even close. Do you understand me?"

He closed his eyes, but I only gripped his face harder. We were alone up here. It was him and me against the world. I needed him.

I needed him to not shut me out.

"You are *good*, Mal." I kissed his cheek, his forehead, his nose. "You are good. And even if you were not good, even if you were the worst fae to ever walk among this world, even if you killed and killed and took whatever you wanted whenever you wanted it, I would still love you the same. Because it's not what you *do* that makes me love you, Malachi. It's who you are. And if you have Erebus's blood in you that makes your wings black, well *good*. Because I like your black wings."

He cracked the tiniest hint of a smile. His wings spread, just an inch. "Really?" he teased. "These wings?"

"Yes," I answered. "Those wings. And don't push it." His wings spread out to their full capacity, almost touching each side of the small stone cave. "You're pushing it."

He laughed, and I laughed with him. It felt strange, laughing when we were in this terrible situation.

Malachi's arms fell around me, and he pulled me onto his lap in one swift motion. My arms settled on his shoulders as I relaxed against him.

"I love you, Jade," he said. "And you could also kill and kill and kill. I'd find that pretty attractive."

I punched him in the arm.

He laughed even harder. "What?" he asked. "It's true! Now I'm thinking of you dripping in the blood of our enemies. That's even sexier."

I punched him harder.

But my stomach fluttered. *Our enemies.*

Whatever we faced in the future, we would face it together. Descendants of Saints or not.

"Do you think Cordelia will be pissed that we never showed back up for training?"

"No," Malachi answered without a second of thinking. "I don't. And I don't care much about what she thinks, anyway."

"You really don't like her," I said.

"She's let her power go to her head. I never liked her, even when we were younger."

The way Malachi talked about Cordelia got me thinking about their past. He clearly had issues with her, and they must have gone through a lot while living here together. There weren't that many people under this mountain to begin with. To be trapped together for years, maybe even decades…

I couldn't stop myself from asking, "Did you ever…?"

Malachi shook his head "Saints, no. Never. Cordelia and I trained together, but we were never even friends. Sometimes, if we were too tired to fight, we were civil. But that's as close as things got between us."

I eyed him carefully. "Okay," I answered. "There's just so much tension between you two."

"Cordelia has a way of doing that. She's not exactly warm and welcoming."

"I hate to break it to you, King of Shadows, but neither are you. You two have a lot in common, you know."

I expected some sort of retort to my comment, but Malachi's eyes had gone into that far away place again. "Something is going on with her and Esther," Malachi said. "They're keeping a secret. I just don't know what it is."

I crawled off Malachi's lap—even though I instantly missed the warmth of him—and began looking for my tunic.

"Where are you going?" Mal asked.

I drew my black tunic over my head. "If you want to find out what they're hiding from us, we have to figure it out ourselves. They won't be serving it to us on a silver platter."

Malachi rolled his eyes. "We shouldn't be sneaking around the temple at night."

I rested my hand on my hip. "Now you're the noble one? What was that you were just saying to me about…oh yeah. *Dripping in my enemies' blood?*"

"Fine," he said after a second. He picked up his sword and strapped it to his waist. "But be quiet. Remember that the fae can hear and see much better than you can. Don't try to sneak up on anybody."

"You can't tell me you never snuck through these tunnels when you were younger. Not even once?"

Malachi remained silent, which was answer enough.

I pushed open the stone door to our room and stepped into the dark, shadowed hallway.

It had to be well past midnight. If we were lucky, most people would be avoiding the main areas.

I wasn't sure what we were looking for. A scroll with all of the plans for my trials would be nice. But I wasn't going to get my hopes up.

"This way," Malachi said. Instead of taking us back the way we usually came from, he turned and walked further into the tunnels. Malachi walked silently, and I cursed myself for not being as careful as him.

But he had been doing this much longer than I had, I reminded myself. He had decades of sneaking through castles and creeping down halls. I only had a few months.

"What's back here?" I whispered. Even with my quieted voice, I felt it echo.

The heat in the pit of my chest, the one that I now knew was connected to my power, flared. As if it wanted to protect me. As if it wanted me to know it could help.

Malachi instinctively reached back. I slid my hand in his.

The wet, stone wall on either side of us grew more and more narrow. "Are you sure there's something back here?"

I asked. Malachi didn't respond, but he squeezed my hand.

The small amount of light that had been giving me the ability to see before was gone. We turned a tight corner, and to my surprise, the light disappeared entirely. I couldn't see a thing.

I squeezed Mal's hand even tighter. *He better not let go.*

A freezing cold breeze hit me out of nowhere. My breath was nearly taken away.

"Almost there," Mal said.

"Almost where?"

The wind grew stronger and stronger until I had to use my hand to catch myself on the stone wall next to me.

A couple more steps forward, and I could finally see again. But it wasn't a lantern that lit the path, nor a fire of any kind.

It was the moon. The sky.

The stars.

Glowing in a way that warmed my soul, that lit a fire of excitement in my chest.

"We're outside?" I asked. Goosebumps erupted over my skin, half from the chill of the air and half from the excitement of what we were doing. "How is this possible?"

"Let's say it's more of a secret spot. More secluded. We're safe up here."

"And how is this supposed to help us learn all of the secrets from our enemies?"

Malachi smiled. His white smile reflected the moonlight above. "It's not."

He stepped forward and wrapped his arms around me,

encapsulating me in his warmth as I stared up at the night sky.

"I didn't notice the stars before," I admitted.

"They're beautiful, aren't they?" Esther's voice behind us made us both jump. Malachi slid away from me, drawing his weapon and pointing it in her direction.

Every sense of mine erupted with adrenaline.

"What are you doing here?" he asked.

"Likely the same thing you're doing here," Esther answered.

"I somehow doubt that."

Esther stepped forward, her pale face becoming illuminated by the moonlight. Malachi tensed with each step she took.

"We need to talk," Esther said.

Malachi finally lowered his sword. "Yes," he said. "We do. Did you follow us here to tell us that?"

"I didn't follow you," she said. "I've been waiting. Silas told me you enjoyed hiding away up here when you were younger. I don't blame you. It's beautiful."

I glanced between the two of them but stayed silent. "You and Silas are awfully close. Would you like to start by explaining what's going on with you two? Are you working together?"

Esther leaned against the stone mountain edge. "Silas isn't who you think he is," Esther answered.

A deep, unsettled feeling grew in my stomach. Were those Malachi's emotions? Was I feeling what he was feeling through the connection of our power?

"Are you telling me you know Silas better than I?" Mal asked.

I thought back to the conversation I had with Esther about Silas. She had known him. She had lived here with him, in fact, after Malachi had returned to Rewyth.

Did Malachi know?

Esther glanced down at her feet. It was unsettling enough that we were having this conversation, but it was even worse that she seemed so nervous about it. Esther, the most powerful witch bloodline to walk this world, was nervous to talk to Malachi.

Something was up.

She took a long, shaking breath before saying, "Silas is your birth father, Malachi."

CHAPTER 11
Malachi

"You lie," I demanded, but the words came out softer than I planned.

"I have no reason to lie to you."

Anger blinded my vision. "You have plenty of reasons to lie to me, I just have a difficult time discovering which of your motives is currently affecting our safety."

My mother stepped forward, a pleading look on her face. "Silas is your father. He has been this entire time. I let the King think he was your father because he would have killed me if he found out. He hated me enough already, Saints..."

No, that wasn't possible. *Silas?* My enslaver, my torturer? The leader of the Paragon?

"That's impossible." I backed up a step, but Jade was there, hands on my back.

"I'm only telling you this now because you need to understand what's at stake."

"Does he know?" I asked. "Does Silas know I'm his son?"

Esther took a long breath. "He does."

"All of that information he told me about Erebus...he told me I had the blood of that wicked Saint. Are you telling me that Silas is a descendent of Erebus, too?"

Another long breath. "I am."

No, none of this made any sense. Even the freezing mountain air couldn't clear my swarming thoughts. "But his wings, Silas has silver wings."

Esther looked away from me again. How cowardly, not able to face your own son with the truth. Jade whispered something behind me but I couldn't hear her through the pulsing anger in my veins.

"We've suspected that his Erebus blood mixed with my powerful witch bloodline is what brought out the black wings again. What he tells you is true, son. You are one of his descendants. And as a descendent of both a Saint and a powerful witch, you have more gifts than you can even understand."

I laughed, and I enjoyed the way Esther flinched at the sound. "You are a cruel, vindictive woman," I growled. "How is telling me this now going to help me? Why have you kept this a secret all this time?"

"He would kill me, Malachi. He would kill me if I told you the truth. He doesn't want you to know how powerful you really are."

"Is that why he brought us here? He doesn't care about Jade at all, does he? He just wants to exploit my power as his son." It all started to add up. The secrets, the attack on my kingdom, his interest in Jade.

Esther let out an exasperated sigh. "If Jade is truly chosen from the Saints, which we all know she is, she will have no problem passing the trials. I'll make sure of it."

"How? How can you make sure of it? Is Silas still blinded by you? Is he so in love with you that he'll do anything you suggest?" My questions were satire, but Esther's face made me reconsider. "You really have him wrapped around your witchling finger, don't you?"

Her face hardened. I didn't care if my words hurt her. Once again, she had blindsided me with a secret. "Silas has watched over you, Malachi."

My temper unraveled. Silas had done many things to me in my life, but *watch over* me? "He brought war to my kingdom!"

"And you walked away alive. Is that not a sign of good faith?"

"My people died. Innocent citizens lost fathers and husbands. The sense of safety in my kingdom shattered. The Paragon..." I took a shaking breath to gather my thoughts. "The Paragon is supposed to *protect* us. Silas's subordinates put a damn blade through my wife!" I reached back and grabbed Jade's hand. She squeezed tightly. "Was that *protecting* her? Was that protecting me?"

"His healer helped her after I brought her back from the depths, Malachi please!" Esther rushed forward with her hands before her. "Please, listen to me now. None of that matters. I'm here because of the trials."

"What does any of that have to do with Jade's trials? It

seems as though they want to toy with us to make themselves feel more powerful. Is that not true?"

"They will push Jade to her limits to ensure that she is powerful enough to be the peacemaker. Silas will create these trials, but he needs witches to bring them to life. He needs us to string our magic into Jade's mind. That's why I'm here, Malachi. I'm here to help Jade."

The world around me spun. "Are you telling me you'll be helping Silas create Jade's trials?"

Esther took another long, shaking breath. Her eyes softened, and in another world I would have actually believed that she felt bad about all of this. "Yes, and I'm going to do everything I can to protect her from herself."

My fists pounded the training bag, stray feathers flying with every hit.

Another punch.

Another punch, harder.

Faster.

More painful.

I didn't remember leaving Jade and walking here to the training room, the only thing I could think of was Esther's voice.

She had betrayed us time and time again.

And every damn time I thought she might be on our side, she shifted.

I punched the bag again.

Again.

"Malachi," Jade's soft, angelic voice filled the room, echoing off the walls between my ragged breathing.

I ignored her. I didn't know what to say. My own mother was going to help Silas perform whatever messed up magical ceremony was necessary to turn his wicked plan into visions that would torture Jade's mind.

How could I face her? How could I look her in the eye after that?

"Malachi Weyland," Jade's voice echoed again, laced with an urgent sense of anger. "Don't you dare shut me out," she said.

I punched again, feeling the skin on my knuckles split.

I grabbed the training bag, stopping it from swinging on the rope it hung from as I rested my sweaty forehead against it.

Her footsteps approached.

Small, delicate hands slid onto my shoulders, just over the base of my wings. It took everything in me not to flinch away from the soft touch.

"Esther's not the one who designs the trials, Mal. You know this. You know she doesn't have much of a choice. We're all at the mercy of the mighty, undefeatable Paragon." The last words dripped with resentment.

I shook my head and pushed Jade's words away. "It doesn't matter," I said. "She's part of it. That's the reason she came here with us, isn't it? So she could help with the trials?"

A beat of silence passed between us. "She brought me back from death. You think she would throw me back at death's doorstep so quickly? She nearly died herself by bringing me back, Mal. It drained her. And you heard what Cordelia said. She disrupted the balance. She wouldn't have done all that just to kill me again when the trials came around."

It didn't make sense. It didn't make *any* damn sense. Why would Esther bring Jade back if she was willing to help Silas put her through the Trials of Glory?

"It's a trick," I thought aloud. "That's the only logical explanation."

Jade gripped my shoulder and spun me around. "Or," she started, "your mother is pretending to be on Silas's side for *our* sake, and plans on swaying his decisions in the trial so I have an easier time. Could that be a possibility?"

Saints, when did Jade become the reasonable one?

I repeated her words in my mind before answering, "It's highly unlikely, but I suppose it is possible."

Jade took another step toward me and picked up my bloody hands. "My wicked, violent husband," she said.

She leaned down and brushed a kiss over my red-stained knuckles.

I put a finger under her chin and lifted her face to mine. "You are too good for me, Jade. You are smart and trusting and true."

She leaned into my touch as I caressed her face. "I am nothing if not yours."

CHAPTER 12
Jade

Mal kissed me, not caring to be delicate. Not worrying if he would hurt me or not. And I kissed him back with an equal amount of aggression.

He gripped my waist and backed my body up until I leaned against the stone wall behind me. Our mouths moved together in a frenzy, giving me the release of emotion that I'd been needing for so much longer than I realized.

Malachi's hands ravaged my body, sliding down my back and up my torso as his hands splayed against my skin.

I lifted myself up to him, wrapping an arm around his neck to hold my body against his. One of his hands slid down my thigh, gripping my skin with need as he hauled my leg around his waist, pinning me to the wall.

"Someone could walk in," I noted as Malachi moved his mouth to my jawline, sending a hot, fiery trail of kisses down my neck and against my now-bare shoulder.

"Let them," he growled. His black wings beat around us, shadowing us even further in the dimly lit training room.

Malachi's mouth didn't leave my body. He kissed me everywhere he could, only pausing for a moment to pull my tunic up and over my head, tossing it to the floor with ease. I didn't remember pulling his shirt off, but soon enough it, too, was gone, our skin igniting with heat anywhere we touched.

"Is this your way of blowing off steam?" I asked, distracted by Malachi's hands as his fingers slipped under the hem of my trousers.

Malachi froze as if I had physically hit him. He pulled away from my body just enough so he could look into my eyes as he said, "Is that what you think this is, Jade Weyland?"

The intensity in his eyes took my breath away, not that I had much left after that type of kiss. "I don't know what this is," I answered honestly.

"Let me tell you exactly what this is, my queen. You," he trailed a finger down my face, pausing them on my now swollen lips, "are the most beautiful creature the Saints have blessed this world with. You are everything I have ever needed, and everything I will need forever. Everything else? The Paragon? Esther? None of that matters." He gripped my face with both hands now, although his body still pressed mine into the stone wall behind me. "I love you, Jade. That's all that's ever mattered to me, even before I truly knew what these feelings I have for you were. And this?" He motioned to the two of us together. "This is me showing you exactly how you deserve to be loved."

My head spun from the mixture of adrenaline and euphoria as I pulled Malachi's face down to mine so I could kiss him again. I didn't hold anything back. I pushed away all of the thoughts in my mind about the Paragon, the trials. I didn't care about any of that. What I cared about was how damn good it felt when Malachi lifted me up again, wrapping both of my legs around his waist this time. What I cared about was the fact that we were moving, his wings pumping for a split second before we landed on a padded mat meant for combat training.

"Malachi, wait," I said, pushing on his bare chest. My trousers were already untied, similar to his, and neither of us had to guess where this was headed. "Are you sure about this?"

A wicked grin spread on his face. "You never, ever have to ask me if I'm sure about you, my queen. The answer will always be yes. Every damn time."

"Well," I said, fighting the rush of emotion that came with his words, "that's good to know, then."

He laughed, and I closed my eyes as I felt the vibrations from his chest transfer to mine, our power linking together at our mere proximity. The magic in my veins pumped, too, harder than it ever had. With more power than it ever had.

I knew Malachi felt this. I could see it in his eyes, like a shining star in a black night.

There were no questions this time. No hesitations. No second-guesses. Malachi and I, made for one another in nearly every way possible, knew exactly what to do. Knew how each other's bodies would react before they did.

Skin on skin, intertwined breath and limbs. I pulled his body to me and held on like he was the last thing I would ever need in this world.

I didn't even realize my power was losing control until it was too late.

The stone room erupted.

A blast of power—not just mine, but Malachi's black, wicked shadows, too—blasted through the room, burning the training equipment, burning the mat under my back, burning it all.

Malachi's wings blasted out to protect me, as if I needed it. As if that would help.

We caused this. The eruption of power came from us.

"Holy Saints," I whispered.

Malachi stayed on top of me until our power settled. It wasn't until he pushed himself away from me that I saw how bad it really was.

We had...we had *burned* the entire damn room.

CHAPTER 13
Malachi

Cordelia laughed.

I couldn't bring myself to look at her until Jade finished telling the story. Jade tried to be as vague as possible as she told Cordelia what happened in that training room, for both of our sakes, but Cordelia only relished in that further, asking questions that I knew would turn Jade bright red in the face.

But it didn't matter. We needed answers.

"If we could go anywhere else to find the answers we're looking for, trust me, we would," I added. Jade exhaled, I could tell she was relieved I joined the conversation at all.

Saints, Cordelia would never let us forget this.

She laughed again. Jade and I waited patiently in her potion-covered bedroom as she finished entertaining herself with our situation.

"Okay, okay. I'm done. I'm sorry, I just..." She covered her mouth again to stifle another fit of laughter.

"If you can't help us," Jade interrupted, "We'll just leave. We don't need to stay here and listen to you laugh at us."

Cordelia cleared her throat and made a half-assed attempt at straightening her expression. "I can be serious," she said, more to herself than to us. "And I think I do know a little something about this."

"We're all ears," I added.

"You're telling me your magic connected? Combined? You both didn't simply lose control at the same time, did you?"

I squinted. "If by lose control you mean…"

"Of your powers, you imbecile! Jade's magic is fairly new, it's possible that you–"

"It wasn't that," Jade stated. "It was more like…more like Mal's power pulling mine from the source. And the same with him. We couldn't control it, I couldn't stop it once it began."

She considered these words. "But neither of you are hurt?"

"We're fine," I said. "But I can't say the same for the training room."

"The training room?" Cordelia asked. "You two couldn't take it back to the damn bedroom? Saints!"

Jade shifted uncomfortably, but I couldn't help the wave of satisfaction that came over me. I was a king, and Jade my queen. I would show her my love anywhere we damn well pleased. It wasn't our fault we happened to be cooped up under this mountain.

"Have you heard of this before?" I asked.

She paced in her bedroom, scanning over her small bookshelf filled with grimoires, spells, and decades of witch history. Cordelia may be sassy, stubborn, and a general stick in my ass, but she was knowledgeable. I had to give her that much.

"Not exactly," she started, "but I've heard of something similar. With your magic, both being so rare, I wonder if..."

She pulled a dusty, leather-bound book from her shelf and flipped through the pages.

"You wonder what?" I pushed.

She ignored me and continued scanning through the pages of her book until she stopped, finger on the page, and read aloud, "Anastasia and Erebus, the Saints of life and death, could not hurt each other. It was unheard of for such powerful beings to not cause damage to one another. But their love, as the prophecy goes, was strong enough to create a lasting protection around each other. Bound by forces beyond our understanding, they were meant for each other. Created for each other. The forces of lightness and darkness could not be separated, for the world knew that they belonged together. For eternity, they would belong together."

I waited for her to say more, but she only shut the book and turned to stare at us.

"What does that mean?" Jade asked, the smallest amount of panic lacing her words. "The Saints could not hurt each other either? Like us?"

"Life magic," Cordelia held a hand out to Jade, "and death magic." Her hand waved to me.

Death magic.

Jade's hand fell over mine.

"Are you saying we're supposed to be together?" I asked.

Cordelia only shrugged. "I can't say for sure, but you two are certainly not normal. Your magic isn't normal, being the peacemaker is definitely not normal. I think it's safe to assume you both possess the same magic as the Saints, and therefore are bonded the same way."

Bonded by the Saints.

It made sense. Before I met Jade, I had felt a deep, needy urge to protect her. My magic reacted to her presence, and I knew hers did the same. It was clear that Jade had been chosen by the Saints to be the peacemaker, so it did make sense that we…

"Bonded?" Jade repeated, interrupting my thoughts. "As in, our magic?"

"Magic," Cordelia answered, "souls, beings. You're already married, but yes. I'd assume you're bonded in all of those ways."

My heart pounded. Jade was not just my wife. Was not just the pacemaker. Was not just my queen.

Jade was a gift from the Saints, a light in my darkness. She was the balanced piece of me, everything I ever needed.

She was my other half.

I was a damned idiot for being nervous.

Jade hadn't spoken since we left Cordelia's bedroom. She didn't speak as we walked down the hallway to our bedroom, either.

The things I would do for Cordelia's mind-reading gift...

"So," I started as we approached our bedroom door. "What do you think?"

Jade shrugged and took a deep breath, which didn't help my nerves. Would she be disappointed by the bond? Angry that she was tied to me? I tried to imagine how I would feel if I were in her shoes. She lost her freedom a long time ago. Marrying me was not part of her plan.

But was this? Was being bonded to me forever part of her plan?

Or was she secretly thinking of any possible way to get out of the situation?

I stepped to the side, letting her walk into our bedroom first. She opened her mouth as if she wanted to say something, but pushed the stone door open instead and headed inside.

I followed.

"It's—It's crazy. Right?" she stammered.

"What's crazy?" I asked, carefully choosing the tone of my voice. I turned to the wall and began unbuckling my weapon belt. *You don't care. You don't care.*

And then she laughed. It was a light laugh, one that bubbled from her chest until she couldn't hold it in any longer. I spun around to find her staring at me with bright eyes.

Damn, I loved those eyes.

"You're laughing," I noted.

She tried to open her mouth to speak, but fell into another fit of laughter. Her dark hair slid over her shoulders as she tossed her head back and continued laughing.

Her laughter spread like a fire, I had to admit.

I stepped forward and grabbed her shoulders, forcing her to look at me. "Please tell me what you're thinking," I said, "because I think I'll lose my mind if you stand here laughing for one more minute."

It took her a few tries, but she eventually straightened and withheld her laughter long enough to say, "It's crazy that we're only finding this out. We've known for a long time that we're meant for each other, Malachi Weyland."

Thank the Saints for that.

The sigh of relief that came from me was involuntary, as was the kiss I couldn't stop myself from planting on her lips.

"What?" she asked as I pulled away. "Did you think this would scare me off?"

I shrugged. "I think it would make a lot of sense if you didn't want to be my other half for the rest of your life, considering the circumstances."

I tried to turn back to the wall but Jade stopped me, pulling my arm until I stood even closer to her than before.

Not a single hint of laughter laced her features now, no humor at all as she said, "If I have to spend every waking day of my life with you, I will do it gladly. Saint or no Saint. Bond or no bond. You are mine, Malachi. And I am yours. Don't think for a second you can scare me off so easily."

When I kissed her this time, I didn't stop.

Mine. Forever.

CHAPTER 14
Jade

I couldn't help the hint of nerves as I prepared for another training session with Cordelia. The hint of burnt magic lingered in the air from my night here with Malachi, but Cordelia didn't seem to notice.

"Why do we need to do this?" I asked, ignoring the way Cordelia's muscles flexed as she rubbed her hands together in front of her body.

"You have no idea what you need to prepare for," she answered coldly. "If you're caught in a physical fight with your enemies in these trials, you'd be as good as dead. Physical combat is equally as important as your magic."

"I don't plan on letting anyone close enough to have to fight them physically," I replied.

"Really?" she teased. "And what happens when you lose your magic? What happens if Silas decides to restrict your power? What then?"

"Why would he do that?" I asked. "The whole point of the trials is to test my power."

She stepped closer to me, fists drawn.

Saints, I didn't want to fight Cordelia. I didn't want to get within three feet of her, actually. Her perfectly sculpted shoulders, her tall yet lean build. She could take me in a fight, I was sure of it.

Cordelia had likely been training for this. She had probably trained dozens of other trial contestants, and she'd likely been fighting for years.

"If you think that's all these trials are for, peacemaker, you have a harsh lesson coming your way."

I didn't have time to think of a reply. Cordelia closed the distance between us and threw a fist directly at my face.

I dodged her hit last second, stepping to the side and spinning around to face her. "What was that?" I yelled.

She didn't answer. Instead, she advanced again, trying to hit me.

This time, her fist flew so close to my face I could feel the breeze as I threw my body to the other side of the room.

Okay, she wasn't messing around.

I didn't love to fight, but I *would*. If my choice was between fighting or Cordelia landing that punch into my face?

I pulled my fists up and paid closer attention. Cordelia took her time crossing the room, moving slowly like a predator stalking its prey.

I wasn't going to let her get the satisfaction this time. I moved first, stepping quickly and punching toward her abdomen.

She dodged it with little effort, snickering as she moved aside.

"Nice try, peacemaker. You'll have to do a lot better than that."

Saints above.

Cordelia had a slim build and fast reflexes, but she was strong. She was quick on her feet. We weren't all that different in size and movements, I realized. She was just fifty times better at fighting than I.

Which meant she would be cocky. She would get too confident.

I took a long breath and focused. Cordelia shook her arms out before pulling her fists back up to her chest, ready to fight.

I moved again, attempting to throw her off guard with my left fist as I punched directly after with my right.

Which left me entirely unguarded.

Cordelia saw this opportunity and landed a hit to my cheekbone.

I hissed in pain, stumbling backwards.

"You bitch," I sneered.

"Get mad all you want," she replied. "We're doing this to help you, not hurt you."

"Right. Not hurting me at all."

I put my fingers to my cheekbone, feeling the nearly split skin there.

Cordelia wanted a fight? She would get a fight.

Focus, Jade. You're plenty capable of doing this.

I thought back to the time I spent training with Malachi. He was fierce, strong, and determined. He taught me how to be all those things, I had simply forgotten.

And Cordelia had underestimated me.

I used the anger that built in my chest and threw myself at Cordelia knocking her off guard and off balance. We both tumbled to the ground, a yell of frustration escaping me.

She hit the ground first, but quickly spun so we were barrel-rolling through the room. Her sharp fingernails dug into my arms, but I didn't let go. I didn't back down.

I widened my hips to stop us from rolling, pinning Cordelia to the ground beneath me. She was strong, yes, but not strong enough to throw my entire body off her.

Her claws eventually lost their grip on my arms as she switched her strategy, clawing at my neck, my face, my shoulders.

I still did not back away. I gripped her wrists and pinned them to the floor behind her head.

Hard.

A satisfied smile spread onto her face when she realized what had just happened. Her breath matched mine, coming out in harsh pants. "Very impressive, peacemaker. It seems you're not all looks after all."

"What is that supposed to mean?" I asked. I let go of her and moved away so she could sit up.

"You were forced to marry him, the deadliest fae in your kingdom. I should have known you'd be a fighter. I should have known they were wrong."

"*Who* was wrong?" I asked, trying not to sound too interested. After everything I had endured, I didn't quite care if strangers held negative opinions of me. They could think of me as weak, as afraid. They could think of me as the poor human girl who had to marry the evil prince.

They could think whatever they wanted. They had no idea what I had gone through, what my life was like.

"Everyone, peacemaker," Cordelia whispered, a twinkle of amusement in her eye. "You should really hear what the rest of the Paragon thinks of you. Saints, they might as well start a wager on how quickly you'll die in these trials."

I stood up and stormed out of the room. I didn't need this. I knew how much of a challenge winning would be. I didn't need it thrown in my face during my own training.

"Wait," she yelled before I reached the door. "You should take some pride in that, peacemaker."

"Why would I take pride in people thinking I am weak?"

"Because," she stood up and stepped toward me, her eyes flickering to the busted skin on my face. "Now, you can prove them all wrong."

CHAPTER 15
Malachi

Two days.

We had two days until Jade's trials began.

She seemed calm. Collected. During the day, she never showed an ounce of concern. She appeared confident and tough, ready for whatever training Cordelia seemed to throw her way. Even when Esther showed up to help, Jade did not falter.

She was ready.

I, though, could see the slight break in her scowl each time Cordelia landed a punch. Each time her magic flared beyond her control. The stress built day after day. I didn't blame her. Two days was not a lot of time to prepare for every possible scenario Silas might throw her way.

The Saints chose her for this, I reminded myself. She would not have been selected by the Saints if she wasn't ready. They would help her. She would get through this.

She had no other choice.

Jade had been training with Cordelia for hours now.

They had the same routine down each day. Wake up, eat, study with Silas, train. Sometimes the training was physical. Sometimes mental.

I began to drop my guard around Cordelia. Not because I wanted to, but because I saw her. I could see how much she cared about Jade's training, how much she wanted Jade to succeed.

Why? I wasn't sure. Perhaps she believed in the prophecy of the peacemaker just as much as the rest of us.

Either way, I figured Cordelia could be trusted. For now.

I, on the other hand, should not have been left unsupervised. I snuck through the dark tunnels of the mountain, careful not to make a single sound as I turned the final corner to Cordelia's bedroom.

I needed that damn book.

Knowing that Jade and I were bonded was just the beginning. I needed to know more about Anastasia and Erebus.

I would have remembered a story like that before. The hours I spent in that library, the thousands of stories I heard about the five Saints.

Was there a reason Silas hid that piece of history? Was there a reason I hadn't heard about the bond of life and death magic?

My senses peaked as Cordelia's bedroom door came into view. It was a large stone door, just like any of the other doors in the tunnel. Still, it felt different. Darker. I ignored the slight uptick in my heart rate as my senses dialed in on the bedroom. I approached the door, placed both hands on the stone, and pushed.

And then I waited. I wasn't sure what exactly I waited for, an alarm? A trap? Some sort of magical force shoving me from the entryway of her bedroom?

But none of those things came. A small bead of sweat rolled down the back of my neck.

I took one step forward, leaving the door ajar as I walked through the threshold of Cordelia's bedroom.

It only took a few small strides to cross the bedroom and reach the bookshelf on the far wall. It wasn't difficult to find the book she had read from when Jade and I visited. The book was wrapped in a thick black leather and a golden string hung from the spine as a bookmark.

I stilled and quieted my breathing, waiting for any sounds coming from the hallway. My fae ears turned toward the open door. Still, I heard nothing.

So I pulled the book from the shelf.

I couldn't take the book with me. If Cordelia saw it missing when she returned, I would be the first one to blame. It was suspicious enough that I had left Jade and her alone to train while I stepped away to scavenge her bedroom.

Instead, I flipped through the pages, looking for any mention of Anastasia and Erebus. Immediately, I knew this was a book I had never read before. Pages and pages of history filled the thick paper, with handwritten notes scribbled into the margins outside of the text.

This book was older than Cordelia. And it wasn't part of Silas's library...

Focus. I didn't have much time.

I flipped through more and more pages, taking in as much information as I could. For the most part, the pages were filled with personal stories of the Saints. Stories of how they got their magic, how they struggled to come to power for so long.

Some of it felt so familiar to me, had been ingrained in my memory for so long. I knew the five Saints so well, I could recite some of the stories in this book.

But the other stories...

Stories of love, stories of loss. Stories of betrayal among the Saints, of uprisings and abused magic.

I had never read those stories before.

My eyes landed on a particular page that had been handwritten and scratched out.

"It scares me, what I'm willing to do for him. He is everything I am not, yet he pulls me to him like I've belonged there all my life."

I re-read it again and again, skimming the pages to follow and looking for any more handwritten notes in the same flowing style. I nearly gave up on the book when I found what Cordelia had read to us before.

The love story of Anastasia and Erebus.

Life and death, the perfect balance. The perfect match. My heart sank as I read the story, burning it into my memory.

The last sentence read, *"To love death is to become it."*

CHAPTER 16
Jade

I never thought I would miss the scandalous dresses in Rewyth, but *Saints*. Looking down at myself in the long black cloak that the Paragon provided, I really, really, missed them.

The black fabric hid my frame entirely, dragging the ground beneath my feet as I took a step. The bruises from training with Cordelia had only multiplied, covering my skin with dashes of red and purple.

"You look amazing," Malachi said. His own black cloak somehow looked fitted and perfectly shaped to his lean, muscular body.

"You have to say that," I breathed. "You're my husband."

He moved closer, and my stomach erupted in heated butterflies as his eyes raked themselves down my body. "I most certainly do not have to," he replied, "but I'd be willing to tell you every day for the rest of our lives, if you're interested."

A teasing smile played on his lips.

"If you're trying to distract me," I said, closing the distance between us and sliding my hands up his chest, "it's working."

Malachi and I had been invited to a feast, thrown in my honor. What a joke, a feast to celebrate what might be my last day alive.

I wanted to laugh. How many times had I thought that? How many times had I thought that this day alive would be my last? I certainly thought that before my wedding, and look where that got me.

"What are you thinking right now, my queen?" Mal asked, pulling my hands from his chest and kissing each of my knuckles.

I watched his plump, perfect lips brush against my skin. "I'm thinking about how badly I don't want to do this. I don't want to eat with them. I don't want to look at Silas for one more second." The words were true, and I knew Malachi felt the same way. We couldn't exactly say *no* to the feast thrown in my honor.

"It's all part of their game," Mal said, lowering my hands to his sides. "They want to appear as your ally before they send you to the wolves."

"The wolves," I scoffed. "You mean the wolves that they create with their own messed up, magic concoction?"

He smiled, but it didn't reach his eyes. "Exactly," he breathed.

I eventually pulled my hands from his and began walking out of our room. "I suppose we should get this over with, then. The night can't last forever, right? We've attended plenty of dinners we wanted no part in. This will be nothing different."

Mal nodded.

We took our time walking to the dining room. I half-hoped that some sort of interruption would stop us from having to go, but it seemed as though we were the only two people walking through the underground tunnels.

Esther, Cordelia, Silas. They would all be there. They would all pretend like they had my best interests in mind, like they were on my side.

I threaded my fingers through Mal's. At least I could count on him. Of everyone that would be attending this feast, Mal would kill for me. He would kill them all. In fact, I wasn't entirely convinced that he wasn't thinking up some fool-proof plan to kill them all in their sleep before tomorrow's trial.

The dining room doors came into view, and even though they were shut, I could hear the cheerful sound of long, rich music coming from within. The loud voices carried out into the hall, voices I hadn't heard before. Voices of cheer and enthusiasm.

I stopped walking.

"Everything okay?" Mal asked.

"Fine, I just...I didn't expect music. The Paragon hasn't banned that luxury yet?"

His smile was real that time. "These wicked fae need something to keep them sane, right?"

With a light tug on my hand, we walked through the doors and into the dining room.

The entirety of the Paragon, over forty black-cloaked

members by the looks of it, stood from the massive wood table and clapped at our arrival. Blood rushed to my cheeks from the wave of attention.

"Our guests of honor! Welcome, Jade and Malachi Weyland!" someone announced in the back of the room.

Silas approached from my left, arms extended in a welcoming gesture. "It's an honor, truly," he started.

Malachi stifled a laugh. "It's not as if we had other plans," he muttered. If he meant for only me to hear it, he wasn't nearly quiet enough.

Silas's eyes hardened for half a second before he returned his ignorantly large smile. "Either way, we're happy to host you. Please, both of you. Have a seat." He motioned to the head of the table, where two large, throne-like chairs awaited us.

"You want us to sit at the head of the table?" I asked. "Isn't that your position?"

Silas's smile remained plastered across his pale face. "Not tonight, peacemaker. Tonight, you two are to be celebrated!"

The entire room, Silas included, watched in anticipation as Malachi and I approached our seats. I could have sworn they even held their breath as they awaited for us to sit.

"Wow," I said as Mal and I sat on the cushioned thrones. "What an elegant way to send me to my death."

A few in the room chuckled, although I knew it was their attempt at being polite and not a real reaction to my comment. There was nothing funny about this situation. This was real, and this was happening.

Silas settled in on the other head of the massive table, feeling miles away yet still somehow much, much too close to us. "I would like to propose a toast!" Silas announced. The members in the room each raised their small, wine-filled glasses. Malachi and I, after hesitating for a few seconds, did the same. "To Jade Weyland, the peacemaker. The saver of worlds. The balancer of magic. The Paragon has been working for decades to ensure that the balance is not disrupted. Fae, witches, humans. We should all be able to live in peace without one species overtaking another with their *gifts*."

I waited for him to continue, my palms beginning to sweat.

"With Jade Weyland as our peacemaker, we will be able to complete the sacred ritual from the Saints to restore power as it once was. Magic will flow freely over the lands of the fae. Every fae will possess gifts, not only a few. Every witch will have access to ancestral magic, not just the powerful bloodlines."

The hair on the back of my neck stood up. I knew that fae and witches were not as powerful as they once were, aside from special instances like Malachi, Esther and Cordelia. Very few fae and witches possessed strong magic.

Humans, of course, had nothing. They would always have nothing.

"Once Jade completes these trials, we will know without a doubt in this world that she is the one. She has been chosen. She will be the one to break the lands of this curse." Silas's voice grew louder with every word until every pair of eyes, mine included, glued onto him in anticipation.

"Raise your glasses, everyone. Tonight, we celebrate the peacemaker."

A roar of cheers filled the room, followed by clinking of glasses as the Paragon members saluted one another, all in celebration of me. Of future peace.

It was an interesting thought that more power would create peace. Why would the Saints need to limit the amount of power in this world in the first place? Were the fae and witches in power truly that greedy?

I thought about Malachi's power, how deadly it could be. In the wrong hands, magic like that could crumble kingdoms. Could overturn kings.

Malachi's warm hand on my lower back brought me back to the feast. "Still with us?" he whispered.

I replied with a reassuring smile, and we all took our seats. The sound of wooden chairs scratching against the stone floor pierced through the chilled air and added to the unsettled feeling that lingered in the room.

The Paragon members, all in the same black cloaks that Malachi and I now wore, didn't even look in our direction. They focused on their own hushed conversations around the dinner table, keeping their heads low and their voices even lower. Everyone, in fact, seemed to lower their heads. Except for Cordelia, naturally, who held her chin up as she glanced between myself and Silas.

She and Esther together found their seats in the middle of the table, equal distance from the two heads.

"So," Silas began, his words slicing like a sword through the low roar of voices, "I take it your training with dear Cordelia has been going well?"

A few Paragon members glanced in my direction. Their gazes didn't last.

"Define *well*," I spat, staring directly at Silas's pale face. "It would be mighty helpful if I knew what I was training for. Right, Cordelia?"

She half-choked on the wine she drank before setting her glass down, re-focusing on the conversation. "Jade Weyland is very talented," she stuttered in Silas's direction. "I have nothing but confidence in her after our training sessions." She winked in my direction.

Silas gave a nod of approval. "Good," he started. "Cordelia here has prepared many of our Paragon members for the trails."

"How nice of her," I sneered. "She seems to be quite an asset to the Paragon."

With Malachi so close, I could feel his warning through that small thread of power. With it, though, came a low purr of satisfaction.

My wicked, wicked husband.

Silas chose to ignore the attitude that laced my words. "That, she is," he replied. "We're honored to host the few of those that still possess gifts in this world. I must say, it was a shame when your husband chose to leave us all those decades ago."

Malachi straightened in the corner of my eye.

"Yes," Malachi answered before I had the chance. "My kingdom needed me."

Silas shook his head, finally breaking eye contact and taking a bite of the food that sat in front of him. "A pity," he started, "that such power can go to waste."

A laugh escaped me at the same time Malachi's power stirred. I felt it in my blood, in my bones.

Yet he held onto it. I admired that about him. Malachi could be temperamental and reckless, but he never lost control of his power. Not even in front of the most deserving of enemies. He only made calculated, deliberate moves with his magic.

I, on the other hand, had not even a portion of control Malachi possessed.

I lifted my chin to the room. "I would not consider becoming King of Rewyth a waste," I chimed in. "Nor would I be ignorant enough to show the King of Shadows a single ounce of pity."

Malachi's hand found mine beneath the table, squeezing gently. Either a warning, or a thank you. Either way, Silas was really pissing me off.

"Well," Silas said, leaning back in his chair and placing both palms on the table beside his plate, "you don't know Malachi like I do."

I wasn't sure why, but I half-expected Malachi to lose control then. Launch across the table, throw the knife through the room, anything. But I waited and waited, and Malachi sat motionless beside me.

I would have killed to know what he was thinking.

Cordelia, who actually had the ability to know what thoughts rummaged around in Mal's mind, stifled a smile in the middle of the table.

"Out of curiosity," I began, "does Cordelia help you turn all of the gifted fae into weapons? Or was that just your son?"

Gasps filled the room. Silas's face morphed in anger. "Watch what you say to me, child."

Malachi's hand tightened around mine again, his free palm smacking down on the surface of the table, rattling the plates around us. "My wife will speak freely."

Another snarl came from Silas. "Such a powerful man succumbing to his own wife. What happened to you, Malachi? You used to be so powerful. Feared across nations. Now you let this girl control you?"

I felt him before I saw him move, the rush of power, feeling almost like a rush of adrenaline in my bloodstream, zipped through my body as Malachi rose to his feet and threw a violent, black-misted ball of deadly power in Silas's direction.

I had seen Malachi's power on a few different occasions. Each time, silence filled the room. Each time, a tiny prick of fear made the hair on the back of my neck stand up. Even though I knew Mal would never hurt me, there was something so feral about the way he wielded his dark power.

But this? Malachi was…Malachi was *furious*.

Although just when the rush of power nearly sliced into Silas's body, a shield of glamour protected him. Not as if he would need it, though. As Malachi explained, Silas could not be killed.

Fueled by adrenaline, anger, and the need to defend my husband at all costs, though, I couldn't help myself.

I, too, mustered my emotions into a hot ball of fury, pushing my hands out in front of me to throw my own power in Silas's direction.

Gasps filled the room again, mixed with a few shouts of

fear. The Paragon members sat in limbo, unsure of what to do, as Silas's bubble of fae glamour protected him in an invisible fortress.

I pushed and pushed and pushed, wanting so desperately to crack that fortress, to rid us all of this pest that was the leader of the Paragon. Glass shattered in the distance.

I felt it, too. I could have cracked it. I could have put all of my energy into that attack and sliced through Silas's barriers to see exactly how unkillable he was.

If it weren't for the strong gust of wind that slammed into me, pushing me from my feet and slamming me against the wall behind us.

Malachi was at my side in an instant, helping me stand back on my feet as we turned to face the room.

"This is how you repay me?" Silas roared. "We throw a feast in your honor, and this is what I get in return?"

My breath came in heavy pants. I couldn't form any words. I knew that anything out of my mouth would only make the situation worse.

Esther whispered something to Cordelia. I could only guess what she said, because a second later, Cordelia walked toward us. "I believe this feast is over," she said in a low voice, more to us than to anyone else. I didn't dare look at Silas again. Neither did Malachi, although I could feel the anger radiating from him. "Come with me."

Nobody said another word. Our footsteps leaving the dining hall mixed with the sounds of ragged breathing as we exited. To my surprise, even Silas remained speechless. I avoided meeting his gaze as we left the room, the heavy doors shutting behind us.

"You two are idiots," Cordelia hissed as we made our way down the tunnel. "Did you know that?"

"That bastard is lucky he had his Paragon servants around to protect him," Mal muttered.

Cordelia scoffed. "Ha! As if he needs them. What was your goal there, anyway? To kill him? You know that's not possible. Unless your anger blinded you to that small fact, in which case you're even dumber than I thought."

"Come on, Mal," I said, gripping his hand and pulling him in the direction of our bedroom.

"Not so fast," Cordelia said. She turned to us with a mischievous smile on her face. "Tonight was supposed to be a celebration. You worked your ass off this week, peacemaker. You deserve at least some final send-off before the trials. You're coming with me."

"For what?" Mal asked.

Cordelia didn't answer. Her smile only widened as she turned on her heel and began walking in the opposite direction.

Mal and I exchanged a glance. "I suppose we don't have much else to lose tonight, do we?" I asked.

He exhaled loudly and wrapped his arm around my shoulders. "I suppose not, my queen."

CHAPTER 17
Malachi

Cordelia took a long, dramatic swig of the emerald glass bottle, her lips dripping with the red wine as she pulled it away and passed it in my direction.

"Is tonight a good night to be drinking?" Jade asked from the stone ground beside me. I glanced back to Cordelia, awaiting her answer.

She had taken us to a small stone cave, hidden in the depths of the temple. Condensation dripped from the cold walls around us, the sound of water constantly filling our silence.

"Trust me, honey," Cordelia answered. "There couldn't possibly be a better time."

I took the bottle from her and drank. The taste of wine had never been my favorite, but dulling my senses didn't sound like the worst thing in the world. Especially after that damned feast.

I passed the bottle to Jade. "Is this fae wine?" she asked. "Or human wine?"

"Drink it," Cordelia ordered. "Either way, it will make you feel better."

If it weren't for the light amount of pity and care that laced her words, I would have snapped at her for telling Jade what to do. But deep down, I started to understand that Cordelia had a soft heart. Even if it was hidden beneath layers and layers of Paragon skin.

Jade drank.

We stayed that way for a while, passing the bottle around and taking sips. The three of us were so different, but I knew that the same feeling of dread and anticipation hung in the air for all of us.

None of us wanted tomorrow to come, yet none of us could do anything to stop it.

"If you knew," Jade said after a while, breaking the calming blanket of silence, "if you knew what my trials would be, would you tell me?" She looked at Cordelia with a heart-wrenching amount of hope in her big, warm eyes.

Cordelia's jaw tightened. She took a long gulp of the bottle before setting it down on the stone ground before us. "Did Malachi ever tell you about my best friend, Tempesta?" Cordelia asked.

I felt Jade's eyes slide over to me, but I averted my eyes. I knew the story of Tempesta all too well, and the last thing I wanted to do was tell Jade about her.

"No," Jade answered softly.

"She was my sister. Not by blood, of course, but in

spirit. She was my other half, my better half. She was kinder than me, smarter than me. I envied her for it, really, but nobody else saw her that way. She was a fae, born and raised. Her magic existed, but she struggled to wield it. She wasn't strong like Malachi and I. She was...she was innocent."

I kept my eyes glued to the floor. Jade remained silent, although I could hear her heartbeat picking up.

"She was raised here in the Paragon, and after only two decades in this world, Silas made her..." Her voice cracked. She cleared her throat before picking up the bottle once more. "Silas made her complete the Trials of Glory. We all saw it coming, of course. Silas is cruel and wicked in ways that don't even make sense."

"Why would he make her do that?" Jade asked, shaking her head. "Why couldn't she leave instead?"

I didn't look at Cordelia, but I heard the smile on her face as she replied, "Tempesta didn't want to leave," she explained. "She had family here. She had friends, she had... she had me."

I clenched my jaw to keep the rush of emotion back. Cordelia and Tempesta were more than friends. Though she would never admit it, Cordelia had looked at Tempesta in a way she never looked at anyone else. Cordelia could be cruel and brutal, but never to her. She never raised her voice, never lifted her sword.

Those weeks before Tempesta's trial caused more pain in Cordelia than I could imagine.

"So I trained her," she continued, pushing past whatever memories surfaced in her mind. "Like I did everyone, like I was told to do by Silas. I taught her to defend herself. I taught her to use whatever tendril of magic she had pulsing through her blood. I begged and begged Silas to tell me, to at least give me a hint. Saints, if he would have just…"

She didn't have to continue. We all knew what she was going to say.

If Silas had given her a single hint as to what Tempesta's trials would be, Cordelia could have saved her life. And maybe, just maybe, she wouldn't be lonely in this damned temple all these decades later.

"None of that matters now," she pushed on. "What I'm trying to say is that yes, Jade. If I knew what your trials would be, I would tell you."

A beat of silence passed between us as the effect of Cordelia's words settled.

"Thank you," Jade whispered. "For helping me, I mean."

Cordelia scoffed, her cold, emotionless mask reassembling on her face. "You don't need to thank me, Jade," she said. "In fact, after tomorrow, you'll probably hate me for not preparing you better."

Jade laughed, and the sound of it alone sent a warm thrill through the icy shield forming in my chest. "Trust me," she sighed. "If I survive these trials, you'll be my best friend on the other side."

Cordelia smiled, a genuine smile this time. Not her usual smile laced with malice and motive.

"Not *if*," I corrected her. "*When* you survive the trials."

Jade's eyes locked with mine. "Right," she replied. "*When.*"

We drank until the bottle dried up, until the fear that connected us faded, until the emotions dulled. Only then could we at least attempt to get any sleep, the weight of tomorrow still looming over every single thought that crossed my mind.

CHAPTER 18
Jade

I stared up at the stone ceiling, unsure if I slept for more than ten minutes. I couldn't quiet my mind long enough to doze off, I was too busy envisioning every possible way today could go wrong.

Malachi stirred next to me. Apparently he hadn't slept much, either.

I didn't blame him.

Today was the day. The first day in the Trials of Glory. It was the last day I would sleep in this bedroom. The last day I would lie next to my husband.

Possibly my last day alive.

No, Jade. I had to stop thinking like that. Saints, I was the peacemaker. I had magic and power that very few others possessed. Had I accessed all of it? No, not even close.

But doubting myself wasn't going to help me.

Trial number one. *The past.*

Part of me couldn't help but think back through my

life, wondering which of my ghosts would haunt me during the trial. Malachi had warned me that everything would seem real. Sorting reality from magic visions would be nearly impossible.

My chest tightened as I thought of Tessa. Her perfect, pale face staring at me. Her bratty voice when she complained to me. Her soft, tiny hands as she clung to me when we were children.

I missed her. I missed her more than anything, and yet I rarely had time to grieve.

Maybe when this was all over I would grieve. I would have time to pity myself, to grieve the life I lost. And maybe, just maybe, I would see her again today during the trial.

Saints, I hoped so. I would do anything to see her face again. I would do anything to hear her say my name.

"You should be sleeping," Malachi mumbled. The grogginess in his voice made my chest ache. I silently prayed that I would be able to hear that voice again, would be able to wake up next to him again, even just once more.

"Can't sleep," I answered.

He rolled over and pulled me closer to him, using his arm to lock me into his chest, creating a fortress of warmth and love that I never wanted to escape. He had a way of doing that, of making me feel safe.

"I'll be there the whole time," he said, nuzzling himself into my neck and reassuring me with his lips. "You're not alone in this, Jade. Even if it might feel that way."

"That doesn't make me feel any better."

"Why's that?" He kissed my cheekbone, my temple.

I took a deep breath. "I don't want you to watch me get hurt. I don't want you to see that."

His hand trailed down the length of my body. "You're not going to get hurt, Jade. The challenges will be simple, and we'll be out of here before you even realize they've started."

"I get that you're trying to make me feel better," I said, "but I can't say it's working." I pushed myself out of his arms and crawled out of the bed. "I should get going. Better to get it over with, right?"

Malachi sat up onto his elbow, his black wings splayed beside him. I was going to miss this; Malachi's sculpted body, shirtless in our bed. His dazed smile and his lazy eyes as they flickered across my body like they so often did.

"I want you to take this," he said. He let go of me and crawled out of bed, reaching for his sword. "For the trials."

I shook my head when he handed it over. "No way," I said. "I can't take that."

"You can and you will. You need a weapon, and I want you to take mine."

"What if you need it?" I asked. "The enemies I'll be fighting are only in my mind. Yours are real, Malachi."

"It might look like they're in your mind from the outside, Jade," he said, "but to you they will be very, very real. And they'll be just as dangerous. Take it."

I held the sword in my hands, wondering how many lives he had taken with it. How many wars he had fought. I flipped the black sheath over in my palms, taking in every detail. "Thank you, Malachi," I said. "This means more than you know."

His features softened in a way that melted my entire heart. "You are everything to me, Jade Weyland. When I wield this sword, it is for you. Not for myself. There is nobody I want to have it more than you. Now, would you do me the utmost honor of accepting this gift, and wielding my own weapon in your Trials of Glory?"

Now I was sure my heart actually melted. "I would love nothing more," I breathed.

I took the sword from his hands. The weight of it shocked me, it was much heavier than the dagger I was used to. It might have been the strong metal used to carve the sharp weapon. Or, it might have been the hundreds of lives taken with one motion.

They held weight. I was beginning to feel it.

"If this doesn't work," I started to say before my voice wavered, my own body betraying me.

"Don't you dare say those words." Malachi pulled me to him with a hand on the back of my neck and wrapped his arms around me. Hard. I basked in the smell of him, the smokey danger that had lingered in his shadow since the moment I first saw him in that forest.

"I don't know how we got here," I said. "I don't know what I did wrong."

"You didn't do a damn thing wrong, Jade Weyland. You did everything right. Every single thing."

"Then how are we here? How did we get to this point?"

Heavy silence lingered. "People who do the right thing in this world don't have good things happen to them. They have the worst things happen, and every single person looks at them as if they deserve it."

I pulled away, choking back tears. I wasn't going to cry. Not today. Today, I had to be strong. I had to be someone else.

The peacemaker.

"How is this peaceful? I want to know who came up with that name," I said. "They should call me the chaos-bringer, or the death-flirter."

Malachi's mouth twitched at the corner. "I don't know, but now isn't the time to look for peace, either. You give them what they deserve, Jade. They've tried to take everything from you." He held my face and forced me to look into his torturous, dangerous eyes. "Now, it's your turn to take everything from them."

"How? They're in control here, Mal. I'm a stupid toy in whatever game they want me to play."

Malachi's jaw tightened. He knew it was true. He had been in this exact situation before.

Except he wasn't the peacemaker. Kingdoms weren't dependent on his survival.

"Show them how powerful you can be. Show them, and let them fear you the way they should. Bring them to their knees, my queen."

A new wave of heat filled me, but not one of anger or desire. One of confidence. One of eagerness.

I thought I wanted victory. I thought I wanted peace.

I realized now that was all wrong. I didn't want any of that. I wanted what Malachi had. I wanted heads to roll the second I walked into a room. I wanted the sound of my name to put a deep, ebbing fear in the hearts of my enemies.

I wanted people to fear me. I wanted people to think twice before they challenged me.

Malachi was right. Today, they would learn. Today, they would think twice.

"Okay," I said after what felt like hours. "Okay, I'm ready."

He kissed my forehead, fierce and harsh. "We should go," he said. "They'll all be waiting."

We both got dressed quickly, and Malachi helped me strap the sword onto my hip. It was bulky and heavy, but I liked it. I wanted a piece of him with me during the trials. Maybe, even in the midst of chaos and magic, I would recognize the gift from him and remember.

"What happens now?" I asked. "I mean, how much time do I have?"

Malachi stiffened, adjusting a black cloak around his shoulders before shoving the stone door to our bedroom open. He held his hand out for me. I took it.

"You'll have to stay in the arena. The arena isn't much, it's just a large stone room. But it won't feel like that when you're in it."

"Why not?"

He nodded. "They'll have the strongest witches and gifted fae working together to create a new reality for you. You won't know where you are, you won't know how long you've been there."

Don't be afraid, I told myself. This is all part of the process. Part of the facade. They want to scare you, they want to see you weak.

Don't give them that satisfaction.

Malachi didn't let go of my hand as we walked through the now-familiar tunnels of the mountain and approached the dining hall.

Silas stood in the middle of the room, clearly expecting us, with a group of hooded men and women behind him.

"Are you ready?" Silas asked. His eyes glared into me with an intensity that made the hair on my neck rise.

"Yes," I lied. Malachi squeezed my hand once and let it go.

Everything happened so fast. I felt as though just yesterday we were fighting against them at the castle of Rewyth.

I didn't want to die.

"Hey," Malachi whispered. "You can do this."

My walls were crumbling. They had been, I realized, for quite some time. But today would be the day the walls came cascading down, and I had nothing but my own magic to protect me. I wasn't sure that would be enough.

I didn't even realize I had stumbled until Malachi caught me in his arms and pulled me to his chest. I wrapped my arms around him, feeling like he was the only thing in this world I had left to fight for. "I'm scared," I whispered, not confident that I had even said the words aloud.

Malachi pulled back and smiled at me gently. "You would be insane if you weren't afraid," he admitted. "But fearful or not, this is the next step. Remember who you are, remember what you can do. And try to remember that it's all magic. None of it is real."

I nodded, drinking in every word; consuming everything he said, devouring the way he said it.

"Come with me," Silas said from behind me, ruining whatever peace I had left in my solitude with Malachi. I immediately stiffened away from Mal and rolled my shoulders back, lifting my chin.

This is how he would want me to act. Unafraid.

Don't let them see your fear.

"I'll see you when it's over," I said. Malachi nodded, and I held his gaze until the gentle smirk on his face faded away, replaced with a dark shadow of unreadable emotion.

I would do this for him. I would survive for him.

My feet moved, or more so glided, to where Silas stood in wait. He had a dumb smile on his face, staring at me as if I were his shiny new toy. "Let's get this over with," I said to him, although the words didn't come out as strongly as I meant them to.

Suddenly, my entire body grew numb. My heart beat, not any faster than it already was beating, but much, much harder. Silas said something to me, but a distant ringing in my ears grew louder and louder. His mouth moved, but I heard nothing.

And then we were moving. Silas put a cold hand on my arm and led me out of the dining hall, through a set of tunnels I had yet to venture down. I meant to look back at Malachi one more time, but my body stilled. Aside from my feet moving slowly, one foot in front of the other, I was frozen.

"Trust yourself, Jade," Silas said, but the words seemed to echo through the walls of my own mind.

Trust yourself. How was that even possible? How could I trust myself, when my entire life all I have done was destroy lives and torment the ones around me?

How?

Silas attempted to place a hand on my back for guidance, but I flinched away from him.

Cordelia stood before me now, and I realized we had entered a small cave in the tunnels. I wasn't sure how long we had been walking or how long we had been standing in the cave.

"Jade?" Cordelia asked. She shook my shoulders, and her hands were much warmer than Silas's. I didn't flinch away.

Time seemed to snap back to me. "What?"

"Were you listening to me?"

The ringing in my ears slowly dissipated, and I began to feel my own body again. "I'm sorry, can you say that again?"

Cordelia's expression hardened. "The trials typically only last a few days, but it will seem much longer to you. You'll have to fend for yourself, feed yourself, find shelter when needed. We cannot interfere with the trials in any way, including Malachi. So once you enter through those doors, you're on your own."

"What's out there?" I asked.

Cordelia ignored me and pulled the cork from a small vial of liquid. "Take this," she said.

"What's that?"

She gripped my jaw and forced my head back, pouring the sweet, purple substance into my mouth.

I swallowed it, not even trying to fight.

"This helps create the setting of the trials for you. To us, it will look like you're running around going crazy in the room. But your body will be affected by what you see in those trials, Jade. If you get stabbed in your trial, your body will bleed out as if you got stabbed here in this room. If you are stuck in the freezing mountains in your trial, your body will freeze to death inside this room. Understand?"

"Where did Silas go?" I asked once I realized we were now alone.

"I'm sure he's in the gallery by now. Nobody wants to miss the show."

My stomach sank. "Show? You mean people will be watching?" No, Malachi shouldn't watch me die. I didn't want him to see me struggle, to see me panic.

She stopped what she was doing and looked me in the eye. "We can sit around and pretend like the Paragon wants to prove you as the peacemaker, or we can look at this situation for what it really is, Jade."

My vision blurred. "And what's that?"

"Entertainment. Silas and the others, they only want a good show."

A show? Was she really suggesting that everything I was about to endure was for entertainment?

"Don't let Malachi watch," I blurted. "I don't want him to see me out there."

Cordelia snorted. "Honey, I don't think I could keep him away if I tried."

My vision swirled again. Cordelia pushed open the massive stone door ahead of me, which gave way to a large cave-like room.

I could hardly see what was in front of me, but I could feel Malachi. I knew he was near.

"Good luck, peacemaker," Cordelia said as I walked through the stone door. "The whole world is counting on you."

CHAPTER 19
Malachi

A few minutes later, I joined the Paragon members on the stone balcony that overlooked the underground arena. The room was not small by any means, but filled with the dozens of Paragon members gathered to watch, it felt miniscule.

I pictured myself in that stone arena below. How small I must have looked back then. How afraid. That was the last time I had truly been afraid. Until I met Jade, anyway. Now, with Jade at risk, it seemed as if everything frightened me. I did not fear for my own life, but for hers.

"It feels like yesterday that you were the one in this same arena," Silas said. "I remember it so clearly, how fiercely you fought."

Every single word out of his mouth pierced like a knife to my gut. I reminded myself to control my anger. He wanted to see me worried. He wanted to see me affected by Jade's pain.

I lifted my chin. "To me, it was lifetimes ago. I'm not the same person I was entering those trials."

Silas stepped closer to me. I fought the urge to throw him through the wall. "And you're a better man for it," he said.

I felt Jade before I saw her, her frightened presence struck like fire igniting in my spine. *Come on, Jade. You can do this.*

Cordelia approached from behind. I wanted to speak with her, but I couldn't tear my eyes away from the arena. Cordelia would tell me the truth. She would tell me how bad it was.

"The Saints have blessed this place," Silas announced. I had absolutely no idea who he was talking to. It's not like Jade could hear him. "This girl is full of power, full of this offering from the most gracious. Three trials will test her heart and spirit; trials confronting her past, her present, and her future. She will see herself for her raw potential, her pure spirit. And thus, the peacemaker will be born."

Paragon members cheered. It made me sick. How long had they been waiting for the trials, waiting to see Jade fail?

"Your nerves are palpable," Cordelia's voice over my shoulder made me tense.

I clenched my fists and tried to calm myself. Her slim body slid through the forming crowd that overlooked the arena and stopped at my side.

"I can't say I care, Cordelia," I replied.

"Your wife will be fine," she said. Her voice was barely a whisper.

Is Jade nervous? How is she feeling? Is she afraid, confident? Saints, I hope she's confident.

"Saints," she mumbled under her breath. "Your thoughts are louder than Silas's annoying voice."

Movement in the corner of my eye caused my heart to sink. Jade stumbled forward, confused and unaware. The effects of the serum finally kicking in.

The arena, as Silas so gallantly called it, was nothing but a stone pit under the mountain. Jade, however, would not see it that way. She would see whatever her mind forced her to see. For the first trial, it would be something of her past. Her father, maybe. Or Tessa. My chest physically hurt at the thought.

Jade was strong. But she had a breaking point. We all did.

Silas and the other Paragon members would be watching her, judging her. They would wait to see how she reacted to pain, to distress.

And based on how my wife reacted under the agony they inflicted, they would decide if she was worthy.

It made me want to vomit. They did not know Jade. They didn't know how strong she could be, how much pressure she could take. They knew absolutely nothing about her, and yet they thought of themselves as messengers from the Saints to test her spirit.

Jade had fallen to her knees on the stone ground, breathing heavily. It wouldn't be long now before the visions started.

"Come with me," Cordelia barked. "You need to get your shit together."

Her sharp fingernails dug into the flesh on my arm as she pulled me backward. I didn't fight her. I followed her out of the crowd, ripping my eyes away from Jade's struggling figure down below.

I didn't want to leave her, but something felt almost violating about watching.

Once Cordelia and I were alone in the tunneled hallway, she shoved me against the wall.

A warning growl was all she got. I had fought with Cordelia more times than I could count, and as much as I hated to admit it, she was a great sparring partner.

But I was angry. She wouldn't win a fight against my anger.

"You know just as well as I do that Silas is doing this to get to you."

His own son. How damned poetic.

Cordelia's face twisted in confusion before her features lightened. Nothing annoyed me more than having my thoughts invaded, but Cordelia wasn't my enemy right now.

"How long have you known that he's my father?" I asked. "I'm sure you've been having plenty of entertainment with this secret, you and Esther."

Her nostrils flared for a second before she smiled, cocking her head to the side. "Actually, yes. Although I must say, I thought you would have figured it out by now. Not so smart these days, are you, king?"

I snapped, hauling myself forward and grabbing the witch by the throat. She hardly flinched, but that didn't stop me from slamming her backward.

"First," I spit back, "you can get out of my damned mind. Second, you can shut up about my mother and Silas unless you have actual useful information you'd like to share. But according to your reaction, you've known this since the beginning. Which doesn't make you my ally, Cordelia. In fact, that makes you pretty damn close to my enemy."

Her brows furrowed in anger. *Good,* she should be angry. "Silas took care of you. He favored you."

I tightened my grip on her scrawny neck. "He ruined me."

She gasped for air when I released her. "You really think so? You think Silas ruined you? He gave you a name, Prince of Shadows. Or is it King of Shadows now, I figure? He sent you back to the kingdom you were born to rule. He made you what you are, Malachi. He made you a *king*."

"He made me a killer."

"And that's any different from the rest of us?" I ignored the way her voice wavered. "Look at me, Malachi," she growled. I glanced up at her, finally looking at her tired, worn out face. "I am many things. Am I your friend? Saints, no. But I, of all the damned people under the mountain, am not your enemy. And *that* you can believe."

My power flared beneath my skin. Saints, I didn't know what to believe. Cordelia had never been my friend, at least she was honest enough about that. But what angle did she have? She was half witch, half fae. Just like me. How could she benefit from either side gaining the power of the peacemaker?

She smiled, and I could have cursed myself for even

thinking the words. "I have no angle," she answered, letting herself wind through my thoughts. "I want nothing to do with your peacemaker."

"Then what is all this?" I asked. "Why are you…"

"Helping you?"

"I wouldn't call it that."

"I would." She lifted her chin. "Maybe I have my own motives, Malachi. And maybe they have nothing to do with you or your fragile, human wife."

"You dig through my mind all day long, witch. Tell me what you mean, I don't have time for riddles."

She glanced toward the arena door. "Not here," she said. I didn't flinch away when she stepped closer. "Trust Esther, and no one else. Not Silas. Not anyone. At this point, I'm not even sure I would trust a Saint himself standing before me."

As if I planned on trusting any of these Paragon members anytime soon. "Am I supposed to know what that means?"

"Your wife's trials are starting," Cordelia said. "Go."

Shit, she was right. I pulled my wings tight against my shoulder blades and turned to the gallery door when her hand fell on my wrist to stop me.

"If your wife dies during these trials, it would be a great mercy."

She was gone before I processed the words.

CHAPTER 20
Jade

I became vaguely aware of a solid surface beneath my knees, but when I tried to look around, my vision darkened. Clouds blurred my eyesight until I couldn't see anything.

Splitting pain in my head made it difficult to open my eyes. The blank, stone arena that I had seen before seemed to morph. It turned slowly from the open nothingness to a forest, one filled with tall, vibrant trees and I could even swear I saw the sunshine above.

No, it wasn't real. The trees, the sun. Malachi had warned me about this. This was all magic, I was in the empty stone arena.

A soft breeze caressed my skin, my loose black hair. Saints, when did my hair get that long? It fell nearly past my waist now.

"Jade?" a familiar voice asked.

When I looked up from my dark locks, I was standing

in that forest. My thoughts grew foggy yet somehow clarified at the same time.

A girl I knew stood before me. Her choppy black hair and tall, lean figure would be identifiable anywhere.

"Sadie?"

Sadie smiled. Her short braids were just as I remembered them, yet she looked...healthier. Happier. "How–"

I stopped myself from asking. This wasn't real. None of it was real. Sadie left when I...when Malachi killed Isaiah.

Right?

I tried to recall who Isaiah was, but my mind lost the thought. I refocused my attention on the girl standing before me.

"I've missed you," she said. "I wasn't sure I would ever be able to see you again."

My chest tightened. "I'm sorry, Sadie. About everything. Did you make it out of the castle okay? Where did you go when you left?"

"Malachi made sure I was able to make it out. I scavenged the woods for a while before I found a small human camp, much like Fearford."

Fearford. It felt like decades ago that I had stumbled into Fearford, the human kingdom where Sadie had once lived.

"Good," I said. "I'm glad you're okay." Sadie stared back at me with a simple, clean smile on her face. "What are you doing here, Sadie?"

"I'm here to help you," she said.

"Help me with what?"

"I'm here to help you survive, Jade. Since that's what you did for me."

I snorted. "I wouldn't say that. If I never would have showed up to Fearford, you would still be there. You would still be happy."

She reached out and gripped my hand. Not a magical touch, not one of air, but a real human touch. Her skin was warm against mine as she held me. "You saved me, Jade. You made sure I was fed, and you forced your husband to show me mercy."

"I'm the reason Isaiah is dead," I admitted.

"You're the reason we aren't *both* dead. Isaiah betrayed you. I would never dream of doing the same."

Birds chirped in the distance, something I hadn't heard for a very long time. Or maybe I had heard it, but I was too busy living in chaos to notice. Sadie and I both looked up, scanning the tree line above before I closed my eyes and basked in the warmth of the sun.

The sun felt nice. Welcoming.

"Do you know where we are?" I asked after a few minutes.

"We're home," she answered. I opened my eyes again to find Sadie smiling at me. In all the time I knew her, I didn't know if I had ever seen her smile so much.

My chest ached. "Home? We're in Rewyth?"

She shook her head. "Your first home, Jade. Your *real* home."

A light flicker of panic threatened me, but I quickly shoved it away. I scanned the trees around us again.

The familiar patterns of the shrubs and trees sparked a

memory of this place. We weren't standing in just any forest. We were standing in my forest, the same one I had hunted in dozens of times. The same one I had cried in, escaped to.

This *was* home.

"Follow me." I began walking through the forest, through the same path that I had walked hundreds of times. Everything came back to me like I had been there all along. The familiar path, the smell of the fresh air. It was different than the forest around Rewyth. The air smelled different, less crisp. More of flowers and less of spice.

But it was still home.

My heart fluttered at the thought of my old house, and who might be inside of it.

Tessa.

My feet moved faster, quickening in pace at the thought of her golden hair, her pale skin. She would be here, right?

Because she was home. If this was truly my home, Tessa would be here.

"Slow down!" Sadie yelled from behind me, but I didn't stop.

I did no such thing. My quick walking turned into a jog, and before I knew it, I was outright sprinting out of the woods and up the path to that first, worn-down house at the bottom of the hill.

My home, the place I had grown up in. The place that caused me so much pain and suffering for years on end, and yet here I was, running to it like a child.

I ripped the rotting front door open. "Tessa?" I yelled. "Tessa, are you here?" I scanned the kitchen and the small bathroom before shoving aside the ajar door to the bedroom we shared.

Empty. All of it empty, not a single sound echoed through the crumbling walls.

But the bed was unmade, something Tessa had a bad habit of doing. And a pair of her favorite shoes sat tossed in the corner.

My heart fluttered once more.

After ensuring she was nowhere in the house, I ran back outside. Sadie waited for me. "She's here," I said. "She's here somewhere."

"Where does she like to go? Where are her favorite spots?"

Sadie spoke as if Tessa was still around, as if she still lived and breathed. I stopped walking and spun around.

Sadie didn't know. She wasn't there when Tessa died, and she would have no way of knowing she was dead.

I thought about telling Sadie, but...what if Tessa *was* alive? What if she was here somewhere, living and breathing like the same girl she had been?

What if nothing had changed? What if this was all normal, and Tessa was simply in town shopping for food?

It was a possibility.

"Come on," I said to Sadie. And the two of us began the walk to town.

I waited for her to ask questions, like how we possibly lived in such houses when they were barely standing or why nobody even looked up when they passed us on the narrow dirt path.

But she didn't. She silently walked beside me, a silent

presence of comfort. "The market is at the end of this path," I said after a while.

"Great."

"Tessa doesn't usually go to the market alone, but if I've been gone maybe she went there to find me. Or maybe she went there to get food."

"It's definitely possible," Sadie said. "I'm sure we'll find her there."

The path grew more and more crowded, each familiar face we passed stared down at the path or at their own feet as we scurried by. It wasn't unusual. People here weren't friendly. Being friendly wasn't part of survival, and that's all that happened in this town. Surviving.

The market came into view, and I recognized the meat seller at the first table. "Have you seen my sister?" I asked as we approached. "Has she been through here today?"

The man scoffed. He wasn't exactly friendly, either. "Move along, girl."

"Excuse me," I said, louder this time. "I asked you if you've seen my sister."

"I'm not a babysitter." The man didn't even look up from the table as he spoke. "If you've lost your sister, I suggest you go find her."

Sadie was already staring at me with a knowing look when I glanced her way. I didn't have to try much to summon my power. It was ready to go, ready for me to use it.

Light flashed around us, directed at the man's table. He screamed and slammed against the wood pile behind him.

Burnt meat turned to ashes before us, completely ravished by my power.

"You crazy bitch!" he yelled. "What are you? A witch?" I pulsed another round of power in his direction, narrowly avoiding his body. He screamed again. "I told you I ain't seen your sister!"

A few others were screaming now, some running for the houses. *As if that would stop me.*

"Has anyone seen my sister?" I yelled as I turned around, surveying the scattering crowd. "Where is she?"

Slight panic turned into a forest fire of chaos. Screaming turned into non-stop cries of fear, and running turned into trampling. Everyone fled the market, running away from a danger they hardly knew existed.

To them, I was Jade. I was the poor girl with the drunken father at the bottom of the hill. They had no idea who I had become, they had no idea how powerful I had become.

"Tessa!" I screamed. Sadie followed tightly behind me as we walked against the sea of panic. "Tessa!"

She was here. She had to be here. *Right?* "We'll keep looking," Sadie shouted over the chaos. "I'll check the rest of the market."

Sadie pushed and shoved the pitiful crowd as she maneuvered herself around the rest of the market.

But I had my eyes locked on one place. One place that a small, heated tether inside of me pulled me to.

The tavern was the one place I hated, the one place I avoided at all costs. I knew what dwelled there, drunks and others who only wanted to escape the lives they had here in this pitiful town. My father dwelled there, often staying there for days at a time before stumbling back home.

I kicked the cracked door open with my dirty boot. And for the first time in my life, I stepped inside the tavern.

A few men turned from their spot at the bar to look at the intruder. "Jade?"

One filthy man in particular stood from a corner table and stepped closer to me. It took me a handful of seconds to recognize him as my father.

Of course he was here. "I'm looking for Tessa," I said. "Where is she?"

He stammered, looking at me as if he were staring at a ghost. "Jade, she's not here."

"What do you mean she's not here? She wasn't at the house, so where is she?"

"She was with you," he explained. "She left to find you."

My stomach twisted in a vile, desperate way that made me sick to my stomach. "When?"

He didn't answer right away. His mouth hung open, and I could feel the way he dug through all of the possible word choices, desperate to find the right one.

Tessa wasn't here.

"Forget it," I mumbled. "You're no help. You never are."

I spun on my heel and left the tavern.

The market had nearly emptied. Sadie stood in the center of it all, looking at me with pity. I hated that. Pity. As if people truly felt sorry for the situation I was in.

But I wasn't sorry. I deserved every ounce of the shit situations I had been put in.

"She's not here," I said.

"What?" Sadie yelled back.

I opened my mouth to say it again, but I didn't have the energy. I couldn't summon the strength to be heard, to repeat those words again. "She's not here," I breathed to myself.

My legs gave out beneath me. I crashed to the dirt pavement, not even feeling the pain that I expected. "She's not here," I breathed again. "She's not here, she's not here, she's not here."

Sadie was beside me, then, holding my shoulders and trying to lift me up. "She's not here, Sadie."

She needed to hear me. This was no use. Coming here was a waste of time. "Tessa's gone."

I tilted my head up to the sun that still warmed my skin. *Why?* Why would such a beautiful, healing light shine down on such a horrendous day?

I did not stop the tears that fell. Sadie spoke to me, but I couldn't make out the words. I opened my eyes and stared at the sun, not caring that it hurt. Not caring if it took my sight forever.

Exhaustion seeped out of my bones as if it had been hiding there, waiting for its time to creep into the rest of my body.

"Jade?" another voice asked, but this time it was not my father.

I looked away from the fire in the sky, and, when my eyes adjusted, saw Tessa standing before me.

CHAPTER 21
Malachi

Her pain cascaded around me, filling the cracks in my exterior. My eyes locked on her body in the arena. She saw something, something dreadful.

She paced around the stone room for a few minutes, talking in a voice too quiet for any of us to hear. Although, by the nasty look on Silas's face, the trial played out exactly as planned.

I hated this. I hated the pain she was feeling, I hated that I couldn't run down there and take it all from her.

But what I hated most was that I couldn't see what she was seeing. I couldn't see what hurt her.

She paced faster and faster before she stopped, stumbling backward with wide, surprised eyes.

"Tell me what's happening," I hissed at Cordelia. "What is she seeing?"

Cordelia rolled her eyes, but leaned toward me and whispered, "She's home. She's looking for her sister."

Dread ran through my body, drying my sweaty palms. "Is her sister alive?" I asked. "Saints, tell me she doesn't have to see her dead sister again." Cordelia's chest rose and fell. Twice. My patience dwindled with every heart-aching second. "Tell me!" I hissed.

My voice echoed, and I felt a dozen Paragon eyes slide in our direction from under their black hoods.

"You're causing a scene," she whispered. "Calm yourself, *king*."

"I don't care if I burn this entire damned mountain to the ground, *witch*. Tell me my wife is okay."

She took a long breath. "Her sister is alive," she answered.

At the same time, the crumbling suffering in my gut dissipated, turning into something much, much more dangerous. Especially in the trials.

Hope.

"I can't watch this," I mumbled. "You people sit around and watch an innocent girl torture herself with her own mind. It's sickening."

This time when I stormed from the room and into the tunnels, Cordelia did not follow.

Each step I took put distance between myself and Jade, and with each step, our connection weakened.

I had never felt so damned helpless in my entire life.

I remembered my first trial, how utterly confused I was. You could understand that this was all fake, that it was all part of the trial, yet still become completely blindsided by what happened down there in that arena.

Of course Jade would see Tessa in the first trial. She

would be confused and hurt and lost. And I couldn't help her. Not in the slightest.

My wings tucked tightly behind my back as I walked, and I didn't even try to get out of the way when others passed me in the hallway.

They didn't care about her. They didn't care if she lived or if she died.

They wanted to exploit her power, humiliate her, and feel better about themselves during the process.

I needed a distraction. I couldn't sit around and watch this, feeling everything she felt through our magic bond.

I had to get my mind off those damn trials.

Rewyth. That would help me.

I ran my hands down my face, rubbing away the tension from the last hour.

Someone was trying to take my throne in Rewyth. Serefin needed me. Before I could register where I was headed, I found myself looking for the one person I had spent the last week avoiding.

Esther.

"No way," Esther said, shaking her head. "He won't allow it."

"My throne is being threatened, Esther, and he kept it from me. He doesn't want me to know about it. Saints, who knows what else he's been keeping from me? It was a damn miracle that little boy got us the first letter."

She stilled in thought. I had found her in her bedroom,

alone in the darkness. It didn't surprise me that she didn't want to watch Jade's trials. She had saved Jade's life more than once, after all. It was an insult that her life was in jeopardy again.

I stepped forward, looking her in the eye, needing her to feel my urgency as I said, "I need to get a message to Serefin. Can you help me? Can you get it past Silas?"

She opened her mouth to reply, but shut it. At least she wasn't blatantly declining the idea.

"It's dangerous," she said. "If he catches us..."

"What?" I asked. "What exactly will Silas do to you, Esther? Tell me, is he still in love with you?"

She looked away from me and laughed quietly. "Love," she sneered. "What a damn waste."

"He's softer to you," I said, trying to quiet my voice. "He cares."

"He may have cared in the past, son, but the Silas I knew is long gone."

I shook my head. "People don't forget love that easily, Esther. If you ask him, he might say yes."

"Or," she pushed, "he'll get angry that we're trying to sidestep him and he'll retaliate. He'll take it out on Jade. Is that what you want, Malachi? Are you willing to risk that?"

Saints. No, I wasn't willing to risk that. But to think of Serefin and my brothers struggling back home, not knowing if we were still alive, not knowing if we were coming to their aid.

"I can't sit back and do nothing," I said honestly.

"I know you can't. Let me do some thinking. I'll find you when I have an answer."

CHAPTER 22
Jade

"Tell me this is real," I begged. "Tell me you're really here right now."

My sister—my frail, perfect baby sister—dropped to her knees in front of me. "I'm here," she repeated. "I'm here, Jade."

As soon as my hands felt her body, everything I thought was real and everything I knew was fake collided. I no longer knew what was tangible and what my mind was forcing me to believe, because what I *did* know was that Tessa—my dead baby sister—knelt right before me.

In the flesh.

And she was no longer deceased, no longer dead because I couldn't protect her. No, we were home, where we should have been all along. Where *she* should have been all along.

"I'm so sorry," I blurted out. "I'm so sorry I couldn't protect you."

"What are you talking about?" Tessa asked. "I'm fine, Jade. Look at me."

She lifted my chin with a finger and forced me to look at her. I dragged my eyes across her untouched face, across her neck that was perfectly *not* snapped.

She was okay. She was back to herself, how she should have been all along. "Where have you been?" she asked me. "I've been looking for you."

"We should get going," Sadie interrupted. I had almost forgotten she came here with me.

Another scream came from the market. I ignored it. "Go where?" I asked.

"Anywhere but here. Come on, Jade. Too many people have seen you."

"What do you mean?" I asked. "I live here, of course they've seen me."

Sadie shook her head, suddenly desperate to get me out of sight.

"What happened to you, Jade?" Tessa asked.

"I–" I held my hands out before me, examining them. I wasn't sure why, but I thought they might look different. "I don't know what happened."

Tessa and Sadie both stared at me then, side by side. They were so different. Compared to Sadie, Tessa looked so pure. So perfect. Sadie, as beautiful as she was, had an edge to her. Her choppy, black hair had blunt edges and messy, stray pieces fell around her chiseled face. Not Tessa, though. Not a single strand of her hair fell out of place.

But they both stared at me like I was the crazy one, like I was the one that needed help. "What is it?" I asked.

They both held their mouths agape, as if they both desperately wanted to say something but couldn't. Then, their eyes shifted to somewhere behind me. Somewhere inside the tavern. I spun around and stood up, searching for what they stared at.

My stomach dropped.

Every single body from the tavern now hung from ropes. Dead.

Including my father. "Saints," I muttered. I didn't wait for Tessa and Sadie before running inside. "Stay back!" I yelled. They didn't need to see this, especially not Tessa. She was too young, too innocent.

I took a few steps forward and entered the threshold of the tavern, now eerily silent.

I should have been surprised or disturbed, but I had already seen this, hanging from the dining hall in Rewyth. The memory came back in flashes. I had seen plenty of death in my life, this shouldn't have phased me.

It wouldn't have, I was certain of it.

If it weren't for my father.

"Father?" I asked. He looked alive, no paler or no more still than usual. He looked entirely normal. But I knew, deep in my soul I knew that he was dead.

Tessa wailed a sob behind me. I ran to her, ran out of the tavern and shut the door behind me.

"Is he—is he—" She fought to get the words out, but I knew where she was going with it. Is he dead?

"Yes," I said, harsher than I meant to. "He's gone, Tessa. They're dead."

She didn't look confused, she didn't seem to even

wonder what just happened inside that tavern. I was certainly wondering. I was just in there a few minutes ago, and everyone was alive.

Tessa looked me in the eyes. And then screamed.

She screamed and screamed and screamed, it was a sound that could not possibly have been human. I tried yelling her name, tried shaking her shoulders to get her to stop.

But the screaming continued, with more force than even possible.

When I could not possibly take the screaming anymore, I looked away from my sister and covered my own ears, trying to drown out the torturous sound.

But when I looked away, Sadie was on the ground. Unconscious.

Over Tessa's nonstop screaming, I dropped to the ground next to my old friend. "Sadie!" I shouted, but Tessa's screams only drowned them out. "Sadie! Wake up!" I placed a hand on her chest, feeling for any sort of heartbeat. Feeling for any movement that would wake me up from this nightmare.

But she wasn't moving. Her skin grew colder with every passing second.

Sadie was dead.

My scream matched Tessa's, and it was only then that her own screams stopped.

Tessa fell to the ground behind me. "Saints," I muttered, scrambling over Sadie's body to get to her. Tessa's eyes were still open, her mouth still agape as if she had stopped breathing mid-scream.

I touched her body, shook her shoulders.

Not again. This wasn't happening again.

Panic overtook me, seeping into each of my senses and constricting my chest like a fist tightening around my heart.

Not again.

"Tessa?" My voice cracked and broke, shattering like the world around me. I laid two hands on her body, feeling for anything. Feeling for hope.

But I knew what had happened.

My father was dead.

Sadie was dead.

Tessa…for the second time in my life, was dead.

I laid my forehead against hers.

And I cried.

Somehow, this hurt just as badly as it had hurt the first time. Even though some part of me, deep down, knew it was coming. Knew that it was too good to be true.

People like me didn't get happy endings. Tessa being alive was…it wasn't real.

Real. Somewhere in my mind, I knew what was real. But this pain was real. This grief that ate at my soul and devoured my heart was real.

My pain morphed into anger, anger that I had let this happen again. Anger that I was back here, back in this saints-forsaken village.

I lifted my head and surveyed the area around me. Everyone had scattered, leaving the place entirely abandoned except for the dead bodies that surrounded me.

Everyone left me. Nobody cared.

My power, the life power, flared within me. I did not

have the energy to fight it, nor did I care to. I took a long, surrendering breath and released the power, letting a large flash of light surround me.

And I did not try to stop it.

Power flooded from my veins, pulsing into the air around me. I did not care much about Tessa's body, or Sadie's. Better they burn to ash by my power then rot in the dirt of this horrid place.

Tears streamed down my face, but the grief within me created a large, gaping hole of emotion. I relaxed into it, relaxed into the void of nothingness.

This was my destiny, I realized. To destroy everything and everyone around me. My power was not one of life. I knew, now, that it was one of death. And so was everything inside of me.

I belonged to the darkness.

I wasn't sure how much time passed. My power eventually fizzed down, reverting to the low void of emotion inside me. I was afraid to look at my sister. I knew I had burnt her body. I knew I had burnt the tavern behind me. The market was ash.

But I didn't quite care.

I didn't care about anything, actually. Not the fact that I was utterly alone. Not the fact that a few strangers had begun to creep around me, looking in horror at what I had done.

It was horrid, wasn't it? What I had done? Who I was?

I closed my eyes and imagined myself back home. Home. This was home, that's what Sadie had said.

But I knew, I knew deep in my bones that home wasn't

here. Home wasn't this worn down, desperate, barely-surviving village of strangers. Rewyth was home. Malachi was home.

Malachi. I missed him. I missed him more than anything, yet my brain couldn't fathom the last memory I had of him. I missed his face. I missed his warmth. How long had it been? How long had it been since I last saw him?

Malachi, my husband. My everything.

Where was he? Wasn't he here? Why would he leave me here alone without–

Blood-curdling screams interrupted my thoughts. And they weren't screaming at me.

I turned my attention to the row of houses down the hill, or more so, the black-cloud of horror that followed.

Deadlings. Deadlings crawled over one another, clawing and destroying everything as they rushed forward up the hill, completely ripping apart everyone they came into contact with. The horrified screams were cut off by the gore of the deadly creatures.

For a second, I froze. Deadlings. The disgusting creatures had no right. It was then that I remembered something, something I must have known before. The deadlings were controlled by someone.

Someone or...something.

I stood, frozen in fear, watching the creatures attack and destroy as they made their way up the hill, closer to me. Closer to the destruction around me.

For a moment, I thought about letting them. I pictured their nasty, inhumane claws ripping my flesh to shreds, bleeding out on the ground until the jaws of the swarm tore out my heart.

But something deep within me resisted the thought, pushed it away. Something inside me wanted to live. For what? I wasn't sure. I didn't have an answer. But I knew that I had to keep going. I had to keep fighting.

The black creatures came closer. They didn't exactly have eyes, yet somehow I knew their attention had been locked onto me. As if they found their target.

I did not feel afraid. Not in the slightest. To be afraid of death, I would have to not welcome it. No, I was angry. Angry at whatever Saint had decided to take my sister away. Angry that my father hadn't died sooner, and angry that Sadie, who I thought I could protect, couldn't be saved, either.

And I was really pissed off that these disgusting creatures were creating even more of a damned mess.

Light burst around me, blocking the deadlings from my view. I found it amusing, how someone—although I couldn't remember who—had suggested my power was one of life. Clearly, my power was one of death. One of destruction, just like those deadlings.

Those deadlings were not as angry as I.

I pushed forward, screaming as I expanded my power. I pictured the deadlings burning to ash, just like I had done with my sister's dead body. I pictured the whole village burning to ash, actually, because I couldn't give any less shits about who lived or died in this damned place.

And when I opened my eyes again, when the screaming

had stopped and the pain had turned from a burning passion of fire to a dull throb, I saw what was left.

I saw nothing. Nothing but burnt ash, not a single house and not a single tree left in the rubbish.

I had ruined it all. All of it, gone, just like everything else in my life. I had nothing left. I closed my eyes, dropped to my knees, and pictured the whole world turning to ash.

CHAPTER 23
Malachi

I wasn't a fan of being in the library alone. The dark shadows that lingered in the corners never let me relax. I couldn't fathom how others actually enjoyed being in here, enjoyed studying of the Saints and history.

That didn't mean I didn't spend my fair share of hours and late nights in this exact room, bent over these books, trying to figure out why the Saints had done this to me.

This curse that disguised itself as power.

I headed for the study when Jade's screams had become too torturous for me to bear. I couldn't listen to them, knowing I was powerless. The Paragon did nothing but watch, nothing but nod along and act as if Jade was doing everything according to plan.

I hated them for it. I hated them for making her do this, for creating visions that only she and them could see.

Although part of me knew that I didn't need the visions to know what Jade was experiencing.

"I never thought I'd see you studying on your own free

will," Silas entered the study. The energy in the air shifted, from one of frustration to one of anticipation. That's how it always felt when he was near. Like death was coming, and he would be the reaper. "What are you looking for?"

"Something I already know the answer to," I answered. Bile grew in my mouth. I quickly swallowed it. "And I enjoy the solitude. See yourself out."

I waited for his footsteps, my eyes returning to the words written on the script in front of me. But instead, I heard quiet, blood-freezing laughter.

"I'm glad this is humorous for you. It seems you're not getting enough entertainment with my wife in that damn arena."

His laughter subdued, followed by the sound of his approaching footsteps. He stood behind me, just a few feet back. "The Trials of Glory is not for my entertainment."

"Really? Could have fooled me."

I tried to bite my tongue, tried to fight back the anger that clawed at my spine and threatened to rip me apart from the inside, but now was not the time. There would be a time for revenge. Once all of this was done, once Jade was safe. I would give them all what they deserved.

Starting with Silas.

"You can be more than this, you know," Silas said. Each word hung heavy in the air between us.

"More than what? More than the King of Shadows? I thought this was what you wanted for me." I took a cooling breath. This was what he wanted from me; to shake me up. To get me angry. But it wasn't going to work. I had changed since my time here. He couldn't treat me like a confused child anymore.

I was a warrior. A king. A killer.

I became too distracted by my own thoughts to notice Silas reading over my shoulder. I slammed my hand over the scroll and stood up, turning to face him. "Why are you here?" I asked.

Silas's face flickered through a few emotions. I had become better at reading emotions since being with Jade. Her emotions, as much as she fought against it, displayed clear as day all over that perfect face of hers.

Silas's tedious smile faltered. "There's something I need to talk to you about."

"Why don't I spare us the formalities? You are my father, after all." Silas's face remained blank, but my own heart pounded like a wild animal in my chest. "Is that why you pulled us back here? Forced Jade into the trials? To get back at me? Was it all because I am your son?"

"Why would I want to get back at you?" he asked, ignoring the other questions.

"Because I left. You taught me everything I know. You taught me how to kill, how to sneak around, how to spy. You turned me into a weapon to use for your own good, and then I crawled back to my own life like a child."

"I trained you because that's what we do here. You needed to live up to your potential."

"And I've done that, right? I became the monster you wanted me to be."

"You're not a monster, and you know that. I took you

in because that's what the Paragon does. We take the gifted and we make them great."

"I suppose that's what your excuse is for my wife, too? You think this will make her great?"

"Your wife..." he laughed again, muffling a cough. A vein on his forehead stuck out. "Your wife does not choose peace, Malachi. Although I'm sure you knew that already. Peacemaker?" He shook his head, as if shaking the very word that just fell off his lips. "The Trials of Glory have just begun. Your wife must face the present and the future before the Saints deem her worthy."

"They've already deemed her worthy!" My voice echoed off the walls. "Why can't you see that? You all sit up here with your black robes, high and mighty amongst everyone in this world, and you don't see it."

"See what?"

"Jade is better than me. Better than you. These trials will only prove that. She is more powerful than anyone who has ever walked here, and in a few days she will harness the power of all Saints, not just one."

Finally, something I said shocked him. His eyes widened for half a second before he stepped forward. After all this time, I think he grew even shorter. I stood a full head taller than him, I looked down at his thin, bald body. I wasn't sure why, all those years ago, this man made me feel so powerless.

I held the power now. And him, along with his power-hungry group of hooded figures, couldn't accept that.

For a fleeting second, I released the power that begged for his life. I unleashed the black threads, aiming them at

Silas, and he crashed to his knees before me in pain. We had fought with magic many times before, until we were both bloodied and bruised. Until we both gave in, accepting defeat.

The truth was, Silas's power alone did not make him strong. It did not make him worthy of being a leader, and it damned sure did not make him the leader of the Paragon. No, his arrogance did that.

That was a hard lesson I learned.

"My wife," I barked, "will beat these trials. She will come out on the other side even stronger than she is now, with an even clearer picture of her gift. And when she does that, when she walks out of that arena after becoming exactly who you all thought she could never become, she will tear down this mountain with her bare hands."

His sounds of pain turned to gruntled laughter. Before I could fathom my next thought, pain slashed through my mind, a knife dissecting every inch of my flesh. I would have cried out in pain, would have screamed against my every will, but no sound would come out.

"You may think you are a king now," Silas said, "but make no mistake; I am the leader of the Paragon. I am the one the Saints speak through. I am the descendant of Erebus, same as you, and his strong, power-hungry blood runs in my veins, too."

I drew in a shuddered breath and clenched my fists.

"You may try to escape. By the glory of the Saints, your wife may just survive these trials. She may survive the depths of her own mind, but you will be the one picking up the pieces and putting them together. She is just a girl,

Malachi. She is not your weapon. She is not stronger than you, and she most certainly is no stronger than me. Than what I have built here."

More pain exploded in my mind. I tried to send out those dark tethers of magic once more, tried to send him crashing back down to the ground where he belonged, but it was no use. I understood why Silas had been so undefeatable all these years. Impossible to kill. Stronger than anyone in the Paragon.

It was Erebus. This whole damn time, it was Erebus's power that Silas wielded.

It took every ounce of restraint in my body to back down from the fight.

"I should have known," I mumbled.

"Speak up," he demanded. "Kings do not mumble words beneath their breath."

Anger dulled my senses. I didn't care what Esther said before. Not anymore. "Did you know that my throne was being threatened?" I asked.

His face didn't change. Not a flicker of surprise, of denial.

"There's nothing you can do about that right now," Silas replied.

I couldn't believe this. I thought maybe—just maybe—Silas wouldn't know. Maybe he had been kept in the dark. Maybe it slipped through his communications, too, that someone was threatening Rewyth. "You want my kingdom to fall that badly?" I asked. "Why? So you can take it for yourself?"

"I don't wish to take your kingdom, son."

"Don't call me that," I argued. "We may share Erebus's blood, but you are not my father."

Silas attempted a smile, but his eyes remained dark. Emotionless. "If Rewyth needs you to return, be my guest. Leave. Your wife will be in great hands here," he spat.

"You know I won't leave her."

He shrugged matter-of-factly. "That's your choice, then. But don't blame me or the Paragon for whatever seems to be happening in your kingdom."

I turned around and ran my hands through my hair, trying to get a grip on the situation. He was never going to help me. He was never going to help my kingdom. Saints, he sure never helped me in the past. He might say he does not want my kingdom to fall, but I knew what he really wanted.

He wanted what he always fought for. Power.

"Fine," I said, turning around to face him. "I won't ask you to send aid to my kingdom, but at least allow me to send a letter to my men."

He considered this for quite some time before giving a silent nod of approval. "Our messengers are slow and I cannot promise anything, but if you wish to send a message to your kingdom, I will not stop you."

What bullshit. He had been trying to stop me ever since our arrival here. Nevertheless, I rushed to the desk behind Silas and found a piece of parchment.

Ser,
Do what you need to do. I can't leave her yet.
- M

I prayed to the Saints that Ser would know what that meant, would know what to do. I couldn't leave Jade. I couldn't leave her here with them, the ones who tortured her mind with every passing second.

Serefin wouldn't have asked me to come back unless it was absolutely necessary. I knew that. I knew that whatever threatened our kingdom likely moved closer and closer to my throne every day.

Still, knowing that my throne was threatened didn't begin to convince me to leave my wife. It wasn't a question.

I was staying.

"Here," I said, folding it and handing it to Silas.

He took it without breaking eye contact, a hint of something amused lingered in his gaze.

"What?" I asked.

He waited a few seconds, my letter hanging in his fingers, before answering, "You would risk your kingdom for this girl. You were right. You're not the same boy who won the trials all those years ago."

CHAPTER 24
Jade

When I woke up, I was back in the stone arena. Something told me I had been there before, but my thoughts were too foggy to focus, and even trying to recall where I had been the last few days put a piercing blade through my mind.

And then, all at once, as I laid there on my back looking up at darkness, I began to remember.

Sadie. Tessa. My father. Everything crashed back into my memory, along with all of the pain. All of the anger.

I had to watch her die. Again.

But Sadie had been there...and she wasn't really dead, was she? And my father wasn't dead, right?

I shook my head, trying to rid the thoughts that crumbled in my brain.

Something caught my eye in the upper corner of the stone arena. It was dark, and I had to rub my eyes to make sure I wasn't seeing things. I still didn't trust my own eyes.

What was that? A small glint of shimmer caught my eye, and it reminded me of the doorway into the Paragon.

That's where I was, wasn't it? The temple of the Paragon?

My chest ached as Malachi's chiseled face came to my mind. I missed him, and I hated myself for missing him. I knew this would be hard on me, these trials. Malachi had tried to prepare me, and he was probably somewhere watching me miss him.

I rubbed at that pain in my chest, trying to push it away. But nothing worked.

"Miss?" A yelp escaped me as I twisted around on the cold ground to see where the voice came from.

A small boy peaked his head through a hidden door in the stone. Wait, I recognized that boy. I had seen him before, he was the one who…who…

No. Maybe I hadn't. My memories faded as quickly as they arrived. The boy came through the same door I had walked through. How long ago was that? How long had I been here?

"Hello?" I asked. My voice croaked.

"I have food for you, miss." He crawled forward, glancing to that portion of the stone that shimmered as he brought a plate of food into the stone room. His feet were bare and dirty, and while he did wear black linens, they were not fashioned in the head-covering robe that others wore.

"How long have I been here?" I asked him. His eyes widened, as if he wasn't expecting me to speak to him.

"It's been two days, miss."

"Two days?" I shook my head. "No, that can't be right."

Two days? Two days since I was forced to drink the elixir, and two days of the trials?

The boy began backing away when I reached out and gripped his arm. "The first trial. What did I do? What happened?"

The boy tilted his head, but didn't try to pull his arm away. "It was like fire," he started. "Everywhere, all over the stone and filling the whole room. We didn't think you would survive it, miss."

I let go of him and staggered back. He pointed in the distance, and I followed his finger to the empty arena behind me.

Burn marks, as if charred from a fire, lined the walls. I rubbed my eyes again. "Was that me?"

The boy nodded, and then gave me a look that caused my stomach to sink. "I have to go. Your second trial will be starting soon, miss. You ought to eat and try to rest."

He backed away and the stone slammed shut behind him.

And once again, I was alone.

I glanced at the plate of meat, but didn't feel the slightest bit hungry. Especially after what had just happened. Although when I tried to remember the specific events...

Forget it, I thought. *It doesn't matter.* If I had used my magic, I probably gave them a show. And that was probably exactly what he wanted.

Silas. Did he know I would see Tessa? Did he play that out specifically so I would have to relive that trauma?

Of course he did. He wanted this, he wanted to see me

suffer. I took a quick scan of my body to make sure I hadn't been injured. Other than the low throb of my heartbeat that I could now feel in the temples of my head, I was fine.

I had survived, and that was enough for now.

Trial one, my past, was done. Two more to go.

CHAPTER 25
Malachi

Memory of my second trial came swiftly and violently in my sleep.

Adonis, Lucien, Eli, and Fynn all sat around the dining table. Something felt strange about the situation, but I couldn't quite put my finger on it.

Adonis laughed, something about Eli's ability to hunt for the family. Or lack thereof, rather. He had never been a good hunter, but we didn't care. Apart from hurting his pride, he had nothing to worry about as long as he lived in Rewyth.

"What are you all going on about?" Adeline asked. She sauntered in the room as if the whole castle were built just for her. She did that frequently, and I was always surprised by the way she could entirely change the mood of any room.

"They're being idiots," Lucien groaned. So typical of him, the buzzkill of the group unless the group's activities involved getting into trouble.

"I can't say that surprises me," Adeline added, setting

down a large plate of food. "Here," she said. "Father won't make it to dinner."

A dull emotion flared, right beneath my chest bone. I didn't care that my father hadn't attended dinner. He rarely had time for dinner, so why was I affected at all?

"Where is he?" I asked. My voice felt raw and distant.

"Politics, I'm sure. I don't tend to ask details when those are involved." She tossed her long hair over her shoulder and sat beside our brothers.

"Malachi?" Fynn asked, his voice as light and innocent as ever. "Are you alright, brother?"

I looked at him, at his sharp cheekbones and pointed ears. Something was different about him. Something was different about all of them, actually.

I didn't answer. Instead, I turned my attention to the room around us. The castle looked spotless. The green vines that threaded through the white stone of the walls looked extra green this time of year. It was my favorite, when the nature around the castle began to swallow it whole. I always loved that part about the castle. We didn't try to rid the nature around us completely. Instead, we became one with it. One with the land and the trees.

Everyone at the table stared at me as I finally quit daydreaming.

"What?" I asked, not remembering the question they were waiting for me to answer.

"I said, are you okay? You're acting strange."

Was I acting strange?

"I'm fine, Fynn."

"Here," Adeline insisted, shoving some food from the

platter onto the smaller plate in front of me. "Eat this. You'll feel better."

I accepted the offer and shoved some of the meat into my mouth. How long had it been since I had last eaten? Saints, I didn't even remember what I had eaten for breakfast.

"Okay," Eli said, setting his own fork down. "We should likely discuss how we'll do it."

"Do what?" I insisted.

Eli scoffed. "How we'll kill you, of course."

I shot my eyes in his direction. Surely, I didn't hear him right. Everyone else continued eating as if Eli had said nothing.

"Kill me?"

"Yes," Eli replied. "We've already discussed this, Malachi. We have to kill you if we want the throne for ourselves."

I glanced at Adeline, who surely would tell Eli to shut up at any second. But she, too, continued casually eating her food.

"You can't kill me, Eli," I replied, still not sure if he was joking.

"Sure, we can," Lucien jumped in. "We've killed plenty of fae before. You'll be no different."

Were they serious?

"I must be exhausted," I said, "because I really can't tell if you're being stupid or not."

Adonis set his fork down and stared me directly in the eye. "It's nothing personal, brother. You've known we would try this for some time now. Just face it. You're not meant to be king. You're not meant to be heir to the fae throne."

Saints above. They were serious about getting rid of me.

My power flared in my blood, very aware of the threat we were openly discussing at the dinner table.

"Adeline?" I asked. "You're okay with this?"

She shrugged. "To be honest with you, brother, I try not to concern myself with the politics of the castle. Much too boring for me."

It was Fynn who picked up his knife, pointing it casually in my direction.

"Put your knife down, Fynn," I ordered. "Let's talk about this."

He didn't. Instead, he laughed. He laughed as if this entire situation were a game, and he had been waiting for the final blow all along.

"There's nothing to talk about," Lucien added. "In fact, it's better if we don't talk at all."

He, too, picked up his knife.

A few stabbings I could handle. But my entire family attacking me with one sole purpose to kill me? That would be a fight.

A fight I wasn't sure I could win.

My power sensed this, too. I let it come forward, engulfing my senses.

"Don't make me do this," I said. "I don't want to hurt any of you."

They all looked at each other, Adeline included, and laughed. As if it were a ridiculous thought that I could hurt them. As if I were weak. Powerless.

Fynn stood up, his wooden chair screeching against the floor as he did.

"We all knew this would happen eventually," he said. "We better get it over with now."

I lost it. My power blasted through the room, strong enough to wipe out any soldier if it needed to.

But there were no soldiers in the room. We were not at war.

My family—Adeline, Fynn, Eli, Adonis, Lucien—they all fell to the ground, screaming in pain.

It wasn't long until those screams stifled, the pain becoming too much to bear.

"I don't want to do this," I said again, more to myself than to them. "I don't want to hurt any of you."

I pulled back lightly, just enough to allow them a breath.

But Adonis, as strong-headed as he was, took this chance to reach for his dagger.

"Don't," I warned, but he ignored me. In one swift motion, he pulled the dagger from his sheath and threw it toward my chest.

I swatted it away effortlessly, but my power saw this as a threat on my life. I could hardly contain it as it pulsed through the room again—full force this time—and did not stop.

Did not stop as the pained groans silenced.
Did not stop as the breathing slowed.
Did not stop as each of their five heartbeats stilled.
Only then, when the room was calm, did my power relax.
A wave of nausea overcame me.
I had killed them all.

CHAPTER 26
Jade

Malachi slept next to me when I woke up, twisted together with me in the silk bed sheets. I couldn't see his face, but I knew it was him. The familiarity, the intuitive comfort.

I rolled over and ran a hand up his bare arm. "Good morning," I whispered, squinting against the morning sun.

He mumbled a groggy response before turning around and wrapping me in his arms, brushing a hard kiss onto my forehead.

Birds sang somewhere on the other side of our open window. These were my favorite days—the days where the morning breeze pulled us from bed.

It felt like it had been so long.

His fingers ran across my cheek, sending a chill down my body. "You're trying to torture me," I insisted.

Malachi laughed, and I tried to soak in the way his vibrations spread across my own body as he pulled me tighter in the bed. "If by torture you mean with my mouth and hands, my queen, then I'll torture you all day long." His hot mouth moved to my cheek, my neck, my collarbone.

But then he pulled back. His features darkened as he looked down on me, holding himself up with his forearms. Concern dripped from his face as his eyes scanned me.

"What's wrong?"

Mal shook his head before answering. "Jade, you're..." he couldn't finish the thought.

"I'm what?" I repeated, sitting up in bed and pushing him back. "What is it, Mal?"

He picked up his hand and dragged a finger across my chest, right under my collarbone. He then turned his hand and showed me what was dripping from his finger.

Blood. Red, ruby blood.

My mouth fell open. I frantically began searching my body, looking for any indication that the blood was mine.

That wasn't the worst part, though. The worst part was the look on Mal's face.

Because he already knew. Deep down, he knew that blood wasn't mine. I knew it, too.

"I need to wash this off," I stammered. "Just...just hold on, okay? I'll go rinse it away and I'll be back."

Malachi didn't say anything. I staggered away from the bed—half naked—and stumbled into the bathroom where I shut the door strongly behind me.

My heart raced, too hard for this early in the morning.

But it stopped beating altogether when I glanced at myself in the jagged mirror before me.

Blood dripped from nearly every inch of my skin, some dried, some glistening with the reflection of the sunlight.

"Saints," I mumbled. My mind raced as I tried to think about where I went last night. Whose blood was this? And why hadn't I cleaned it away before crawling into bed with Malachi?

Pain pierced my temples, and I massaged them with my red hands to subdue the pain. I couldn't remember. Saints, I couldn't even remember whose blood was covering my own body.

I stepped into the stream of water that fell from the other side of the bathroom and tried not to think.

It was an accident, I told myself. An accident, or maybe it was self-defense. Either way, I wouldn't have killed someone if they hadn't deserved it.

I wasn't even sure I had killed someone. Maybe the blood was part of a ritual of some sort, where it was required that I dump blood over myself. Maybe that was it.

The water that ran off my skin ran red.

I knew that wasn't it, though. I had killed someone last night. And I was so much of a monster, I couldn't even remember who.

Malachi stood dressed when I exited the bathroom, free from a single drop of a stranger's blood. Maids had already begun stripping away the bed sheets, the ones that I had smeared the red substance across in my sleep.

"Busy day today?" I asked, leaning against the wall with my hair still dripping wet.

Mal barely met my eyes. "No more busy than usual."

I nodded and tried to smile, but Mal had no interest in being polite, it seemed. "Mal," I said, stepping forward. He flinched—actually flinched—away from me. "Mal," I said, more gentle. "Can we at least talk about this?"

"There's nothing to talk about," he replied with a king's voice. "You're covered in blood, and now it's my job to find out whose blood was spilt in my kingdom last night."

I reeled back, shocked that he would speak to me with that voice. He was always so gentle with me, so adoring.

Not anymore, it seemed. Something had changed. I wasn't that ignorant human that needed him to save me around every corner.

No, I was something else now. Something powerful. Something deadly. I felt it, deep in my bones I felt it.

And Malachi couldn't even look me in the eyes because of it.

"I should come with you," I said before he could storm off. "I should come so I can explain."

He looked at me with a sigh, his eyes like daggers piercing into mine, but at least he was looking at me. "Can you?" he asked. "Can you explain, Jade? You're covered in blood, and my guess is you have no clue what even happened. You could have slaughtered the entire kingdom while I slept." Exhaustion dripped from his words. Exhaustion and something else, something that hurt me as much as a punch.

Mal's jaw clenched as he shook his head, thinking something that I really had no interest in hearing. "Come on," he said after a few torturous moments. "At this point, I can't trust you enough to leave you here alone."

He didn't even wait to see if his words had hurt me. He stormed out of the bedroom, not slowing for me to catch up.

I slipped on my black boots and followed like an idiot after him.

His black leather wings tucked tightly behind his shoulder blades as we sauntered the halls of Rewyth.

I walked behind him, happy to be in his shadow. Happy to walk in his footsteps. I was never going to be his equal, I knew that. But times like this reminded me of how royal Mal was. How good.

His job as King was to get rid of threats. And I was becoming the biggest threat to this kingdom.

He stopped walking, and I almost ran into the back of him before I stopped myself, too. It took me a few seconds to realize that we were no longer in the castle. When had we walked outside? We were now standing in the tree-covered lagoon, one that I had been to a time or two before. Although now, I couldn't remember when, or with who.

But the lagoon still glittered with beauty.

Mal spun on his heel to face me, which forced me to rip my attention from the beautiful surroundings.

"Malachi?" I asked. He looked at me with something I had never seen from him before.

He looked at me with hatred.

The hair on the back of my neck stood straight up. "Mal, what's going on? Why did you bring me out here?"

His jaw tightened even further, and his nostrils flared in a predator's preparation. His pointed ears twitched out slightly from his mess of curly black hair, and I watched as he absentmindedly placed a hand on the hilt of his sword.

"You know why, Jade," he said through gritted teeth.

"Tell me," I insisted. I didn't even care that I sounded like a desperate child.

Every inch of my body told me to run. Malachi wouldn't hurt me. He would never lay a finger on me, I knew that.

Still, alarms blared in my mind. Something wasn't right here. Why would he want to get rid of me just because I had blood on my skin? He had blood on his too, right?

I took a slow step backward, away from the king before me. I tried to think of a time that Mal had killed someone, that Mal had been covered in blood.

But again, my mind fell blank.

He was perfect. He was golden and innocent and good, and I was the splatter of blood staining his perfect white kingdom.

"I don't want to hurt you," Mal said. His voice cracked, and in that moment I would have given anything to take away his pain, even if I were the one causing it.

Malachi deserved the world. I would give him anything.

I'll do it myself, I wanted to say, but I didn't get the chance.

I heard them before I saw them—sudden rustling in the trees around us. Too much, too many.

I spun around, searching the shadows of the tree line, only to find that we were completely surrounded.

By hundreds of silver wings.

"Mal," I pleaded. "What are they doing here?"

When I looked at him, his jaw was set, but a single tear slid down his tanned skin. "They're here to help you, Jade."

Weapons raised against me, but I knew they wouldn't need to use them. I was no match against a fae. I never was.

"You ordered them to get rid of me?" I asked. "Because you couldn't do it yourself?"

"Don't make this harder than it needs to be," he said. I didn't recognize him. Not anymore. Those chiseled cheekbones seemed dull. Those dark eyes fell distant.

This was not the same Malachi I fell in love with. This was not the strong, protective fae who pulled me back from the edge of darkness.

This was a coward.

One of the silver-winged fae to my left stepped forward. Out of nowhere and without my permission, a rush of anger flooded my senses.

"Don't do this," I pleaded to him. "It's not what you think. I can be better, Malachi! I can change!"

He didn't even look me in the eye. "You'll never change, Jade. You'll always be this helpless. This violent."

"No!" I argued, but the fae had already approached me, encircling Mal and I both in the tight circle of the lagoon—the one place I actually thought was peaceful.

I couldn't believe it, yet somehow I wasn't shocked at all. Malachi Weyland—the one fae who would once protect me with his life—was going to kill me.

CHAPTER 27
Malachi

I mindlessly wandered through the tunnels of the mountain, not wanting to go to bed. Not strong enough to see Jade in that arena. Her second trial had started, I could feel it deep in my body. I could feel her emotions rolling like waves in the ocean.

No, I couldn't be near her.

Instead, I staggered through the underground, not caring where I ended up. Not caring if I got lost.

Saints, if I were lucky, I would find a way out of this place. Perhaps there would be a hidden entrance, one not monitored by glamour.

"Don't even think about it. You can't escape. You know that." Cordelia's voice pierced my thoughts.

"Get out of my head," I ordered. "Do you ever mind your own damn business?" I spun around to see her standing in the tunnel a few feet away.

"Usually," she purred. "But your thoughts are so entertaining. You really think you can escape with not only your life, but your precious wife's?"

"I've done it before," I replied. It was the truth. The last time I was here, I was able to leave without a single interruption.

"No," Cordelia corrected. "You left. You didn't escape. There's a difference."

My gut twisted again. I had been so sick just a few moments ago, I vomited three times. Something wasn't right. It was my magic—I knew it.

And I really hated it. Jade felt terrified and...*betrayed*. Her emotions came to me as clearly as if they were my own.

The second trial wasn't even over. Jade had to survive this, and then an entire third round of challenges before she was deemed worthy.

Worthy. What a pile of shit.

"You're sassier than I remember," Cordelia added, still clearly poking around in my mind.

"What are you doing here?" I hissed. I pushed past her and entered the hallway, facing the direction of Jade's trial.

She took a deep breath and followed after me. It was rare for her to watch what she was about to say. I had grown used to her blurting out whatever thought first crossed her mind. She glanced over her shoulder before answering, "I'll help you."

"Help me what?"

Her eyes narrowed before she answered, "I'll help you kill Silas."

I finished dragging her by the arm into the bath house where the running water at least attempted to cover our voices. "Please tell me you didn't just say that out loud."

"Trust me," she started. "They're occupied. Besides, if anyone were listening to us I would hear their thoughts. Now, do you want my help or not?"

"I don't...why would you want to help me? What's in it for you?" If I knew anything about the half-witch, I knew she always had an ulterior motive.

She shrugged and broke eye contact. "You're not the only one who's tired of his antics, you know."

"Explain."

She closed her eyes while she took a deep breath before she continued. "He's changed, Mal. He's power-hungry, even more so than he used to be. He gets...he gets these twisted thoughts, like he doesn't even care about the Paragon. He just wants to stay on top."

"He's the leader of the Paragon, by definition he's already on top."

"It's not just that. With Jade...he..."

My stomach dropped. "He what?"

"He sees her as a threat. Not as a tool. Not as the peacemaker, who has literally been in the prophecies of the witches for centuries now."

"Well that's not exactly groundbreaking news, Cordelia. He sees everyone as a threat these days."

"My point, exactly."

"So what? You want to kill him because he wants to kill Jade? I'm not buying that."

I moved to walk out of the bath house and back to the arena to check on Jade, but she caught my arm and forced me to stay. "Jade is no longer a human, Malachi." Her grip tightened on my arm. "Hear me when I say this, because I won't explain it again. Your wife is not human. Not anymore. What Esther did to save her life…"

This topic had a strange way of coming up at the worst times. Jade had died, we all knew that would have consequences. But to hear Cordelia say this with such urgency…

"What is she, then? A witch?" I asked.

Cordelia's nostrils flared. "It's complicated. But Silas knows."

Silas. He was the first one to whisper to Jade that she might not be human. Of course he knew.

"How? How could he possibly know what my wife is before I know myself? Is it another part of his gift?"

"Esther told him. She knew as soon as she brought Jade back from death."

Everything clicked into place, all my messy thoughts and rough intuitions finally piecing together.

Esther and Silas were working together. Jade wasn't human.

And I wanted to kill that bastard more than anything.

"We aren't so different, you and I," Cordelia said. "We want the same things."

I scoffed. "I doubt that, witch."

I ripped my arm from her grasp and turned around

again. "Half-witch," she barked, her voice stronger than I had ever heard it. "And you forget how powerful I really am, *king*."

I turned to see her scowling at me, a fierce emotion in her eyes. Her silver wings flared on either side of her, as if she were trying to remind me that they were there. "Tell me what you really want with Silas and Jade."

My temper was beginning to tether out, but I didn't care enough to control it. She knew this about Jade and she was only now telling me. Even worse, she knew that Esther had kept a secret from me yet again.

"I want to see Jade rule by your side as leader of the fae," she started. "And I want Silas out of the picture so magic can finally flow freely. Witches have been in hiding for decades now. It's time we all live how we once did. How it should be."

I couldn't deny the chill that flickered down my spine. How it should be.

Jade deserved to rule. If what Cordelia was saying about her not being human were true...

She was born for great things. I had known that for some time now. The others were the ones who couldn't see. They refused to accept her for what she was—the peacemaker. The most powerful entity of our time.

Jade held the power of the Saints.

She could win these trials, and then we would be gone. We would leave this damn temple and never come back, never have to see Silas or any of the Paragon members again.

We could hold out until then.

"It's too risky," I said to Cordelia. "Jade will rule beside me, but we can't kill Silas. Not yet, anyway. She'll win these damn trials and we'll be gone before the week is over."

CHAPTER 28
Jade

"How?" I asked. "How can you live with yourself knowing you're killing your wife. We took vows, Malachi! You promised me!"

His face remained blank. Any amount of sadness he had been showing before now covered by the mask of emotionlessness.

"You're dangerous, Jade. If I don't handle the situation now, you'll be the end of us all."

The fae around us moved closer. With every step they took, with every inch of space around me that disappeared, I grew closer and closer to my own demise.

What I didn't expect, though, was my own power having a fighting instinct. Heat of power fueled my body, pumping through my veins. I stared directly at Malachi, straight into those dark, endless eyes, and held my palms on either side of my body.

"Don't fight this, Jade," he said, as if he could feel what

I was about to do. "It's best for everyone if we get it over with now."

"You mean it's best for you!" I yelled. "Dammit, Malachi! Think about this for one second!" More power pulsed to the surface. It was ready to defend me, ready to save my life.

But the result? They would die. They would all die.

My power flashed around me, defending me from the one person I never imagined having to use my power against.

And as that light encapsulated us all, my heart cracked in two.

Screams of surprise came from the silver-winged fae. Not from Malachi, though. He wasn't surprised.

And he also wouldn't be affected by my magic.

I pushed my magic out with strength I didn't expect to have. It was fueled by something, though. Anger. Anger fueled my power, pulsing it through the screams of the fae until those screams turned silent.

Until those screams were drowned by my own thoughts, my thoughts that were directed at just one thing—Malachi.

"Is this what you wanted?" Mal screamed. I pulled back my power and saw the result of my actions—the hundreds of fae around us dead, their silver wings covering half their bodies as they lay on the floor of the lagoon. "Was this your plan all along?"

I stepped toward him. He stepped back. "No," I said, shaking my head. "You don't understand, Mal. I had to protect myself."

"Oh, I understand," he said. The way he looked at me... as if I were something disgusting. As if I were nothing but a pest in his kingdom. "You hate the fae, Jade. You hate what we stand for. You hate that we live in this castle, lavishing away at anything we want. You hate it. Have you been planning this all along? Have you been planning your revenge this entire time?"

Where was this coming from? This wasn't the Malachi I knew. This wasn't my husband. "Mal, I–"

"Don't call me that."

"I don't–"

"It's King Malachi," he corrected. "And you've just murdered nearly half of my royal guard!" Anger, feral and hot, flashed through his features. His pointed ears flickered in emotion, and his lips curled in a wicked snarl. "You are no longer welcome here, Jade," he said.

"Malachi, please!" I was crying now, although I couldn't remember when my anger had morphed into anything else. Nothing made sense. Not anymore. "Don't do this! We're supposed to protect each other, remember? We're supposed to look out for one another!"

"You're a stranger to me," he said, each word twisting that dagger he had already pierced through my heart. "Get out of my kingdom."

"So, that's it?" I begged. "You try to kill me, and when I retaliate, I'm banished?"

He said nothing. He turned on his heel and began walking deeper into the forest, away from the lagoon. I followed, stepping over the fae bodies in my way.

"You're a coward," I snapped. "If you want to get rid of

me so badly, you'll have to kill me yourself." My voice shook, but my words held steady.

How did it get to this? How did we become these people? I couldn't remember a time before today that Malachi even looked at me with a single ounce of distaste, let alone the disgust that practically evaporated off him now. "Kill me, Malachi." I gripped his arm and spun him around.

He shrugged me off. "Get out of here."

"You're a coward!" I yelled. "A coward and a sad excuse for a king!" Part of me regretted the words as soon as I said them, but part of me didn't care at all. That part of me wanted to hurt him, wanted to inflict pain on him just like he was inflicting on me.

I wanted *him* to hurt.

"Kill me," I said again.

He shook his head.

"Kill me, you coward."

He stormed away again, mumbling something I couldn't understand.

His dagger through my chest would hurt far less than his words.

A wildfire of anger and sadness took control of my body, my thoughts. I couldn't hold it together. Not anymore. What was the point, anyway? I wasn't welcome here. I had nowhere else to go.

A scream ripped through the trees around us. It wasn't until my throat began to sting that I realized the scream was mine.

But Malachi didn't stop walking. He didn't care. I kept

screaming as if that would make the pain go away. As if that would make any of this better.

I screamed until I ran out of breath.

Malachi stopped walking.

"Does this make you happy?" I yelled after him with a hoarse voice. "Does seeing me in pain bring you joy, King Malachi?"

He turned to face me and the blood in my veins ran cold.

Malachi—his dark eyes, his chiseled face—it was all gone. Malachi was morphing, right before my eyes, into a deadling.

"No," I breathed. "Mal, what's happening?"

He twitched and snarled, his fae wings disappearing and his sharp ears melting away. Until all that was left were black, disgusting claws and skinless features across his scrawny, boney body.

He—no, *it*—dropped its sword. The deadly creature took one step toward me.

Adrenaline like I had never felt before pulsed inside me, telling me to run, telling me to get out of there as fast as possible.

Malachi was deadly, yes, but a deadling? They had the one thing Malachi did not possess. They had a strong, unrelenting need for blood.

"Mal, please!" I yelled. It took another step toward me. I took another step back. I didn't want to run away. I didn't want to run from this thing as if my husband wasn't standing in its spot just seconds ago.

But this wasn't Mal. Not anymore.

Which meant this deadling could also be affected by my magic. I could kill it right now. I could kill him.

"No," I said to myself. "Malachi, I know you're in there," I whispered. "Please, don't make me do this. I don't think I'm strong enough."

Tears fell freely down my face now, dripping off my chin and down my chest. I froze, daring the creature to come closer.

Please. Please don't make me do this.

"I love you, Malachi!" I yelled. The words felt strange, almost as if they weren't real. "I love you!"

The creature didn't give any sign that it understood me. Power buzzed under my flesh. "Don't make me do this," I said again.

I decided then that I wasn't going to run. I wasn't going to let these creatures chase me through the Kingdom of Rewyth like I was a helpless animal.

I fell to my knees on the rough forest floor. I held my hands out to my sides.

"Is this what you want?" I asked. I knew the thing couldn't hear me, couldn't understand me. "Come on, then."

The creature stepped toward me slowly, as if confused as to why I wasn't running. "Come on!" I screamed.

Two seconds passed. And then the nasty thing launched itself at me.

I didn't plan on fighting. My plan was to let this thing —this remnant of Malachi—destroy me. Kill me like he had planned to do all along.

But when the creature sank its teeth into my shoulder, when its long, deadly claws grazed my skin, I lost control.

Another snarled scream escaped me as my power exploded, disintegrating everything around me with its last attempt at self-preservation.

I shut my eyes tight, blocking out the scene around me. I didn't want to look. But when the sting of the teeth in my flesh disappeared, when I could no longer feel the weight of the creature leaning on my body, when my power pulled back an inch, letting me know I was safe once again, I opened my eyes.

I expected to see a deadling. The ashes of a deadling, actually. The trees around us were flattened, nothing but dust left where they used to stand. The sun of day warmed my skin, now that the thick green leaves were no longer shielding me.

And in front of me, lying on the ground with not even a scratch, was Malachi.

"Mal?" I asked. His eyes were closed, his face pale. "Malachi?" I reached out with a trembling hand and brushed his cheek.

And then yanked my hand back with a gasp. He was cold. Too cold.

"Mal!" I pleaded. My hands hovered over him, wanting to touch him but too afraid to. "Don't leave me, Mal. Don't do this to me."

I watched his chest, waiting for it to rise and fall like it always did. I loved the way his breathing was always steady, even when he was angry. Even when he was tired. His chest would rise with a breath, and then fall. Always.

But I watched and I waited. And when nothing moved, when he didn't take a breath for I don't even know how long, I crumbled completely.

"Come back to me," I sobbed, my words hardly audible. He couldn't hear me, though. He was gone, I had killed him.

I killed Malachi.

Another sob wrecked my chest, but the sound of the pain—the sound of the emotion and regret and hatred for myself crawling out of me—changed something inside me.

No, I couldn't do this. I couldn't be this person. I couldn't live without him, even if he did want me dead just a few moments ago.

He was everything to me. He saved my life. He deserved more than this.

I rested my head on his still chest. "Come back to me," I repeated. "I swear to the Saints I'll change. I'll be better. I'll do better."

My heart broke—shattered entirely into irreparable shards.

I was nothing without him, I realized. Nothing without the man who saved me, who resurrected me from a dying life.

Malachi was my life. I could not lose him.

I lifted my head and screamed to the Saints, screamed to the world for taking him from me. It was a scream that shook the trees around us, rippled the water of the lagoon.

I screamed and screamed and screamed. I screamed until my throat burned, my voice ran dry.

I screamed until Malachi...Malachi *moved*. Just slightly, small enough that I barely noticed it.

"Mal?" My voice was hoarse and raw. "Mal, wake up!"

His eyes moved under his closed eyelids. I placed my hands on his chest, willing him back. Willing him to return to me, to return to this world.

He blinked his eyes open—those deep, marvelous, pain-filled eyes—and looked at me.

"Jade?"

CHAPTER 29
Malachi

After my conversation with Cordelia ended, we both headed up to the gallery to watch Jade's trial. I didn't want to watch her suffer, but leaving her alone with those bastards watching her every move made me sick to my stomach.

So I watched. I watched as she fell to her knees and cried, shouting something we couldn't hear.

I couldn't even begin to imagine what she was seeing, but I could feel it. In that tether of magic, I could feel her pain. Her suffering. Whatever was happening, it hurt her. Badly.

Come on, Jade. You're almost done.

Suddenly, my vision blurred. I gripped onto the stone railing of the balcony to steady myself. Saints, something wasn't right. A few seconds later, my legs collapsed beneath me. I crashed to the floor, no breath in my lungs.

"Malachi?" Esther asked, rushing over to me. When did

she get here? She must have decided to watch the trials, after all. "What's happening?"

I tried to inhale, tried to take a deep breath, but my lungs were paralyzed. Seconds passed, panic began to creep into my body.

Jade. My vision blurred, and I shook my head as an image of myself flashed through my mind. Me, but different. I lay dead on the forest floor of Rewyth.

No, I shook my head again, clawing at my chest. I couldn't breathe.

"Malachi!" Esther yelled. She knelt next to me and gripped my face in her hands. "It's her, isn't it?" she whispered. "It's Jade."

I couldn't bring myself to even nod. At the mention of her name, another vision flashed through me. It was me again, but I wasn't alone. Jade knelt above me, crying and chanting in a language I didn't understand, gazing up at the sky and pleading.

Pleading for...*my* life.

"Stop this!" Esther yelled to Silas. "Can't you see? Whatever torturous disaster you're putting that girl through is affecting him!"

Silas paid us no attention. His gaze was locked down in the arena, on something I couldn't see. But I knew what was happening.

Jade was pleading for my life in her trial.

Dark shadows swarmed the room around me. I needed air. I needed to breathe.

I willed my lungs to expand but...nothing. Not even a

hint of relief came. My body began screaming, demanding air. Demanding that I live.

But there was nothing I could do.

Everything began to fade. Esther still knelt beside me, but I could not feel her hands on me.

Silas laughed in the distance, something dark and evil. It was the last thing I heard before I let the shadows take me.

I stumbled through the forest, not entirely sure how I got there in the first place. I wasn't in the mountains of the Paragon, and I didn't recognize the forest around me as anywhere in Rewyth. The trees were different, the smell was different.

My third trial. It had to be.

The sun blazed overhead. It was hot out, so hot that even the breeze did not bring any relief. Sweat formed over every inch of my skin as I stumbled forward.

At least I still had my wings. They tucked strongly behind my shoulder blades, comforting me as I pushed forward. I had to find out where I was.

I found a small clearing in the thick woods, one where the sun shined into the forest floor in a large, circular form. I walked forward until I felt the heat of the sun above on my skin, and just as I was about to launch myself into the air, a woman appeared.

She had long dark hair that fell in loose curls to her waist. She looked young, maybe two decades old, but her eyes...

I stepped forward so I could get a better look.

Though she looked young, the woman's eyes appeared old and tired.

"Malachi?" she asked, cocking her head to the side.

How did she know my name?

"Who are you?" I asked.

The woman looked me up and down, taking in every inch of me as if remembering an old friend. Her eyes wandered from my black boots to my now-expanded wings.

"You don't know who I am?" she asked.

I was certain I had never seen her in my life. I would have remembered eyes so deep, beauty so radiant.

"No," I answered honestly.

"Come here," she said, holding her arm out. She smiled softly, and my body reacted to it without my permission. I stepped closer to her, allowing her to turn my body and face the forest around us. "Look there," she said.

I focused on the area she pointed at, surprised to see...her.

"What am I looking at?" I asked.

The clone of the woman—the one in the forest—held a knife out in front of her. She was hunting, by the looks of it, but she couldn't see the wolf that approached.

I wanted to scream. I wanted to tell her to turn around, to look.

"We have to help her," I said.

"You will," the woman beside me spoke. "Trust me, you will help her in ways you cannot yet comprehend."

I didn't know what the woman meant, but I quickly quit caring. I watched as...as myself appeared behind her in the woods.

"Is that me?" I asked.

"It is. Keep watching."

So I did. My heart raced, my blood pounded through my veins. More wolves appeared. The clone of myself relaxed, leaning against a tree and waiting for the right moment to help, to jump in.

I watched the encounter in awe. It wasn't a memory, no. I would have remembered. But it felt so…familiar.

The encounter between the two ended too quickly. I turned to the woman beside me, waiting for an explanation.

"Do not forget this moment, Malachi Weyland," the woman said. "You will see me again, and you'll help me save the world when you do. But you must be careful."

"Careful? Why?"

"Many people will have a target on my back. Many people will want to take my life. Some your enemies, some your friends."

My jaw tightened.

"Who are you?" I asked again.

The woman, shining with a light from somewhere within her and practically glistening against the sun with her beauty, only laughed. "I am your wife, Malachi. My name is Jade Weyland."

"Wake up, dammit!" Cordelia's voice pulled me out of my memory.

She and Esther leaned over me as I woke up, they both breathed a sigh of relief when I opened my eyes.

"What's going on?" I pushed myself up to my elbows. We were still in the gallery of the arena. Still surrounded by Paragon members. Still with Silas. "What happened?"

The two witches looked at each other before returning their gazes to me. Shit. That couldn't be good.

Silas moved in the corner of my eye. He ran his hands across his head and shoved the black hood down, exposing his face. He was smiling.

Definitely not good.

"Is Jade alive?" I asked.

"Jade is fine," Esther answered. Cordelia sat back on her heels, jaw set. "The trials are going as planned." Esther sent a strange glare to Silas.

Going as planned? As in, Jade was being exploited for her magic?

"Explain," I mumbled.

"Maybe you should get some rest," Cordelia chimed in. "You're clearly being affected by these trials."

Affected by the trials? How would I be...

I remembered the darkness, the fighting to breathe.

Jade leaned over me, pleading with someone. It hurt to see her that way. I knew that feeling all too well. I wouldn't wish that upon her. Not ever.

"I died in Jade's trial," I guessed. The look on their faces confirmed.

Silas sauntered over to us, finally peeling his eyes from Jade down in the arena. I hated that he even looked at her. "Quite a turn of events, isn't it?" Silas sneered. "Jade is the one in the trials, yet somehow, you're being physically affected."

I jumped to my feet, ignoring the dizziness that followed. "You're behind this somehow," I argued. "What are you doing to her? What are you doing to me?"

He laughed, and I never wanted to punch him in the face more. "That's the intriguing part, really. I'm not doing anything." He stepped closer to me. "This is all on you."

I clenched my fists at my sides as my mind began to churn through the possibilities. I could feel what was happening in Jade's trial. The trials weren't real, they weren't physical challenges. Would Jade feel the physical effects? Yes. That's what made them so dangerous. But for others to feel it? For the mere figments of her imagination to feel the side effects?

Impossible.

That is, it should have been impossible. But clearly something terrible had just happened. I saw it in my vision, and Silas confirmed it now.

"What did she do?" I asked Silas.

Silas stared me straight in the eye while that wicked, arrogant smile grew on his face. He stared at me without talking until I was sure I was going to rip his head off.

But then he said, "The power of life, Malachi. Your wife brought you back."

CHAPTER 30
Jade

My face rested against a cold surface when I woke up. I didn't know how long I stayed like that—listening to the sound of my breath. Not opening my eyes.

I didn't want to know what reality looked like. That trial...it felt so real. So painful.

When I had the strength, I rolled onto my back. I cracked my eyes open to see nothing but darkness above. Darkness, and that small, shimmering corner of the arena.

My hand drifted to my heart and rested there, feeling my heartbeat. It was real. This was real, right?

The truth was, I wasn't sure. I wasn't sure what was real, if any of this was real. The more I tried to decipher the truth, the more pain I felt splitting through my head.

Warm blood trickled from my shoulder, reminding me of the deadling that bit me there. Pain began to radiate down my arm, sharp and fierce. His teeth had dug into me, and in the adrenaline of the moment, I barely noticed. Barely cared.

I looked down to see the row of disgusting, jagged teeth marks denting my skin, red with blood.

A single tear slid down my cheek.

I wanted to cry more, to heal that crack I felt in my chest. But my mouth grew dry as cotton, and I wasn't sure I had it in me to shed another tear.

What was the point? What was the point of any of this? Did they really think I was going to let Malachi kill me in that damned trial? Roll over and let the fae take my life?

Of course they did. They wanted to see me as weak, as defeatable.

Saints. If Silas had a mission to make me look out of control with my power, I imagined it was working.

I could see it now. The black-hooded figures of the Paragon laughing and chatting about how I tried to kill them all...how I couldn't see the greater good.

If the greater good had to do with Malachi wanting me dead, I didn't want any part of it.

A fresh wave of grief washed over me.

It was all so terribly wrong. My thoughts mixed and swirled together, images of what I perceived as reality washed through my mind. Malachi would never hurt me. Never. He would cut down anyone who lifted a finger against me.

So why did I see *that*? Why would the Paragon want me to see Malachi against me?

Against me and dying in my arms.

I couldn't believe it. I begged for him to come back, and

just when I thought I had lost him for good, he came back to me.

I wasn't sure which Saint had blessed us enough to help, but I was damn grateful for it.

That was no Saint, girl, a voice pierced through my mind, echoing within my skull. My hands immediately clamped on my temples.

"What?" I asked.

You're the one who brought the King of Shadows back.

No. This isn't real. None of this is real. I must still be in the trials. "Who are you?" I asked. "What do you mean *I* brought him back?"

Silence.

Your power is one of life, child. You willed him to come back, and so he did.

"No," I said out loud this time. "That's not true. If I could bring people back with mere will, my sister would not be dead!"

You were human when your sister died. You've passed onto something else, something with more power.

The female voice sounded steadfast and calm, even with my rising agitation.

"I...I couldn't have." I couldn't have. Right? "I cannot resurrect from the dead. That is impossible."

Although I couldn't hear it, I felt the presence of laughter and amusement somewhere in the echoes of my mind.

The peacemaker, they call you. Do you want to know what we call you, Jade Weyland?

"Who is *we*?" More amusement came from the space neither here nor there.

We, the voice continued, *are the five Saints that walked before you. We are the powerful beings that once ruled these lands. And we've been waiting for you, Jade Weyland.*

My mind spun, too much pain. Too much confusion. Too much fog.

Vita Queen

"What?"

The queen of life. Vita Queen. That is who you are, Jade. That is who you will rise to become.

I felt a strong, overwhelming need to protect myself. To get away from the voice, to end it all.

This had to be part of the...part of the trial? Right? That someone was testing me, someone wanted me to be tricked by the voice.

"Stop!" I yelled. I pushed myself up to my knees, peering into the darkness. "Just stop!"

My power came easily. Effortlessly. In fact, when the darkness around me became nothing but white, blinding power, I did not try to stop it. I did not try to pull back my power.

I blasted it until I had nothing left, had no voice left to scream. Had no energy left to fight. I blasted and blasted and blasted my power out around me until the source of it, deep in my soul and burning like fire, had depleted itself entirely.

And then I laid down, placing my head back down on the cold stone floor.

I couldn't stay awake any longer. I wanted it all to end, the pain, the torture.

I closed my eyes and filled my thoughts with images of Malachi until darkness silenced the voices echoing through my skull.

CHAPTER 31
Malachi

Silas and the others retired for the evening. They had enough of staring and laughing at Jade—helpless and alone—in that arena, I supposed.

But I stayed. I wanted to be closer to her. I wanted her to feel me there somehow, to know that she wasn't really alone. She would never be alone again.

I stared into the arena, not caring that my eyes were dry and burning from staring for so long. I wasn't quite sure how much time had passed, anyway.

It didn't matter.

Jade slept on her stomach with her arm propped under her, the sword I gifted her beside her. Someone had brought her food, but she didn't touch it. I didn't blame her for that. The trials weren't exactly an appetite churner.

She looked so small in the large stone arena. So...fragile. Although I knew she wasn't fragile, not really. Especially if she wasn't human anymore.

Saints.

I had to get to her. I had to talk to her, at least to let her know that I was still here, I wasn't going anywhere. I was okay. I just had to get down to that arena door, and I could sneak in for only a minute.

I would have killed to have someone visit me during my trials. To know that I wasn't really going crazy, to know that it was almost over. I remembered the way I lost track of time. I wasn't sure if it had been days, weeks, or months since I experienced something real. Visions morphed with dreams. I wasn't even sure I was out of the trials until weeks later when the fog began to lift.

No. Jade didn't have to feel that way. I slid out of the gallery and into the dark hallway.

Silas wasn't stupid. He would have guards at the very least, ensuring that I didn't try to break her out.

He wasn't stupid. But neither was I.

I crept through the dark tunnels, only passing a few Paragon members. Like always, they kept to themselves, their hooded faces not even budging as I walked past.

The tunnels grew more and more narrow. I knew I was getting close. I could feel it, I could feel her, her pain and her hunger and her confusion. I walked faster until I turned left in the darkness.

"I know you're not this idiotic," Cordelia said.

Saints. She pushed herself off the tunnel wall ahead. "Why are you always lurking in the shadows, witch?" I asked.

"To save your ass from dooming us all!" she hissed. "What's your plan here, Malachi? Swoop in and carry your bride off into the sunset? I hate to break it to you, but the sun has already set."

"I'm not trying to escape with her," I explained. "I only want to talk to her."

She scoffed. "Like anyone will believe that."

"Well, aside from you, nobody else knows. And nobody else will know. It's harmless."

She took a long breath, her curious eyes blaring into mine. "You're asking her about your resurrection, aren't you?" she asked.

There was no point in lying. She could read my thoughts. It wasn't my goal to ask Jade about what happened during her last trial, but I couldn't deny that I was interested. Silas was interested, too, which put her in even more danger.

"I'm going to see my wife," I growled. I shoved past her and continued walking down the tunnel. Cordelia's hair-pulling footsteps lingered behind me.

"If you want to know what she's been thinking," she whispered as we turned down yet another tunnel, "you can ask me, you know."

Ask her. I didn't want her poking and prodding through Jade's thoughts. I didn't want her anywhere near Jade, actually. I didn't want anyone near Jade when she was like this, hurt and confused.

"I have no intentions to hurt the peacemaker," Cordelia said.

"Saints, you can be damn annoying. Did you know that?" I kept looking forward, but I imagined her shrugging and rolling her eyes behind me.

We reached the end of the tunnel. We were close, I could sense it. If I focused enough, I could even hear Jade's heartbeat, slow and steady and peaceful, even if it were just for a few moments.

"If you don't want my help, fine," she complained behind me. "But you will soon. And I'll be right here to laugh at you when you realize how big of a mess you've got on your hands. This way," she said. She switched directions, leading me through a tunnel I did not even know existed. The dark stone pathway became darker and darker until I saw a small crack in the stone. It had to be the opening.

"Go," Cordelia said, nodding toward the crack. I rushed forward and pushed it open.

And the stone opened into the arena.

"Stay here," I ordered Cordelia. "I'll be right back." I didn't wait for her response before stepping into the arena and closing the door behind me.

"Jade," I whispered. She twitched lightly in response but didn't open her eyes. "Jade, it's me."

Again, she didn't move.

I moved to her side and knelt next to her. She looked so pale and skinny, as if she had been in this arena for weeks. Saints, I hated it. I hated all of it.

I reached out and tucked a piece of her black hair behind her ear. Only when my skin brushed hers did her eyes flutter open. She looked at me for a few seconds with absolutely no reaction, no recognition, nothing.

And those few seconds were enough to terrify me. "It's me, Jade."

Jade flinched and scrambled away from me, shrieking quietly with wide eyes. "Get away from me," she hissed.

I held my hands out in surrender, trying to hide the crack of emotion that pierced my chest. "It's me," I said again. "It's Malachi."

She shook her head violently, squeezing her eyes shut and pushing her palms against her temples. "This isn't real," she said, rocking back and forth on the stone ground. "This isn't real, this isn't real."

It took every ounce of control I possessed to stop myself from carrying her off that mountain. Whatever happened in that last trial had hurt her. Badly. Blood soaked he shoulder of her tunic, already drying against her skin.

"Look at me," I said softly. "Open your eyes and look at me."

We sat that way for a few minutes, Jade slowly pulling her hands away from her face as her breathing settled. It broke my heart to see her in so much pain.

"Do you remember me?" I asked.

"Malachi."

"Yes," I replied. "I'm your husband and I'm here to see you."

She pushed herself to a sitting position. Her brows drew together as she stared at me. "What are you doing here?" she asked. Saints, her *voice* even sounded weak.

"I came to check on you," I answered. "I came to make sure you were okay. You've been doing a great job, Jade. It's almost over."

Her attention shifted to the arena around us as she took

it in. I watched a storm of emotions cross her eyes. "Is this real?" she asked.

I held her cold hands in mine. "This is real."

Without looking back at me, Jade began to laugh. It was a quiet laugh, a tired laugh, but a laugh nonetheless.

"Jade?"

She continued to laugh, but the sound of it only pained me. It wasn't a laughter of happiness. Not in the slightest. "You have one trial left, okay? One trial and this is all over."

"One trial left?" she asked.

"Yes."

She shook her head again, trying to hide from my words. "I've done them all," she replied. "I've done all the trials."

"You have one left. It will start tomorrow. Just hang on a bit longer, Jade, and when this is all over, we go back home."

Her eyes slid to mine. "Rewyth?"

"Yes, we can go back to Rewyth?" She smiled and shook her head. "What is it?" I asked.

"Sorry," she stammered. "Something someone else said. Not you."

"Someone else—what are you talking about, Jade? Who else have you been talking to?"

Her brows drew together again, and I watched as she took a breath and crumbled as she exhaled. "So many people. I can't tell if they're real."

Ah, the trials. "That's normal," I explained. "You'll be confused for a bit, and that's okay. When this is all over, I'll help you understand. I'll help you decipher what's real and what's not real. Okay?"

She tightened her grip on my hand. "I want to go home, Mal."

"I know you do."

"I don't want to do it again. I don't want you...I killed you, Mal. I killed you and you were dead."

The strain in her voice told me she was seconds from falling apart. And she couldn't afford to fall apart, not yet. Not when we were this close.

"Look at me," I said. I slid forward and gripped her small shoulders. "I am right here. I am alive and warm and with you. You cannot kill me. You'll never be able to kill me, Jade. Even if you could, I wouldn't let you. You and I are together now. Forever. Do you understand?"

Her eyes strained. "Yes, I understand."

"Good."

Jade attempted a smile, but damn. She looked so tired. I leaned forward and placed a gentle kiss on her forehead.

"The Saints don't need me to finish these trials," she whispered so quietly I barely heard her.

Time froze. "Why would you say that?" My heart pounded, every tendril in my chest tightening as soon as those words left her mouth.

"They told me," she replied. "The Saints told me this is just a show, and I must keep moving forward. But Mal, I don't know if I can do it again. It's all too much."

She began rocking again, her eyes focusing on something that didn't exist. She was confused. That was the only explanation for this. She couldn't decipher reality from visions.

"We're almost done with the trials, Jade," I said. "You have one left, and then we're out of here."

"One more trial," she repeated. "The Saints do not care for the trials."

A knock came from the stone door, causing her to jump. "Who is that?" Jade asked.

"That's Cordelia. It's time for me to go. Just hang in there, okay? I'm not going to let you die here, Jade. I swear it."

Jade nodded. I brushed a quick kiss onto her dry lips before I stood and left her, alone and exhausted, in the Paragon's arena.

Cordelia waited on the other side of the door, a knowing look on her face. "Don't say it," I growled before she could open her mouth.

She only smirked. "I don't have to. You already know I was right. And someone's coming."

Damn. Even with my fae ears, I could only pick up so much. Cordelia, though, could hear thoughts from a mile away if she wanted to. I suppose she had some useful qualities, although keeping her mouth shut wasn't one of them.

"Let's go," I said. I gripped her arm and dragged her through the tunnels into the darkness. We walked in silence until we reached the study.

"She loves you," Cordelia said. "I could feel it."

I scoffed, ignoring the first part of her statement. "Feel it?" I questioned. "Or did you peer into her mind again and dig around as you pleased?"

"Does it matter? She loves you, Malachi, and that trial nearly killed her."

I slammed my hands down on the wooden table. "What do you expect me to do about it, Cordelia? I can't escape with her, you said so yourself. I don't see a choice here!"

She stepped forward, unfazed by my outburst. "Answer me honestly, Malachi. Do you think she'll survive another trial? After what happened to her in the last one? After what happened to you?"

No, I wanted to say. Jade was losing her grip on reality. She wouldn't survive a third trial. I could tell simply by looking at her.

Jade was losing her mind.

"Get to your point," I barked.

"You know what I'm thinking. There's one person in this entire temple who benefits from this."

Silas. And what if what Jade said was true? What if the Saints did not actually need her to complete the trials? What if this entire charade existed for Silas's wicked games?

Cordelia tilted her head. "My offer still stands. We can kill him and get Jade off this mountain before he can cause any more damage. He's killing her, Malachi." She turned to leave the library. A desperate, clawing feeling gnawed at my chest as I watched her walk away.

This was my chance. I had wanted to kill Silas for decades now. If Cordelia truly had a way to do it...

Her eyes met mine, determined and angry.

I had to save Jade's life.

"What's your plan?"

CHAPTER 32
Jade

My third trial would start soon. That's what Mal had said, right? That I had already completed two. I just had...I just had one left.

That was real, right? Mal was really here?

I brushed my fingers across my lips. The kiss felt real. His hands on my face felt real.

Then again, him dying before me felt real, too. And it wasn't. At least...I didn't think it was...

That stone door opened, and the young boy from earlier walked inside. "I'm not hungry," I said before he entered.

He walked in anyway, carrying the same small plate in his hands. He shut the stone door behind him before moving to set it down next to me.

"I have to bring you the food anyway, miss. It's my job."

"Really?" I asked. My voice was dry, and I realized then

how thirsty I had been. "You have quite a peculiar job, don't you think?"

The young boy shrugged. His dark hair had been shaved recently, I caught myself wondering what it looked like before. "I don't mind," he said. "I'm usually bored."

"Huh," I sighed. I couldn't bring myself to say anything else.

The boy stared at me with pure curiosity. "Are you a fae?" he asked.

I laughed, it felt like the first time I had laughed in ages. "No," I answered. "I'm not fae."

"Then what are you doing here?" he asked.

What was I doing here? Saints, I wished I had an answer for that. "Someone wants to see how much power I possess," I said.

"Oh, so you're a witch?"

I shook my head. "I don't think so, kid."

He stared at me for a few more seconds, rocking back and forth on his feet. "I should go," he said. "I'm not really supposed to be talking to you."

"What's your name, kid?" I asked. I shouldn't have. I instantly regretted it. The second I knew this kid's name, I would actually care. And caring about anyone but Malachi in this damned temple was a death wish.

But the boy's eyes lit up, as if nobody had ever asked him that before. "Dragon," he answered.

My eyes widened. "Dragon? That's an interesting name."

He nodded while the grin on his face grew.

"Well," I said. "I'm not going to eat this." I pushed the

small plate of bread toward him. His eyes instantly widened. "Would you like to help me with it?"

Dragon couldn't help the smile that lit up his face. I couldn't help but wonder how long it had been since he ate a proper meal. Was anyone looking out for him here?

He slowly picked up a piece of bread, as if confirming that I really wanted him to have it. I nodded at him, and he scarfed the entire piece down in less than two seconds.

I smiled so wide, my lips cracked. "It was very nice to officially meet you, Dragon. I hope we can talk again when I get out of here."

He turned on his heel and walked toward the door, swallowing his food. It wasn't until he had one hand on the stone that he turned to face me, eyes bright and hopeful. "I can help you, you know," he said. "I know a way out of here."

"I—what did you just say?"

"If you want to, I mean. I don't think it's very nice that you have to stay down here. You're dirty, and you kind of stink."

The weight of his words bubbled in my chest. "You can get me out of here? Without anyone knowing?"

The boy nodded. It was ridiculous, trusting a child. But then again, this entire situation was ridiculous. Thinking I could survive another trial was even more ridiculous.

I could get out of here. I could find Mal and get off this damned mountain.

And I didn't see another option.

I squeezed my eyes shut and tried to focus. This wasn't another trial, was it? This was real?

"Okay," I said to the boy. "But the man I came here with? My husband? We have to find him first."

The boy thoughtfully considered my words, his gaze falling to his feet, before he asked, "Do you know where he is, miss?"

Yes, I wanted to say. I knew where Malachi was. He would be somewhere in this temple waiting for me, waiting for the next trial, or maybe planning our escape.

But the truth was, I didn't really know where Malachi went. This temple was massive with endless amounts of winding tunnels and turns. I would get lost in a heartbeat.

"No," I answered. "No, I don't know where he is. He's somewhere under this mountain."

"I'll find him," the boy said. "Wait here in case they come to check on you. I'll find your husband with the black wings and I'll bring him with us."

Joy bubbled in my chest, joy and something else, something cruel and delightful. Hope.

"Okay," I nodded, not able to contain my smile. "Okay, Dragon. That sounds like a great plan."

I turned around and walked back to the arena, no longer terrified that I wouldn't survive. No longer fearful of what I could not see.

Vita Queen.

I ignored the female voice that echoed through my mind again as the boy closed the stone arena door behind himself.

Vita Queen, it said again.

"What?" I hissed. "What do you want from me?"

I want you to stop running away from who you are, child. Leaving this place will not solve your problems.

"Do not take offense to this, but I hardly think you'd know what will and will not solve my problems."

I waited for an argument, but the calm, steady voice said nothing.

CHAPTER 33
Malachi

There were two times in my life where I had attempted to kill Silas. The first was ages ago, the first week he had brought me to the temple.

I did not plan on killing him. But the younger me had a bad temper, even worse than the temper I had now. And Silas, as self-righteous and all-knowing as he was, pissed me off like no other.

We had been training, and I was just beginning to understand the potential of what my power could do. I had brought down a few grown men at that point, and I knew I could take Silas. He wasn't the height of most grown men, anyway. He was so scrawny, so old.

So, one day, while we were sparring after dinner, I threw all my magic at him. I mustered up every ounce of strength I possibly could, determined to kill that man. Determined to bring him to his knees and more.

But of course, it was useless.

I didn't know it at the time, but Silas could not be

killed. *Why?* I still wasn't entirely sure. I had built up my theories over the years, of course, but they were just that. Theories. Cursed by the Saints, I thought. Perhaps he made a deal and sold his soul. That option made plenty of sense. Or, maybe it was his magic. Maybe his magic had created an impenetrable force, saving his life every time a fae like me tried to take it.

It didn't make sense.

The second time I tried to kill Silas was one week before I left the mountain. I had seen what he was doing. He wanted power more than anything, and everything about him was so fake. He kept the peace, he would claim. He creates equality between fae and witches, balancing the power.

I knew how much bullshit that was the first time I heard it. I just had no idea it would all come down to this— to my wife risking her life to prove that she was the most powerful one here. Not him.

Jade would change the world. Not him.

Jade was blessed by the Saints.

Not him.

"You're sure this will work?" I asked. Esther stared at me with a blank face. When Cordelia first insisted that we needed her to move forward, I shut the idea down.

But even though Esther had lied to me, she did know Silas more than anyone here. Including me.

Her eyes focused on something that wasn't there. "It will work," she replied, her voice barely a whisper.

"If this goes wrong, it's all of our lives on the line. Including Jade's," I said.

Cordelia scoffed from the back of the room. "I think your wife is perfectly safe, Malachi. Silas's power will be no match for hers."

"I'm not particularly excited to find that out," I replied. It was possible. In fact, somewhere inside myself I knew Jade would become stronger than Silas. But did Jade know that? Did Jade believe in herself enough to stand up against him alone?

"And you're sure you're up for this?" Cordelia asked Esther. "This can't be undone, Esther. Once we begin the ritual…"

"I'm sure," Esther said. She took a long, shaking breath. Her eyes had dark shadows under them, and her face had sunken in slightly, her cheekbones jutting out. "He wasn't always this way, you know," she said. "In the beginning, he truly wanted peace."

"I find that hard to believe," I scoffed.

"It wasn't until he got a taste of power that he wanted more. When I found out I was pregnant with you…" She trailed off, a ghost of a smile flickering onto her face. "When I knew you were on the way, I knew I had to get out of there. You were going to be a powerful fae, I could feel it in my bones. But he had already been showing signs of hunger for power. One night, when Silas had left the mountain on some sort of mission, I wrapped you in my arms and left. And I did not see him again until he came for you all those years later in Rewyth."

Saints. Part of me already knew this story, had pieced together the parts that made sense. I clenched my fists and shook the memories away. The past wasn't going to help me today.

I pushed myself up from the table, tearing my gaze away from Esther's sea-filled eyes. "Stick to the plan. We all must be fully committed in order for this to work. This could be our only chance at getting rid of him for good. Let's get this over with."

The others were silent as I walked out of the room and into the tunnels, aiming for one thing.

My wife.

Our bond grew stronger with every step I took. She was close, so close that I had to remind my power that we would save her. We would protect her.

"I'm coming for you, Jade," I whispered to myself, hoping that somehow she would know. Somehow she could sense me.

Cordelia followed tightly on my footsteps. This was the first portion of the plan, to get Jade. This was also the most important part, and frankly, it was the only part I cared about.

When we came to the stone door of the arena, I didn't hesitate. I had so much adrenaline pumping through my body that it took only a single shove to open, and we were inside.

My fae eyes quickly adjusted to the darkness. "Jade?" I

asked. She flinched—painful and soul-aching—away from my voice.

Those damn trials.

"You're okay now," I said softly, taking a step in her direction. She looked at me as if she were staring at her enemy.

"Get away from me," she whispered.

I dropped to my knees next to her. I wanted to give her time. I wanted to explain that I was real, the trials were fake. I wanted to be gentle.

But we were running out of time. We had a small window to escape, and that window closed with every passing second.

"Jade, look at me." Her glazed eyes scanned the room frantically, not settling on any one thing. I grabbed her head with my hands and forced her to look into my eyes. "You're safe, Jade. We're getting you out of here."

"No," she repeated. "This isn't real. It's not real."

"It is real. We're going to kill Silas. We need to get out of here before the other Paragon members realize what's happening."

She pulled out of my grasp and began shaking her head. "She said this would happen."

"Who?"

"That Saint. She told me I would be tested and that I, and that I had to remain true. *Straight ahead*, she said."

Saints, I had no clue what she was talking about. She shook with a nervousness I had never seen before. "When did you talk to a Saint?"

A harsh laugh escaped her. "More like the Saint talking at me. She's not a great listener."

I gripped her face again. "Listen to me, Jade. Whoever you've been talking to doesn't understand what's happening right now. You and I are going back to Rewyth. We're going home."

Her brows drew together. "Rewyth?"

"Yes, Jade. Come with me now or I'll have to throw you over my shoulder and carry you out."

Her hands came up to hold my wrists. "You're dead," she whispered. "I killed you."

"No," I said. "That was part of your trial. It wasn't real, Jade. It was all in your head."

"I...I can't tell. I can't tell what's real, Malachi. I don't even know if this is real."

I brought my lips to hers and kissed her, fierce and quick. She seemed confused at first, but quickly began moving her mouth against mine.

"I'm real. I'm here, and I'll never leave you. This is happening. Do you trust me?"

Her lip quivered. "I trust you."

I picked up the sword I had given her and secured it at my hip. "Good. Now let's go."

"Wait!"

Saints. "What's wrong?"

"There's a little boy, he told me he could help us. He told me he knew a way out of here."

"A way off the mountain?"

"Yes. We can't leave without him, Mal. He's lonely and

he doesn't deserve to stay here with these people. He said he could help us get out of here."

"Where is this boy?"

Her eyes unfocused. "I don't know."

I ran my hands through my hair in an attempt to straighten my thoughts. "We can't wait, Jade. If we see him on our way out we can take him with us, but it's too risky. I won't put you in danger again."

Her eyes held mine for a few moments, and I could almost feel the turmoil inside of her. If this boy even existed, Jade wouldn't be able to leave him.

I grabbed her hand and intertwined our fingers. "Let's go, my queen. Cordelia is waiting."

This time, when I pulled her hand to follow me, she didn't object. One obstacle down. Dozens to go.

The tunnels remained quiet, our labored breaths were the only sounds echoing off the mountain stone walls. That, and our constant footsteps, one after the other, over and over again.

"Where is everyone?" Jade whispered. "Shouldn't there be guards or something?"

Yes. This was all too easy. Finding Jade, the silence, the lack of Paragon members in the halls.

Something was off.

"Stay behind me," I ordered.

Without the boy that Jade said somehow knew a way out of here, there was only one other survivable way off this mountain. And it was the same way we had entered it, in the middle of the dining room with a wide open view.

If anyone was there to stop us, it would be nearly impossible to escape without a fight.

But I was ready for a fight. Saints, I had been ready for a fight for decades now.

My grip on Jade tightened, unfaltering. My black wings tucked as tight as possible behind my shoulders.

Something waited for us. I could feel it, like a tether of adrenaline and anticipation, but not from me. Not from Jade, either. Her emotions felt sweeter in my body. This was the anticipation of the Paragon, of our enemies.

As if on cue, Esther jumped into view. I nearly ran directly into her in the confines of the tunnels.

"What in the Saints is—" Silas stepped into the tunnel after her. His body practically buzzed with anger as he realized what we were doing. The air stilled around us.

Jade tensed behind me. I would be damned if I let him hurt her again.

"We're leaving," I said, loud enough that my voice echoed through the stone walls.

Confusion, anger, and resentment morphed together in flashes on Silas's face. Enough to where I was already drawing my sword, already summoning my magic.

I saw Cordelia duck out of the way from the corner of my eye.

Saints save us, we were really doing this.

I needed to distract him. Esther and Cordelia would do their ritual to bring him as close to death as possible. All I needed to do was distract him long enough.

"Get back, Jade," I ordered.

I widened my wingspan, filling the tunnel from wall to wall to shield her.

But Silas clearly did not care. His magic, dark and sinful, pulsed through the tunnels. Not directed at me. Not directed at Cordelia.

Directed at Jade standing behind me.

A scream of pain escaped her, and I didn't have to turn around to know she had fallen to her knees.

I roared, angry, desperate, and sick of this bastard ruining my life. Sword out, I charged him.

Silas, though, wielding the power of Erebus, only held out one palm. One motion with his hand, and I froze in time.

I couldn't move an inch. I could hardly breathe.

Jade stopped screaming, though. Silas apparently could not focus on us both.

"You thought this would work?" Silas growled. Esther moved behind him. I didn't look away from his empty, evil eyes. "You cannot kill me!"

I tried to thrash against his invisible grip, but I didn't budge an inch.

"You deserve worse than death," I managed to get out.

Esther and Cordelia began to chant.

It was a blood-chilling, repetitive, demonic chant. One I did not even wish to understand. Cordelia and Esther had only discussed it vaguely before, and I was the furthest thing from interested in whatever sacrifice they were about to make.

Silas's grip on me disappeared.

I stepped back, putting space between Silas and myself and getting as close as possible to Jade behind me.

"What are you–" Silas was interrupted by his own scream as the chanting increased, echoing off the stone walls and creating a chamber of magic.

Of witch magic.

It only lasted a few seconds, but it felt like hours. Days. The chanting was endless. I barely noticed Esther pulling out a dagger, the dagger that would entrap Silas, the dagger that would remove his immortal ability.

Would it outright kill him? No.

But he would be very close to dead with no magic, no power. And we would never see him again.

Jade mumbled something behind me.

"What?" I asked, turning to see what she was talking about.

She only shook her head, and we both turned in time to see Esther slam the dagger down into Silas's heart.

The chanting stopped.

Esther, who I expected to show some signs of remorse, only stared at him with clenched fists and dark eyes.

Silas's body fell to the ground, eyes wide. I wondered what was going through his mind in that moment, what he was thinking. *Did he regret it? Underestimating us?*

Thinking Cordelia and Esther would defend him?

Thinking I wouldn't try to end him? To save my wife?

I hoped so.

His eyes glossed over, his head hit the stone.

He could not talk. He could barely breathe.

Small footsteps approached, quickly enough to tell me someone ran in our direction.

I pulled Jade's body closer to me just in time for the small boy that delivered my message from Serefin to step into the tunnels.

"This way!" he yelled in a hushed whisper. "We have to go! Now!"

Esther and Cordelia glanced at each other, not moving. I didn't move, either. Did this boy realize what just happened?

Jade let go of my hand and pushed herself in front of me. "Dragon!" she yelled. She knelt before him and held his hands in hers. He smiled at her, warm and genuine. "Are you sure you know the way out of here?" Jade asked him.

His eyes glanced to the three of us who now stood behind Jade, waiting. He stared at us all for a few seconds before nodding.

"Good," Jade said, giving him a reassuring smile. She stood and turned to us, still holding his hand. "This is Dragon," she announced. "He's coming with us, and he knows the way off this mountain."

"Thank the Saints for that," Cordelia mumbled.

"Come on," Esther said. "Let's leave him here to rot before he can cause any more damage for us."

CHAPTER 34
Jade

Malachi, Dragon, Cordelia, Esther, and I huddled together around our dwindling fire, attempting to shield ourselves from the wicked weather of the blizzard-filled mountain. We had managed to climb far enough down the mountain that the assortment of trees now partially hid us, creating cover while we rested up for the remainder of our journey.

"We should have dragged one of those wind-wielding Paragon members with us. Would have really come in handy right about now," Cordelia said.

"You're the witch," I replied. "Can't you and Esther pull your magic together and do something?"

"After what we did to Silas back there?" Cordelia replied. "Not likely."

"We have to save our strength," Malachi chimed in. "This fire is warm enough. In two days, we'll be warm in our beds at Rewyth."

Rewyth. The sound of the name on Malachi's tongue

was enough to warm me from the inside. I leaned over and rested my head on his shoulder, holding my bare hands out to the flames in front of me.

"This feels like a fever dream," I said. "I can't believe we made it out. I can't believe Silas is dead."

"Dead enough," Esther said. It was the first time she had spoken since we left the temple.

"As far as we're concerned, he isn't our problem anymore," Mal said.

The howling wind overtook the conversation, which was a relief. I didn't want to talk about Silas. I didn't want to talk about how we practically killed the man who could not be killed.

And I certainly did not want to talk about the damn trials.

Malachi's wings curled around us, blocking our bodies from the cold. His presence at my side was the thing I needed more than warmth, more than the fire, more than hope itself.

"We should all get some sleep," Cordelia said after a while. "I'll keep first watch. We'll need our energy if the Paragon decides to come after us."

"The Paragon is nothing without Silas," Mal said. "We'll be safe. But you're right, we need to rest."

Dragon had already half-drifted to sleep closest to the fire, nuzzled against Esther as if his life depended on it.

Esther didn't seem to mind, though. She rested her head against his, eyes watching the flames as if she expected to get some answers from them.

"You need sleep," Malachi said, low enough that only I could hear.

"I don't think sleep is coming to me any time soon," I replied. "My mind won't rest."

His hand ran up the length of my arm, a delicate, loving touch. "This is all real," he answered. "This is all happening. I'll remind you of that every minute of every day if I have to."

I exhaled a long breath, letting his words sink in. After what happened to him during my trial, I wanted to soak in every single moment like this. I never wanted to forget how it felt with his arm around my body, with his sweet words meant just for me lingering in my ears.

"I understand now," I breathed.

"Understand what?"

"I understand how scary it was for you. When I died that night in Rewyth. When you held me as the life faded from my veins, wondering if there was anything you could possibly do to get me back. I get it now."

His calming hand on my shoulder stilled. "You brought me back in your trial," he said. It wasn't a question.

"Yes."

"When that happened, when I died in your visions, I felt it," he said. "I could feel the pain, physically in my body. I couldn't breathe. I couldn't think."

My heart stopped beating. "You could feel what was happening to you? I thought you weren't supposed to be affected, nobody but me was supposed to feel those things."

He shook his head. "I wasn't. But I did. It's our magic, Jade. Life and death, connected for eternity. I can feel you,

you can feel me. When you brought me back to life during your trial that day, *Saints*." His voice trailed off as he dragged his free hand down his face. I twisted in his arms, looking up at him with intense eyes.

The light from the fire reflected off his now-pale skin. I watched as his nostrils flared, his eyes searching in the darkness for answers that weren't there. But I knew the answers. I knew what Mal was about to say.

"I brought you back, too," I finished.

His eyes snapped to mine. "You did," he confirmed.

I breathed deeply. "How? How is this possible?"

"It must have been some awakening when Esther brought you back from death. You're different now, Jade. They say you're not human anymore. This could change everything for you."

A quiet laugh escaped me. "I can't even say I'm surprised," I admitted. "With everything that's happened to us, it wouldn't even surprise me if I grew wings out of my back tomorrow."

Mal's black wings flickered in response. "That would be a sight," he growled in my ear.

He placed a delicate kiss on my cheek, warming the skin there. I gripped the front of his shirt with my hands, pulling him closer, taking him in.

Wings would suit you, the voice dormant in my mind said. I jumped at the sound of it, almost forgetting that someone or something had been speaking to my mind.

"How long did it take you?" I asked Mal, "When you completed the trials, how long did it take you to know what was real?"

He shrugged. "Some days I still have to remind myself."

Great, so I would have to listen to this insane voice for the rest of my days?

"Have you ever…" I started. I wanted to ask him about the voice, about the Saint who claimed to be speaking to me. I wanted to ask him if he had ever spoken to a Saint, had ever known someone who had. Because I needed some sort of validation that I was not, in fact, crazy. That I wasn't actually losing my mind. But what would he think? What if I really was just going crazy? He would worry, even more than he already did—which was saying a lot. "Never mind," I said instead.

He only pulled me further into his chest, letting me rest my head against his warm body. "Sleep," he insisted. "Your worries will still be here in the morning, too."

Nothing had ever been more true. I took one last glance at Esther and Dragon, both fast asleep, and one last glance at Cordelia, who sharpened her dagger with her back to the fire, before closing my eyes.

Your worries will still be here in the morning.

"Thank you, Mal," I whispered with my eyes closed.

"Why are you thanking me?"

"For not leaving me. For dragging yourself to that temple with me when you didn't have to. For backing me up always, even when I'm not right."

I felt him smile. "Always," he said.

Sleep came swiftly.

R*un.*
Get up.
Run.

My eyes shot open. We were still in the dark forest, the sun was just beginning to rise in the distance. "What?" I asked aloud.

Malachi was already staring at me, worry in his eyes. "I didn't say anything," he said. "Bad dream?"

Run. Get out of here.

That calming female voice now practically yelled against my skull. "Wake up!" I yelled to everyone. "Wake up, we have to go! Now!"

Everyone woke up slowly, but nobody moved. Nobody ran. "Jade, what are you talking about?" Malachi asked.

I jumped to my feet and pulled him after me. I didn't know which direction to run, I wasn't even sure what I was running from. But I could feel that thread of fear pulling me to move, to act. "She told me to run, Mal, we have to—"

The next words escaped me. Every inch of my body pricked with adrenaline as a few snow-covered twigs snapped in the distance.

Someone—or something—was coming.

"Run!" I hissed, and they actually listened this time. Everyone sprang to their feet, desperate as I was to get away from whatever approached in the distance.

"Let's go!" Malachi ordered in a hushed whisper. "Head down the mountain, go!" We waited until the others were in front of us, Dragon holding tightly to Esther's hand, before we followed suit.

"What is that?" I whispered over my shoulder to Mal. "Did someone follow us here?"

"I don't know," Mal replied. "But I'm not sure I want to find out."

We half-ran, half-stumbled down the mountain. It wasn't until Esther and Dragon stopped dead in their tracks that we halted, too.

"What's wrong?" I yelled to them.

Esther held a hand out in waiting.

One painful second passed.

Two seconds.

I was about to urge them all to keep moving forward when that same voice echoed in my mind, *Now you fight.*

And then chaos.

Cordelia yelled first—a battle cry filled with anger and frustration.

And then deadlings came into view, one at a time. They weren't moving quickly, but they were certainly targeting us.

Cordelia cut one down with her sword.

Then another, slicing its head clean from its body.

Esther pulled her dagger out and shoved Dragon behind, pushing him safely in the center of our circle.

Mal and I both spun around.

We were surrounded.

Deadlings came at us from every direction, slowly clawing and barring their razor-sharp teeth as they moved after one thing—our flesh.

Mal drew his sword next to me.

"Shit," he said. "I've had enough of these damned

creatures." He stepped forward and sliced down, cutting through two bodies and watching them fall into the snow.

"Damn Silas!" Cordelia yelled as she killed another. "He couldn't have taken these rancid things with him when he died?"

"What are you talking about?" I asked. My power prepared itself within me, ready to take out all of them if I had to. As long as I knew the others were safe...

"Silas is the one controlling these damn things! His disgusting little pets," Cordelia answered.

I replayed those words in my mind, ensuring I heard them correctly. Silas was the one controlling them?

"What do you mean, *Silas controls them*?" Mal sliced down another.

Cordelia did the same. "I mean, he controls them! His wicked magic blood or something. He's the one that makes them attack in numbers."

Anger washed over me—hot and feral—as I realized exactly what she was saying. All those times the deadlings came to Rewyth, all those times they attacked, all those times they randomly showed up in mass numbers.

It was no mere accident.

Malachi had told me once that something must control them, something must tell them to attack as if they were a controlled army.

Now it all made sense. This was his last attack, his last piece of damage in our lives.

"His dying wish was to make these creatures kill us all?" Malachi growled. He must have felt the anger, too, because with one swing of his sword he cut through four deadling bodies.

"He can damn well try," I mumbled. "Cover them, Mal! Now!"

I didn't have to explain further. He knew exactly what was about to happen. I gave Mal a few seconds to duck behind me and flare his wings out, covering the three with his large wingspan.

And then I took a long, calming breath, fueling that anger and frustration into one place. Into one overwhelmingly hot, fiery place deep in my soul. My power responded with a flicker of delight, ready to act however I willed it too.

I didn't even realize I was screaming, not until my magic poured from me like blood, lighting up the icy forest around us. I held it there, letting it pull from that place of anger and betrayal and hatred, until I finally felt like myself again.

And then I pulled it all back.

"Saints," Cordelia muttered from behind me.

I turned around to find them unharmed, each with open mouths as they surveyed the area around us.

All except Malachi, who stared at me with an adoration that made my toes curl in my boots.

"Amazing," he said, his dark eyes filled with a primal heat under his thick lashes. "Absolutely stunning."

And for the first time in a long time, I actually felt that way. I looked around us, at the piles of ash that were left in the place of the deadlings. It had been so easy to kill them all, so easy to tear down our enemy.

I lifted my chin. It hadn't been that long ago that I was

the helpless, poor girl who could do nothing but scream in the face of danger.

Not anymore. My enemies would turn to ash before me. My challengers would meet the Saints before they ever drew my blood.

Malachi knew this, too. He rose and stood beside me, placing a hand on my shoulder.

Vita Queen, the voice whispered, so quietly I almost didn't hear it.

Malachi's breath tickled my ear as he whispered, "You'll bring entire kingdoms to their knees, my queen."

The warm kiss on my temple was enough to send a thrill of fire through my body. That, and the unsettling truth of his words.

Entire kingdoms on their knees.

For Mal, I would deliver any kingdom. If power was what he wanted...

I would be the one to give it to him.

CHAPTER 35
Malachi

Silas controlled them. It made so much sense, I grew more and more angry with each passing minute that I hadn't figured it out sooner.

Of course, Silas controlled those creatures. They were spiteful and disgusting, just like him. Hopefully with him dying, the deadlings would no longer be a problem. If we were lucky, he would already be dead.

Jade walked in front of me, not the slightest bit weary from using her power. It was unheard of to have an ability like that, to turn an entire army of deadlings to ash.

It wouldn't be just deadlings, either. She could kill anyone she wanted to, anything that rose against her.

My chest swelled with pride. She was much more powerful than I was, that much was clear to anyone who paid a single second of attention.

She felt it, too. She felt power. I could feel the tiny bead of emotion deep in my core, my lifeline to her that was growing stronger and stronger with each day we spent together. It was almost as if I could read her thoughts, could sense what she was going to do before she did it.

And when she used her power without holding back, without fear of what might happen, Saints, she was marvelous.

"We have to be getting close," Esther sighed. "Rewyth isn't more than a two day's walk from the temple."

"You would know," I sneered. "Tell me, how long have you been traveling back and forth from these woods to meet with him? How long have you been spying on us for his benefit?"

She stopped dead in her tracks, and the others continued as I nearly tripped over her. For the first time that I could remember, anger lit up her eyes. "Have I not proved my loyalty to you?" she hissed in a whisper. "I helped you kill him. I..."

"You what? You loved him? Is that what you're going to say? Because considering your ability to betray him so easily, I'm not too sure about that."

"Easily?" She scoffed. "You think the choice I made came easily, son?" She shook her head and broke our eye contact, smiling at something imaginary. "You know nothing about the choices I've had to make."

"I think I know enough to know that I would never betray Jade. Not if it cost me everything."

"And what if it cost you your child?" she asked. The words were unexpected, they hit me with a force like a punch. "What if you had to choose between the one you loved lifetimes ago, and the one you love now?"

Shit. My mother had done plenty to prove her loyalty

to myself and Jade, yet each time I began to trust her, something else happened. Some new information turned up.

Like the fact that Silas was my father, Erebus's blood ran through my veins.

I brushed past her and began walking after the group, slow enough that Esther could catch up. "He was evil and twisted," I muttered. "We're all better off now that he's gone. Including you." It was the closest thing to sympathy I could muster for her.

Esther stepped into stride beside me, feet crushing against the icy forest floor. "There's a reason I did what I did, son. I meant what I said about Jade being the peacemaker. She's going to change everything for us."

"If you know anything else about my wife, I suggest you tell me now."

Esther paused in a way that made my stomach drop. "You already know."

"Know what, exactly?"

I couldn't help but stare at Jade as I waited for Esther's response. My wife. Human. Magic. The peacemaker. Something else entirely. Esther once told me that Jade would save us all.

Maybe it was time for that. Maybe Jade really would save us all.

I had no doubt that she could do it.

"Jade has made it out of the trials, but there's still a great sacrifice that must be made," Esther replied. "The stories of what the peacemaker can do aren't stories with happy endings."

"You told me we could avoid this. You told me you would help us save Jade's life, that there was another way."

I couldn't even look at her. I was certain if I did, my world would erupt in anger. Esther was only alive, had only lasted this long because she held a promise. She would protect Jade from her fate. She would make it so Jade, as the peacemaker, would not have to sacrifice herself.

But now this?

"There is another way," Esther replied. "But that doesn't mean she will not suffer greatly."

I was about to lose my temper, was about to scream and demand that Esther tell me exactly what Jade needed to do, when Jade's voice interrupted my thoughts.

She still walked on ahead of us, and probably had forgotten that I could hear her low muttering with my fae ears.

"I can't do that," Jade whispered to herself. "I'll never be strong enough to restore the balance of power. They don't respect me. A year ago, I was nothing more than a useless human living in poverty."

Esther must have sensed this too, her magic allowing her to hear much further than a human.

"No, no," Jade argued with nobody. "They won't believe that. This is all insane, all part of my trial. Saints, get out of my head!"

My blood froze over, an eerie chill raising the hair on the back of my neck. Jade thought we were still in the trials?

"Stop here," I yelled loud enough for everyone to hear. "The sun is setting. Let's get some rest and finish the final journey to Rewyth tomorrow morning."

Saints. I hated that we were stopping for one more night, but I didn't hate it as much as what I had just heard coming from Jade's mouth.

Esther gave me a knowing look before walking away to talk to Dragon.

A bitter feeling grew in my chest watching them together. I was happy that Dragon was out of the temple. I was happy that he was being taken care of, and that Jade cared enough to try and save him.

But watching my mother take care of him when she did nothing but abandon me? I didn't expect it to upset me, but it did.

"What's going on?" Jade asked as she walked up. "If we walk through the night, we'll be there by sunrise."

The sun was beginning to drop below the horizon, nothing but a red glow in the distance giving us light.

"We need our rest," I said. "We don't know what we're coming home to, and I don't want to push you any harder than I already have."

The harshness in her face slipped away with each second that passed, replaced by heavy, tired features.

"Fine," she said. "Just for a few hours, though."

"Whatever you say, my queen."

She flashed me a mocking smile and turned to find a large tree trunk to lean against. It hurt me to see her grimace in pain, barely making it to the ground without releasing a grunt. She stuck her legs out, using her hands to help lift each one, before finally resting her head on the tree bark behind her.

"Come on," I said to the others. "Let's start a fire."

Nobody spoke as we collected wood, brushing off the dirt and throwing it into the pile. Even Cordelia kept her mouth shut, which could only mean she was far too exhausted for any snide remarks at this hour.

I didn't mind it, though. After everything we endured, a moment of silence was necessary. To gather my thoughts, to react from the chaos.

Even as we all found our place around the fire an hour later, we were silent. Nobody complained about the cold. Nobody complained about the hunger. We all sat still, staring into the fire.

I eventually looked up from the fire to see Jade staring at me from across the flames.

"Tell him," Cordelia said. She stared at Jade with her brows drawn. Jade ripped away from my gaze and shook her head.

"Stay out of my head," Jade mumbled, but her voice trailed off.

"Tell me what?" I pushed. Whatever Cordelia found by sniffing around in Jade's mind, it had to be important.

Cordelia only rolled her eyes and stood from her spot around the fire. "Come on," she said to Dragon and Esther. "These two lovebirds need to discuss something in private."

Esther and Dragon stood up silently, following Cordelia into the woods. Which was entirely pointless, by the way, because I knew they would be eavesdropping.

"What's going on?" I asked Jade. I moved to sit closer to her. "What do you need to tell me?"

"Cordelia's gift can be very annoying," Jade mumbled. "I didn't want to bring this up right now."

"It's okay," I reassured her. "We don't have to discuss anything you don't feel comfortable–"

Her hand fell onto my thigh. "No," she said. "It's okay." I waited in silence for her to continue. "During those trials, you were right. It all felt so real." Her voice cracked. I waited for her as she took a shaking breath and continued, "After I killed you, something changed. Something…something hardened inside of me. And that bond that connects us? The bond of life and death, or whatever you want to call it. It's stronger now. I can feel it so much more, even though you didn't really die."

I gripped her hand. "You were amazing in there, Jade. You brought me back. You saved me. I could feel your terror as if it were my own. I would trade places with you in a heartbeat if I could. You should never have to go through something like that."

She turned her body to me as her eyes searched my face. "You actually died?" she asked. "I really killed you?"

I placed my hands on the sides of her face and forced her to keep looking at me as I explained, "You could never hurt me, Jade Weyland. You are a miraculous, astonishing woman. You brought me back from death, Jade. You can resurrect lives." I let the words sink in, urging her to hear me. "You do not need to worry about hurting me. Ever."

I still wasn't convinced that she knew how much I meant those words, but I let go of her face anyway.

"Is that what you wanted to talk to me about?" I asked her.

An unreadable expression crossed her features. She opened her mouth, but shut it again. Turmoil swarmed her eyes. I wasn't going to push her, though. Not after everything she went through.

"Yes," she answered. "I just...I just can't lose you, Mal."

I put my arm around her and pulled her closer to me. "You'll never lose me, Jade. I swear it. I'll be by your side until the end, until Erebus himself pulls you from my cold, dead hands."

She leaned her head on my shoulder. "Saints, save us," she whispered, barely audible.

"Saints, save us."

CHAPTER 36

Jade

The castle of Rewyth was bigger than I remembered.

The footsteps from my damp, filthy boots echoed against the stone walls. And white—so much white—sharply contrasted with the greenery that somehow still grew throughout the estate, even though winter chilled my bones.

Yet each time I found myself returning to this place, it felt more like home.

Disguised in the darkness of night, Malachi had snuck us all in through one of the many hidden entrances in Rewyth, which I became very grateful for. He had shown Dragon, Esther and Cordelia to the servants' rooms down the hall before leading me back to our bedroom.

My entire body sagged in relief. I wanted to do nothing more than drop onto that massive, beautiful bed and stay there for weeks.

But Malachi's hand fell onto my lower back. "I hate

this," he whispered. He tugged the edge of my sleeve, causing it to expose my bare shoulder. When I looked, I saw the bite from the deadling in my trial.

"It's not as bad as it looks," I said, but the words weren't true. The bite itself might not have been that terrible, but the memories...

"You're safe now," Malachi replied. "He can't hurt you anymore."

His body behind me became a wall of support as I leaned into him. "I'm so tired," I admitted, barely hearing my own words out loud.

"I know you are, my queen. We're home now. You can rest."

I closed my eyes and replayed those words over and over again in my mind. Malachi helped me peel my shirt from my dirty, bruised body. He pulled my boots from my swollen feet. He guided me into the bath in the other room, filling it with steaming water.

We didn't have to talk. He had experienced the trials, too. He knew what I had gone through. For over an hour, he sat there with me in the bathroom, not asking a single question. Not demanding any information.

I almost told him about the Saint who spoke to me, but my body grew too tired to form words.

Once the hot water had turned cold and my skin had finally been rubbed clean, Mal helped me out of the bath and into our bed.

"Tonight, we rest," he said, pulling the sheets around my body. "Tomorrow, we fight for what's ours."

Yes, we will.

The next day, after a full night of rest and a massive breakfast, Malachi gathered Esther and Cordelia for a court meeting.

They walked behind us as we descended the halls of the castle. I held Malachi's hand so tightly, I couldn't tell if it was his hand sweating or mine. I held his hand until the force of someone's body hitting mine nearly knocked me off my feet.

Gentle yet urgent arms wrapped around my neck.

It was Adeline, nearly suffocating me and half-squealing as she embraced me. I hugged her back, not realizing how desperately I had missed her, how desperately I had needed my friend.

"Thank the Saints you're okay," she whispered as she held me. "I've been worried sick about you!"

She pulled away to smile at me for only a second before throwing herself at Malachi, hugging him equally as fierce.

Malachi chuckled with a warmth I hadn't heard in quite some time. "We missed you too, sister," he muttered.

I fought back a surprising wave of tears, not wanting any of them to see me cry. Not anymore. Not after everything. Adeline pulled back before surveying Cordelia and Esther behind me.

"It looks like you've all made it back in one piece."

Cordelia scoffed but said nothing, which only resulted in a raised eyebrow from Adeline.

"We have a lot to discuss with you," Malachi said from beside me. His king voice was now turned on, back in these halls where we had real responsibilities and people relying on us every day. "Where are my brothers?"

Adeline turned on her heel and began sauntering down the hall. "They've been waiting for you. We have a lot to discuss, too."

She left us scurrying after her, a sinking feeling weighing me down with each step.

Malachi tensed the second he heard the name. *Seth of Trithen.*

The man who should be dead, the man who threatened us all, the man who killed Fynn, Malachi's brother.

"And you're telling me he's still alive?" Malachi asked, fury radiating from every word.

"He's not alone," Serefin explained. "He came with an army of *gifted* fae."

"Gifted?" I asked.

"They have magic," Lucien chimed in from the table. "They've been camped right outside the kingdom for a few days now. We couldn't risk a war, not knowing what type of power they brought with them."

I scoffed. Seth was bluffing. Gifted fae were rare, and *exceptionally* gifted fae were nearly nonexistent these days.

For now, anyway. Until I reclaimed magic to how it once was.

"Besides," Serefin chimed in. "The last thing we want is

Silas and the rest of the Paragon on our asses for killing the King of Trithen."

Malachi and I shared a glance. Cordelia laughed quietly somewhere in the back of the room.

"He won't be a problem for us anymore," Malachi explained. I glanced down at my worn, dirty shoes, not wanting to look anyone in the eye.

"And why is that, brother?" Adonis asked.

"We may have killed him. Or put him in an eternal death-sleep. However you'd prefer to view it," Mal explained.

"You did *what*?" Adonis paced back and forth in the empty dining hall as Malachi replayed the events of the last week.

The trials, Malachi nearly dying, my magic through our strange power bond somehow bringing him back to life.

And yes, *Silas*.

"It needed to be done," Cordelia said. Surprisingly enough, she had been the one with enough presence to make Adonis back down during his outburst. "Who knows what he would have done after Jade completed the trials, and who knows what he would have done to her. To her power."

I watched in amusement as Adonis's nostrils flared. He paced the dining hall once more, his hand rubbing his chin.

The other brothers, Eli and Lucien, sat down at our table, silently taking in all of this information.

A strange feeling washed over me as I watched them sit together. They were still brothers, of course, but it was different now. They weren't really related, not in blood.

The one thing holding them together was the old king's blood, the blood that we now knew did not run in Malachi's veins.

It explained a lot, honestly. Like the fact that Malachi had black wings. Like the fact that he held such a strong magical gift when the others did not.

Adonis stopped pacing long enough to calmly place both his palms on the large wooden table. "None of you thought that this might end badly for us? That the fae would turn against you for what you did? I mean, Saints, Malachi. That's treason!"

"Treason to whom?" Cordelia once again spoke up before Malachi even opened his mouth.

I needed a damn drink.

"I think my brother is capable of answering for himself, *witch*," Adonis spat.

Saints, things really had changed in the weeks I had been gone. Adonis had always been the even-tempered one, the calm one.

Cordelia smiled and put a hand on her hip in a way that reminded me of Adeline, who sat silently at the table next to me.

"*Half*-witch," Cordelia corrected. Her decadent silver wings flared on either side of her, reminding us all they were there. "And you'd be wise to remember that, *prince*."

"Enough," Mal barked. "None of us have the energy for this. We did the right thing by killing him, he would have ruined us otherwise."

"You mean ruined her!" Adonis's finger pointed

directly at me, I didn't need to look at him to feel the attention.

A low growl came from Malachi. "Watch what you say, brother. We've been down this path too many times before."

"Because you continue to choose her over your kingdom!"

Malachi erupted, his chair falling behind him from the force of jumping to his feet as he replied, "We have no kingdom without her! Do you not understand that? Can all of us please get on the same page here and understand that Jade is our future?"

Now, I really felt the attention.

Every single pair of eyes in the room slid to me, and if it weren't for Adeline's hand that slid softly into mine, I would have bolted for the door.

"He's not wrong," Esther spoke up. "The time is coming. Jade will have to perform the sacrifice and fulfill her duties as peacemaker."

"And what duties are those, exactly?" Adeline asked. "Since you seem to know so much."

I could have sworn I heard Cordelia chuckle at that one.

Esther took a long breath as we all waited for her response. I glanced at Malachi, whose night wings were tucked tightly behind his shoulders and whose brows were pulled together with concern.

Perhaps I should have been feeling more concern for myself, for what Esther was about to say.

Somehow, though, I didn't. Because I knew my reality, I knew that whatever my fate was, I would be wanting to change it not for my own sake, but for his. Because I knew how much pain it would cause if I left him, and I couldn't do that to him. Not again. Not after experiencing it myself.

For him, I would fight.

When I finally turned my attention back to Esther, she was already staring at me. Her eyes held something that looked like pity, although with her, I never knew.

She doesn't know about us, the voice said. *She doesn't know I speak to you.*

Great. Now was not the time for an imaginary Saint to be speaking to me. My mind spun, a mixture of dreams and reality flashed as images in my memory.

Cordelia turned to face me, her eyes locked on me.

Shit. I had forgotten about her gift to hear thoughts.

She raised an eyebrow, as if listening to that, too. "Who is that?" Cordelia asked me.

Everyone, including Esther and Malachi, continued to stare.

"Who?" I asked.

"Don't play dumb," she said. "How long have the Saints been speaking to you in your mind?"

Pain burst through my temples. I wasn't sure if it was really happening. I wasn't sure if it was real, or how long they had been talking to me. It was part of the trials, wasn't it? It was part of my mind, part of the visions.

Like Mal dying. Like Sadie dying. Like Tessa...

I dropped my head into my hands and tried to focus.

This is real, the Saint spoke. *The sooner you accept that, the sooner we can move on.*

"Jade?" Mal asked.

My eyes slid over to his, dark and concerned, before I nodded my head. "I–"

"She couldn't tell if it was real or not," Cordelia answered for me. Normally, I would have felt invaded with a half-witch poking around in my mind. Today, though, I was grateful. "The trials have botched her mind, Malachi. She didn't know."

Shame crept up my neck, red-hot with digging claws.

"Saints," Mal whispered. "What do they say? What do they want with you?"

"They want her to fulfill her destiny!" Esther finally said.

"She hasn't told me what she wants," I answered.

"*She*?" Malachi asked, his features dripping with concern.

I shrugged. "The voice is female, I'm assuming it's one of the female Saints."

The room erupted, a chaotic mess of arguing over what to do next, what the Saints could possibly want, and what I had been hiding.

I barely heard any of it. I focused on my own thoughts, on that angelic voice that only came so often. I waited for her to chime in, but she didn't.

"Enough!" Malachi yelled after the fighting went on for a few minutes. "This conversation is beyond inappropriate to be having. Jade is sitting right here! We can discuss the Saints with her later. Right now, we have bigger issues."

I looked at everyone in the room. They once hated me. I remembered it so clearly. Most of them, besides Adeline and Serefin, had at one point wanted me dead. Would they still sacrifice me so quickly? Or would they think twice, knowing I had life magic?

"This has gone on too far," I said. "Esther, tell us exactly what is expected of me as the peacemaker. You said before I had to give my life. What's changed?"

"Nothing has changed," Esther said. "Nothing has changed, except for the fact that you are no longer human. You can no longer die a mortal death."

My ears rang.

"To fulfill your duties as the peacemaker, you must perform a ritual. A ritual that, under normal circumstances, would require your life. But your life is no longer mortal, child. You will perform the ritual, and you will restore magic in this world."

"To the fae or to the witches?" I asked.

"You are the peacemaker," Esther explained. "Only you can decide who is worthy of the magic."

"This is ridiculous," Malachi mumbled. "Serefin, stay here with Adeline and the witches. The rest of you are coming with me." He turned toward the door and began walking out of the room.

"Where are you going?" I asked.

"I'm going to get rid of our current problem."

CHAPTER 37
Malachi

"Slow down!" Jade yelled from behind us. Adonis, Lucien, and Eli marched me in the direction of Seth and his men near the back wall of Rewyth. "Not all of us have fae legs and height!"

"Go ahead," I ordered my brothers, stifling my laughter. "I'll catch up."

"We count on it," Adonis remarked before the three of them walked ahead.

"Saints," Jade breathed, finally slowing herself down to a normal-paced walk. "If only I could have gotten some of your fae speed when I came back from death."

Only Jade could make jokes in this type of situation.

"Trust me, Jade," I said. "We are in no rush."

I wrapped my arm around her shoulders and began walking, my brothers in view ahead.

"How are you feeling?" Jade asked. "About seeing him again, I mean."

I shrugged. I didn't want to tell her that every ounce of

my body burned with anger and hatred when I heard his name again, but I'm sure Jade had already felt it through our connected power.

"It will be a miracle if I don't kill him on sight," I said.

"After what he did to you and your family, I don't blame him. I'm surprised your brothers haven't taken care of him already."

"If it weren't for the damn gifted fae, I'm sure they would have." I knew they would have. Either that, or they respected me enough to leave the kill for me. Either way, they wanted that bastard dead. I wasn't about to let him walk out of this kingdom without paying for what he did to Fynn.

"What type of gifts do you think they have?" Jade asked me. If she was nervous about my answer, she hid it well. Genuine curiosity was the only thing I heard beneath her words.

I shook my head. "Nothing I would worry about, and certainly not something you need to worry about, Jade. Do I need to remind you of who you are?"

She smiled and shrugged my arm from her shoulder. "You're arrogant," she mumbled. "Did you know that?"

I put a thoughtful finger to my chin, pretending to consider her words. "You know, I believe someone has told me that before. But she was ruthless and fierce, so I didn't pay her much mind."

She spun to me, preparing to counter my banter, but the beginning of Seth's men came into view ahead of us.

Maybe one hundred men, camped out and settled in right here on the outskirts of Rewyth.

Wow, Seth really had some guts.

Did he expect us to let this happen? To not retaliate?

My pace picked up the closer we got, but Jade easily kept up this time. I knew she was eager, too. Eager to confront him. Maybe as eager as I was to kill him.

My brothers unsheathed their swords ahead.

It was only when we reached their side that I saw Seth, standing behind a wall of men that I only assumed to be his 'gifted' fae.

His eyes widened when he saw us approaching. Clearly, he didn't expect me to come home any time soon.

"I can't say it's a pleasure to see you again," I spat.

"Our presence here is nothing personal," Seth shouted from behind his protectors. "We were told that the King of Rewyth no longer resided in his kingdom. A shame, really, that nobody was left to lead your people."

He had always been such a damn coward. At least that hadn't changed.

"We should have killed you when we had the chance," I barked, remembering the short period of time we spent in Trithen. I had never trusted him. I ignored my instinct when my heart told me he was a snake. A traitor.

And look where that had gotten us.

Seth, King of Trithen, deserved to die.

"Did you bring these gifted fae here to protect you?" I asked, waving a hand to the men that stood before him. I recognized some. Had spent days training them in Trithen with my own sword, my own skill set.

"I am no fool," Seth replied. I laughed along with my

brothers behind me. "I knew your people would be angry. It is only wise that I bring my own protection."

"Well," I said. "You are here now. My men tell me that you've made your intentions very clear. You plan to take my throne." My power rumbled like thunder in my veins. "*My. Throne.*"

Seth opened his mouth to speak, but I cut him off. "Not only did you march all the way here to attempt an impossible task," I pushed, "but you brought these fae, these gifted fae, along with you. Did you think they would be stronger than myself? Than my wife?"

A few of the fae standing before us shifted uncomfortably. One of them, in particular, even flared his silver wings.

If they were smart, they would stand down. They knew what my power could do. Unmatched and derived from Erebus himself, they could not—*would* not—defeat me.

It was animalistic, the instinct they would have to bow to me. To not turn against me.

I let a small amount of my power flare, not enough to hurt anyone, just enough for the deadly black tendrils to expand around my body for a few seconds.

Their eyes widened as they stared at me.

"Everyone standing before us today," I announced to the crowd, "I do not hold you to the crimes that your leader has committed. Join me. Join us. Claim me as your king, and my wife as your queen, and live. But those of you who do not join me..."

I sent my dark, seeking power of death in Seth's direction. Beyond the fae wall that protected him, he collapsed in pain, withering on the ground.

"Those of you who do not join me will die here, today, with your leader."

A low murmur spread through the crowd of men around us. I was about to send the blast of death through my tendrils of power when Jade's hand fell onto my arm.

"Let me do it," she whispered to me. "Let me end this."

Never in my life had I given up death so easily.

CHAPTER 38
Jade

"Move aside," I ordered the silver-winged fae before me. They hesitated, glancing at each other to see who would move first.

Cowards. They were all waiting for the first one to falter. For the first one to give in.

They needed a push.

Mal's power was on the verge of exploding, I felt it as truly as I could feel my own body. He held back, for whatever reason, he held back.

He felt bad for these fae. I knew he did. He had been in that same position many times before, standing up for the wrong man because that's what he had been told to do.

Me? I did not have the same challenge. I did not have that same conflict.

I held my hands out before me and summoned a small ball of light energy, life power. "Life magic," I said aloud, "I'm told is as rare as the Saints." The fae around me jolted with surprise. "I'm told it can resurrect life as well as take it.

Men," I addressed the men protecting Seth, "you each have special gifts, I am told. That's also rare. You should be proud. Now, which of you would like to test your gift against mine?"

I grew the ball of pure life wider, brighter, until it illuminated against their faces. One of them would test me. The hair standing up on the back of my neck warned me of it.

Malachi stood tall and strong at my side. He was not afraid of my magic. He could not be harmed by it. But everyone else...

Even Malachi's brothers backed up, giving me space. Not out of fear, but out of respect.

Just when I thought I had proved my strength to them all, a gust of wind shot at me, strong and fierce. Air magic was a rare gift, yes, but it was no match for mine.

Or Malachi's.

Malachi rushed to my side, keeping me upright. It took me half a second to identify where the gust of magic had come from, and even less time to aim my power in the fae's direction.

He disintegrated while the fae beside him screamed.

My breath came out in pants. Power fueled me, inflamed me. "Anyone else?" I asked. "Or are we done pretending you all have a fighting chance?"

"Do not back down!" Seth ordered. "That's what she wants!"

I stared into their eyes, into the souls of the men before me. I did not necessarily want to kill them, but I would. For Malachi, I would.

The men directly in front of Seth stepped aside, heads lowered.

I could not stop my own smile.

I stepped forward, Malachi at my side, until I stood only a few feet away from Seth. Malachi would make sure the fae did not change their minds, but I had a strong amount of confidence in them.

If they wanted to live, they would stand down.

Power seeped from every pore in my body. I let myself get angry, remembering everything that happened those days in Trithen. Remembering what Malachi had to do to save my life, what we all had to do to survive.

"Did you think I wouldn't react?" I asked Seth, half-yelling. "When you had Isaiah lock me in a cage with a deadling, did you think I would let that go?"

Power pulsed from my body, like red-hot fire that could not be controlled.

Seth stumbled backward.

"Or did you think, like most of my enemies, it seems, that I would back down? That I would submit to you?"

Malachi's sword touched the back of his neck—just barely—reminding him he was still there. Seth could not run. He could not hide.

"You, King of Trithen, have threatened me too many times to still be standing. What's worse, even, is that you threatened my husband."

More power erupted, a small ball of it even grazing the side of Seth's face. He squealed in horror, his skin burning to ash anywhere my power touched him.

Good. I wanted him to be afraid. I wanted him on his knees, begging for my mercy.

I'm sure he thought I would give it to him. I was nothing but the stupid, weak human girl who played directly into his hands.

"Well?" I asked him, demanding an answer.

Seth's eyes slid over my shoulder, to Malachi's brothers that stood behind me.

"Don't look at them," I barked. "They won't help you. Look at me." His eyes met mine, wide with terror.

"Please," he stammered. "Please, Jade–"

"Queen," Malachi corrected from behind him.

"Queen!" Seth yelled. "Please, Queen Weyland! I made a mistake!"

"You did," I agreed. "And unfortunately for you, I am not one to easily forget."

My power blasted forward, eagerly and effortlessly seeking its target. The tenseness I felt in my body slowly dissipated as I let Seth's body burn and burn with my light, ridding the world of his evilness.

And when it was done, when nothing remained but ash, I took a long, relaxed breath and withdrew my power.

"Saints," Lucien muttered behind me.

I turned my attention to Malachi, who stared at me with nothing but adoration and pride.

I lifted my chin, turning to face the others. "Anyone who betrays us dies. Anyone who threatens my husband dies. Anyone who hurts my kingdom," I pointed to the castle behind us, Adonis, Lucien, and Eli standing close by, "dies."

CHAPTER 39
Malachi

Days later, the entire kingdom stood before us. I recognized each and every one of them, even the ones I had only seen once or twice in passing.

Each one of them stared up and me with wide, expecting eyes. Before, I would have worried that they hated me. Hated my reign. Hated the fact that I killed my own father—who I thought was my father.

But I stood before them now with pride. With certainty.

And Jade stood next to me.

Beautiful and terrifying, she looked out at my people. Our people.

No longer human, no longer fickle or weak. She was powerful, stronger than even me.

And our people knew it. They could feel it, not in the same way I could, but in the same way that we could sense when a storm brewed nearby.

Even my brothers—Adonis, Eli, and Lucien—stared upon her with awe.

The past two days blurred together. Seth's men retreated to Trithen after swearing loyalty to their new king and queen. We would have repercussions, I was sure of it. We would have resistance from other kingdoms claiming what we did was wrong.

But I knew the truth. Killing Seth was justice.

Now, we stood before our kingdom, overlooking each loyal member from the stone balcony we stood on, to announce what we all had known for some time now to be the truth.

"Fae of Rewyth," I declared, "we have all struggled over the last few months. We lost our king, we lost a prince, we lost countless soldiers in battle, and most importantly, we lost the sense of peace and freedom that used to dwell in these lands." Jade's hand fell onto mine. "But I can say to you right now, as your king, that nobody will ever be a threat to us again."

The crowd roared, erupting in a sea of applause and shouts of agreement.

"I stand before you with my wife, Jade Weyland, Queen of Rewyth. The same queen whom many of you doubted just weeks ago, and the same queen who has sacrificed her life for this kingdom. Jade stands before you now with the magic of Saints, more powerful than any fae or witch who walks among us."

Again, the crowd roared.

"Together, we will protect this land. Together, we will

put out any threat to our kingdom. And together," I lifted Jade's hand in the air, intertwining her fingers with my own, "we will rule the fae!"

CHAPTER 40
Jade

I thought I would feel out of place standing before the kingdom of fae. It was never my place, although Malachi had said dozens of times that it was.

It never felt right.

Until today. Until every single one of them stood before me, paying us their respects. Adeline, Adonis, Lucien, Eli, my father. I scanned these faces with a knowing certainty that they would support me for who I was. For who I could be.

And the power I used to kill the King of Trithen, the power that sent every fae before me bowing on their knees, still pulsed through my veins.

Malachi felt this, too. His satisfaction lit up the inside of my chest as if it were my own happiness.

You should be careful with him, the voice in my head interrupted. My fingers, still interlocked with Mal's, tightened.

Why? I thought back. The crowd before us continued to roar with applause at Malachi's words.

He has the power of Erebus running through his veins, the voice said. *You should know better than anyone why that could be detrimental.*

He is my other half, I thought back.

An amused sensation washed over me. *He is your downfall, just as Erebus was mine.*

My chest tightened. I didn't need to know the name of the Saint who spoke in my mind, because the clues were easy enough to put together. Anastasia, Saint of life.

I nearly laughed. From the stories I had read, I knew I was nothing like her. I was no Saint.

I held Malachi's hand tighter and listened for the voice of Anastasia that spoke in my mind, but she was silent. *Good.*

There was only me and my wicked, glorious husband.

His hand tightened around my own in a silent promise. Nobody would defeat us. Nobody would stand against us.

With Silas gone, we would be the future. We would be the decision-makers.

A dark shadow tickled my mind, delighting in my thoughts.

We would be the end.

It wasn't until the crowds dwindled and the cheers subsided that the voice came back with a fierce sense of urgency.

He is your downfall. He is your downfall. He is your downfall.